THIEVES' WORLD™

is a unique experience: an outlaw world of the imagination, where mayhem and skulduggery rule and magic is still potent; brought to life by today's top fantasy writers, who are free to use one another's characters (but not to kill them off...or at least not too freely!).

The idea of Thieves' World and the colorful city called Sanctuary™ came to Robert Lynn Asprin in 1978. After many twists and turns (documented in the volumes), the idea took off—and took on its own reality, as the best fantasy worlds have a way of doing. The result is one of F&SF's most unique success stories: a bestseller from the beginning, a series that is a challenge to writers, a delight to readers, and a favorite of fans.

Dramatis Personae

The Townspeople

Cappen Varra—Itinerant minstrel. Rumored to be the only honest man in town.

Dubro—Bazaar blacksmith and husband to Illyra.

Hakiem—Storyteller and chronicler of Sanctuary's hidden stories.

Hanse Shadowspawn—Young thief. A bitter supporter of the lost glory of Ilsig.

Illyra—Half-blood S'danzo seeress with True Sight.

Jubal—Ex-gladiator and lynchpin of Sanctuary's organized crime.

Moonflower—S'danzo seeress. Teacher of Illyra and friend of Hanse.

The Rankans

Prince Kadakithis—Charismatic but naive governor of the town. Exiled here for safe-keeping by his half-brother, the Rankan Emperor.

Molin Torchholder—Vashanka's archpriest in Sanctuary and, next to the Prince, the highest ranking imperial official in Sanctuary.

The Hell-Hounds—Zalbar, Quag, Razkuli, Armen and Bourne: the Prince's personal bodyguard. Highly trained soldiers responsible for keeping the peace.

The Gods

Dyareela—Ancient blood goddess whose worship was suppressed by both the Ilsigi kingdoms and Rankan Empire.

Ils—Supreme deity of the vanquished Ilsigi pantheon.

Sabellia—Savankala's consort. The patroness of most Rankan women.

Savankala—Supreme deity in the Rankan pantheon. The source of imperial authority.

Vashanka—The Rankan Stormgod. Patron of their conquering armies.

TALES FROM
THE VULGAR UNICORN

Edited by
ROBERT LYNN ASPRIN & LYNN ABBEY

ACE FANTASY BOOKS
NEW YORK

"Spiders of the Purple Mage" copyright © 1980 by Philip José Farmer
"Goddess" copyright © 1980 by David Drake
"The Fruit of Enlibar" copyright © 1980 by Lynn Abbey
"The Dream of the Sorceress" copyright © 1980 by A. E. van Vogt
"Vashanka's Minion" copyright © 1980 by Janet Morris
"Shadow's Pawn" copyright © 1980 by Andrew J. Offutt
"To Guard the Guardians" copyright © 1980 by Robert Lynn Asprin

TALES FROM THE VULGAR UNICORN

An Ace Fantasy Book / published by arrangement with
the editors

PRINTING HISTORY
Ace Original / November 1980
Fourteenth printing / January 1986

ISBN: 0-441-80585-X

Ace Fantasy Books are published by The Berkley Publishing Group,
200 Madison Avenue, New York, New York 10016.
PRINTED IN THE UNITED STATES OF AMERICA

TALES FROM
THE VULGAR UNICORN

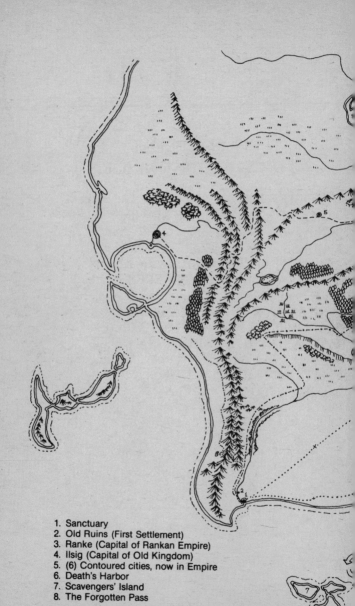

1. Sanctuary
2. Old Ruins (First Settlement)
3. Ranke (Capital of Rankan Empire)
4. Ilsig (Capital of Old Kingdom)
5. (6) Contoured cities, now in Empire
6. Death's Harbor
7. Scavengers' Island
8. The Forgotten Pass

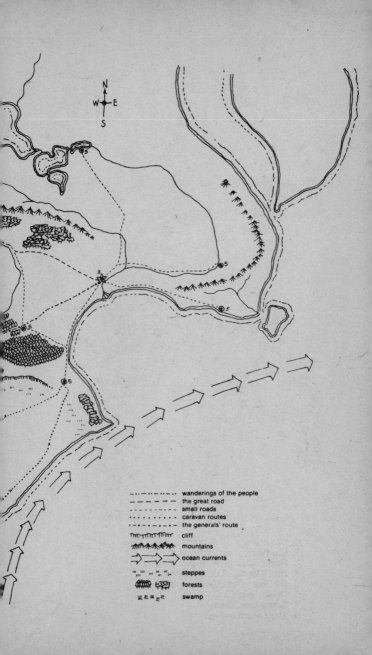

wanderings of the people
the great road
small roads
caravan routes
the generals' route
cliff
mountains
ocean currents

steppes
forests
swamp

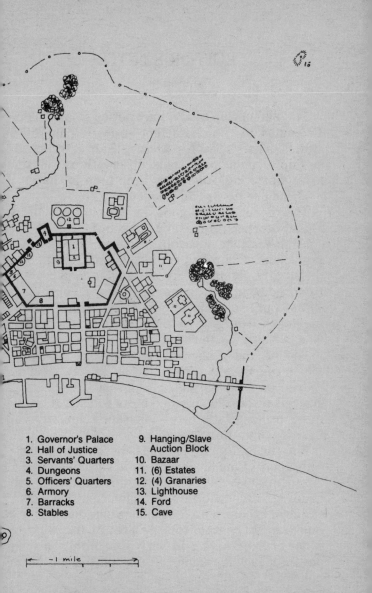

1. Governor's Palace
2. Hall of Justice
3. Servants' Quarters
4. Dungeons
5. Officers' Quarters
6. Armory
7. Barracks
8. Stables
9. Hanging/Slave Auction Block
10. Bazaar
11. (6) Estates
12. (4) Granaries
13. Lighthouse
14. Ford
15. Cave

|← ~1 mile →|

EDITOR'S NOTE

The perceptive reader may notice small inconsistencies in the characters appearing in these stories. Their speech patterns, their accounts of certain events, and their observations on the town's pecking order vary from time to time.

These are not inconsistencies!

The reader should consider the contradictions again, bearing three things in mind.

First; each story is told from a different viewpoint, and different people see and hear things differently. Even readily observable facts are influenced by individual perceptions and opinions. Thus, a minstrel narrating a conversation with a magician would give a different account than would a thief witnessing the same exchange.

Second; the citizens of Sanctuary are by necessity more than a little paranoid. They tend to either omit or slightly alter information in conversation. This is done more reflexively than out of premeditation, as it is essential for survival in this community.

Finally, Sanctuary is a fiercely competitive environment. One does not gain employment by admitting to being "the second-best swordsman in town." In addition to exaggerating one's own status, it is commonplace to downgrade or ignore one's closest competitors. As a result, the pecking order of Sanctuary will vary depending on who you talk to . . . or more importantly, who you believe.

INTRODUCTION

Moving his head with minute care to avoid notice, Hakiem the Storyteller studied the room over the untouched rim of his wine cup. This was, of course, done through slitted eyes. It would not do to have anyone suspect he was not truly asleep. What he saw only confirmed his growing feelings of disgust.

The Vulgar Unicorn was definitely going downhill. A drunk was snoring on the floor against the wall, passed out in a puddle of his own vomit, while several beggars made their way from table to table, interrupting the undertoned negotiations and hagglings of the tavern's normal clientele.

Though his features never moved, Hakiem grimaced inside. Such goings on were never tolerated when One-Thumb was around. The bartender/owner of the Vulgar Unicorn had always been quick to evict such riffraff as fast as they appeared. While the tavern had always been shunned by the more law-abiding citizens of Sanctuary, one of the main reasons it was favored by the rougher element was that here a man could partake of a drink or perhaps a little larcenous conversation uninterrupted. This tradition was rapidly coming to an end.

The fact that he would not be allowed to linger for hours over a cup of the tavern's cheapest wine

1

if One-Thumb were here never entered Hakiem's mind. He had a skill. He was a storyteller, a tale-spinner, a weaver of dreams and nightmares. As such, he considered himself on a measurably better plane than the derelicts who had taken to frequenting the place.

One-Thumb had been missing for a long time now, longer than any of his previous mysterious disappearances. Fear of his return kept the tavern open and the employees honest, but the place was degenerating in his absence. The only way it could sink any lower would be if a Hell Hound took to drinking here.

Despite his guise of slumber, Hakiem found himself smiling at that thought. A Hell Hound in the Vulgar Unicorn! Unlikely at best. Sanctuary still chafed at the occupying force from the Rankan Empire, and the five Hell Hounds were hated second only to the military governor, Prince Kadakithis, who they guarded. Though it was a close choice between Prince Kitty-Cat with his naive lawmaking and the elite soldiers who enforced his words, the citizens of Sanctuary generally felt the military governor's quest to clean up the worse hellhole in the Empire was stupid, while the Hell Hounds were simply devilishly efficient. In a town where one was forced to live by wit as often as skill, efficiency could be grudgingly admired, while stupidity, particularly stupidity with power, could only be despised.

No, the Hell Hounds weren't stupid. Tough, excellent swordsmen and seasoned veterans, they seldom set foot in the Maze, and never entered the Vulgar Unicorn. On the west side of town, it was said that one only came here if he was seeking death . . . or selling it. While the statement was somewhat exaggerated, it was true that most of the people who frequented the Maze either had nothing to lose or were willing to risk everything for what they might gain there. As rational men, the Hell Hounds were unlikely to put in an appearance at the Maze's most notorious tavern.

Still, the point remained that the Vulgar Unicorn sorely needed One-Thumb's presence and that his return was long overdue. In part, that was why Hakiem was spending so much time here of late: hope of acquiring the story of One-Thumb's return and possibly the story of his absence. That alone would be enough to keep the storyteller haunting the tavern, but the stories he gained during his wait were a prize in themselves. Hakiem was a compulsive collector of stories, from habit as well as by profession, and many stories had their beginnings, middle, or ends within these walls. He collected them all, though he knew that most of them could not be repeated, for he knew the value of a story is in its merit, not in its saleability.

SPIDERS OF THE PURPLE MAGE

Philip José Farmer

1

This was the week of the great rat hunt in Sanctuary.

The next week, all the cats that could be caught were killed and degutted.

The third week, all dogs were run down and disembowelled.

Masha zil-Ineel was one of the very few people in the city who didn't take part in the rat hunt. She just couldn't believe that any rat, no matter how big, and there were some huge ones in Sanctuary, could swallow a jewel so large.

But when a rumor spread that someone had seen a cat eat a dead rat and that the cat had acted strangely afterward, she thought it wise to pretend to chase cats. If she hadn't, people might wonder why not. They might think that she knew something they didn't. And then she might be the one run down.

Unlike the animals, however, she'd be tortured until she told where the jewel was.

She didn't know where it was. She wasn't even sure that there *was* an emerald.

But everybody knew that she'd been told about the jewel by Benna nus-Katarz. Thanks to Masha's blabbermouth drunken husband, Eevroen.

Three weeks ago, on a dark night, Masha had returned late from midwifing in the rich merchant's eastern quarter. It was well past midnight, but she wasn't sure of the hour because of the cloud-covered sky. The second wife of Shoozh the spice-importer had borne her fourth infant. Masha had attended to the delivery personally while Doctor Nadeesh had sat in the next room, the door only half-closed, and listened to her reports. Nadeesh was forbidden to see any part of a female client except for those normally exposed and especially forbidden to see the breasts and genitals. If there was any trouble with the birthing, Masha would inform him, and he would give her instructions.

This angered Masha, since the doctors collected half of the fee, yet were seldom of any use. In fact, they were usually a hindrance.

Still, half a fee was better than none. What if the wives and concubines of the wealthy were as nonchalant and hardy as the poor women, who just squatted down wherever they happened to be when the pangs started and gave birth unassisted? Masha could not have supported herself, her two daughters, her invalid mother, or her lazy alcoholic husband. The money she made from doing the more affluent women's hair and from her tooth-pulling and manufacture of false teeth in the marketplace wasn't enough. But midwifery added the income that kept her and her family just outside hunger's door.

She would have liked to pick up more money by cutting men's hair in the marketplace, but both law and ancient custom forbade that.

Shortly after she had burned the umbilical cord of the newborn to ensure that demons didn't steal it and had ritualistically washed her hands, she left Shoozh's house. His guards, knowing her, let her through the gate without challenge, and the guards of the gate to the eastern quarters also allowed her to pass. Not however without offers from a few to share their beds with her that night.

"I can do much better than that sot of a husband of yours!" one said.

Masha was glad that her hood and the darkness prevented the guards from seeing her burning face by the torchlight. However, if they could have seen that she was blushing with shame, they might have been embarrassed. They would know then that they weren't dealing with a brazen slut of the Maze but with a woman who had known better days and a higher position in society than she now held. The blush alone would have told them that.

What they didn't know and what she couldn't forget was that she had once lived in this walled area and her father had been an affluent, if not wealthy, merchant.

She passed on silently. It would have made her feel good to have told them her past and then ripped them with the invective she'd learned in the Maze. But to do that would lower her estimate of herself.

Though she had her own torch and the means for lighting it in the cylindrical leather case on her back, she did not use them. It was better to walk unlit and hence unseen into the streets. Though many of the lurkers in the shadows would let her pass unmolested, since they had known her when she was a child, others would not be so kind. They would rob her for the tools of her trade and the clothes she wore and some would rape her. Or try to.

Through the darkness she went swiftly, her steps sure because of long experience. The adobe buildings of the city were a dim whitish bulk ahead. Then the path took a turn, and she saw some small flickers of light here and there. Torches. A little further, and a light became a square. The window of a tavern.

She entered a narrow winding street and strode down its center. Turning a corner, she saw a torch in a bracket on the wall of a house and two men standing near it. Immediately she crossed to the far side and, hugging the walls, passed the two. Their pipes glowed redly; she caught a whiff of the pungent and sickly smoke of *kleetel*, the drug used by the poor when they didn't have money for the more expensive *krrf*. Which was most of the time.

After two or three pipefuls, the smokers would be vomiting. But they would claim that the euphoria would make the upchucking worth it.

There were other odors: garbage piled by the walls, slop jars of excrement, and puke from *kleetel* smokers and drunks. The garbage would be shoveled into goat-drawn carts by Downwinders whose families had long held this right.

The slop-jars would be emptied by a Downwinder family that had delivered the contents to farmers for a century and would and had fought fiercely to keep this right. The farmers would use the excrement to feed their soil; the urine would be emptied into the mouth of the White Foal River and carried out to sea.

She also heard the rustling and squealing of rats as they searched for edible portions and dogs growling or snarling as they chased the rats or fought each other. And she glimpsed the swift shadows of running cats.

Like a cat, she sped down the street in a half-run, stopping at corners to look around them before venturing farther. When she was about a half-mile from her place, she heard the pounding of feet ahead. She froze and tried to make herself look like part of the wall.

2

At that moment the moon broke through the clouds.

It was almost a full moon. The light revealed her to any but a blind person. She darted across the street to the dark side and played wall again.

The slap of feet on the hard-packed dirt of the street came closer. Somewhere above her, a baby began crying.

She pulled a long knife from a scabbard under her cloak and held the blade behind her. Doubtless, the one running was a thief or else someone trying to outrun a thief or mugger or muggers or perhaps a throat-slitter. If it was a thief who was getting away from the site of the crime, she would be safe. He'd be in no position to stop to see what he could get from her. If he was being pursued, the pursuers might shift their attention to her.

If they saw her.

Suddenly, the pound of feet became louder. Around the corner came a tall youth dressed in a ragged tunic and breeches and shod with buskins. He stopped and clutched the corner and looked behind him. His breath rasped like a rusty gate swung back and forth by gusts of wind.

Somebody was after him. Should she wait here? He hadn't seen her, and perhaps whoever was chasing him would be so intent he or they wouldn't detect her either.

The youth turned his face, and she gasped. His face was so swollen that she almost didn't recognize him. But he was Benna nus-Katarz, who had come here from Ilsig two years ago. No one knew why he'd immigrated, and no one, in keeping with the unwritten code of Sanctuary, had asked him why.

Even in the moonlight and across the street, she could see the swellings and dark spots, looking like bruises, on his face. And on his hands. The fingers were rotting bananas.

He turned back to peer around the corner. His breathing became less heavy. Now she could hear the faint slap of feet down the street. His chasers would be here soon.

Benna gave a soft ululation of despair. He staggered down the street toward a mound of garbage and stopped before it. A rat scuttled out but stopped a few feet from him and chittered at him. Bold beasts, the rats of Sanctuary.

Now Masha could hear the loudness of approaching runners and words that sounded like sheets being ripped apart.

Benna moaned. He reached under his tunic with clumsy fingers and drew something out. Masha couldn't see what it was, though she strained. She inched with her back to the wall toward a doorway. Its darkness would make her even more undetectible.

Benna looked at the thing in his hand. He said something which sounded to Masha like a curse. She couldn't be sure; he spoke in the Ilsig dialect.

The baby above had ceased crying; its mother must have given it the nipple or perhaps she'd made it drink water tinctured with a drug.

Now Benna was pulling something else from inside his tunic. Whatever it was, he molded it around the other thing, and now he had cast it in front of the rat.

The big gray beast ran away as the object arced toward him. A moment later, it approached the little ball, sniffing. Then it darted forward, still smelling it, touched it with its nose, perhaps tasted it, and was gone with it in its mouth.

Masha watched it squeeze into a crack in the old adobe building at the next corner. No one lived there. It had been crumbling, falling down for years, unrepaired and avoided even by the most desperate of transients and bums. It was said that the ghost of old Lahboo the Tight-Fisted haunted the place since his murder, and no one cared to test the truth of the stories told about the building.

Benna, still breathing somewhat heavily, trotted after the rat. Masha, hearing that the footsteps were louder, went alongside the wall, still in the shadows. She was curious about what Benna had gotten rid of, but she didn't want to be associated with him in any way when his hunters caught up with him.

At the corner, the youth stopped and looked around him. He didn't seem able to make up his mind which route to take. He stood, swaying, and then fell to his knees. He groaned, and pitched forward, softening his fall with outstretched arms.

Masha meant to leave him to his fate. It was the only sensible thing to do. But as she rounded the corner, she heard him moaning. And then she thought she heard him say something about a jewel.

She stopped. Was that what he had put in something, perhaps a bit of cheese, and thrown to the rat? It would be worth more money than she'd earn in a lifetime, and if she could, somehow, get her hands on it. . . . Her thoughts raced as swiftly as her heart, and now she was breathing heavily. A jewel! A jewel? It would mean release from this terrible place, a good home for her mother and her children. And for herself.

And it might mean release from Eevroen.

But there was also a terrible danger very close. She couldn't hear the sounds of the pursuers now, but that didn't mean they'd left the neighborhood. They were prowling around, looking into each doorway. Or perhaps one had looked around the corner and seen Benna. He had motioned to the others, and they were just behind the corner, getting ready to make a sudden rush.

She could visualize the knives in their hands.

If she took a chance and lost, she'd die, and her mother and daughters would be without support. They'd have to beg; Eevroen certainly would be of no help. And Handoo and Kheem, three and five years old, would grow up, if they didn't die first, to be child whores. It was almost inevitable.

While she stood undecided, knowing that she had only a few seconds to act and perhaps not that, the clouds slid below the moon again. That made the difference in what she'd do. She ran across the street toward Benna. He was still lying in the dirt of the street, his head only a few inches from some stinking dog turds. She scabbarded her dagger, got down on her knees, and rolled him over. He gasped with terror when he felt her hands upon him.

"It's all right!" she said softly. "Listen! Can you get up if I help you? I'll get you away!"

Sweat poured into her eyes as she looked toward the far corner. She could see nothing, but if the hunters wore black, they wouldn't be visible at this distance.

Benna moaned and then said, "I'm dying, Masha."

Masha gritted her teeth. She had hoped that he'd not recognize her voice, not at least until she'd gotten him to safety. Now, if the hunters found him alive and got her name from him, they'd come after her. They'd think she had the jewel or whatever it was they wanted.

"Here. Get up," she said, and struggled to help

him. She was small, about five feet tall and weighing eighty-two pounds. But she had the muscles of a cat, and fear was pumping strength into her. She managed to get Benna to his feet. Staggering under his weight, she supported him toward the open doorway of the building on the corner.

Benna reeked of something strange, an odor of rotting meat but unlike any she'd ever smelled. It rode over the stale sweat and urine of his body and clothes.

"No use," Benna mumbled through greatly swollen lips. "I'm dying. The pain is terrible, Masha."

"Keep going!" she said fiercely. "We're almost there!"

Benna raised his head. His eyes were surrounded with puffed-out flesh. Masha had never seen such edema; the blackness and the swelling looked like those of a corpse five days dead in the heat of summer.

"No!" he mumbled. "Not old Lahboo's building!"

3

Under other circumstances, Masha would have laughed. Here was a dying man or a man who thought he was dying. And he'd be dead soon if his pursuers caught up with him. (Me, too, she thought.) Yet he was afraid to take the only refuge available because of a ghost.

"You look bad enough to scare even The

Tight-Fisted One," she said. "Keep going or I'll drop you right now!"

She got him inside the doorway, though it wasn't easy what with the boards still attached to the lower half of the entrance. The top planks had fallen inside. It was a tribute to the fear people felt for this place that no one had stolen the wood, an expensive item in the desert town.

Just after they'd climbed over, Benna almost falling, she heard a man utter something in the raspy tearing language. He was nearby, but he must have just arrived. Otherwise, he would have heard the two.

Masha had thought she'd reached the limits of terror, but she found that she hadn't. The speaker was a Raggah!

Though she couldn't understand the speech— no one in Sanctuary could—she'd heard Raggah a number of times. Every thirty days or so five or six of the cloaked, robed, hooded, and veiled desert men came to the bazaar and the farmers' market. They could speak only their own language, but they used signs and a plentitude of coins to obtain what they wanted. Then they departed on their horses, their mules loaded down with food, wine, *vuksibah* (the very expensive malt whiskey imported from a far north land), goods of various kinds: clothing, bowls, braziers, ropes, camel and horse hides. Their camels bore huge panniers full of feed for chickens, ducks, camels, horses, and hogs. They also purchased steel tools: shovels, picks, drills, hammers, wedges.

They were tall, and though they were very dark, most had blue or green eyes. These looked cold and hard and piercing, and few looked directly into them. It was said that they had the gift, or the curse, of the evil eye.

They were enough, in this dark night, to have made Masha marble with terror. But what was worse, and this galvanized the marble, they were the servants of the purple mage!

Masha guessed at once what had happened. Benna had had the guts—and the complete stupidity—to sneak into the underground maze of the mage on the river isle of Shugthee and to steal a jewel. It was amazing that he'd had the courage, astounding that he could get undetected into the caves, an absolute wonder that he'd penetrated the treasurehold, and fantastic that he'd managed to get out. What weird tales he could tell if he survived! Masha could think of no similar event, no analog, to the adventures he must have had.

"Mofandsf!" she thought. In the thieves' argot of Sanctuary, "Mind-boggling!"

At that moment Benna's knees gave, and it was all she could do to hold him up. Somehow, she got him to the door to the next room and into a closet. If the Raggah came in, they would look here, of course, but she could get him no further.

Benna's odor was even more sickening in the hot confines of the closet, though its door was almost completely open. She eased him down. He mumbled, "Spiders . . . spiders."

She put her mouth close to his ear. "Don't talk loudly, Benna. The Raggah are close by. Benna, what did you say about the spiders?"

"Bites . . . bites," he murmured. "Hurt . . . the . . . the emerald . . . rich. . . . !"

"How'd you get in?" she said. She put her hand

close to his mouth to clamp down on it if he should start to talk loudly.

"Wha. . . ? Camel's eye . . . bu. . . ."

He stiffened, the heels of his feet striking the bottom of the closet door. Masha pressed her hand down on his mouth. She was afraid that he might cry out in his death agony. If this were it. And it was. He groaned, and then relaxed. Masha took her hand away. A long sigh came from his open mouth.

She looked around the edge of the closet. Though it was dark outside, it was brighter than the darkness in the house. She should be able to make out anyone standing in the doorway. The noise the heels made could have attracted the hunters. She saw no one, though it was possible that someone had already come in and was against a wall. Listening for more noise.

She felt Benna's pulse. He was dead or so close to it that it didn't matter any more. She rose and slowly pulled her dagger from the scabbard. Then she stepped out, crouching, sure that the thudding of her heart could be heard in this still room.

So unexpectedly and suddenly that a soft cry was forced from her, a whistle sounded outside. Feet pounded in the room—there *was* someone here!—and the dim rectangle of the doorway showed a bulk plunging through it. But it was going out, not in. The Raggah had heard the whistle of the garrison soldiers—half the city must have heard it—and he was leaving with his fellows.

She turned and bent down and searched under Benna's tunic and in his loincloth. She found nothing except slowly cooling lumpy flesh. Within ten seconds, she was out on the street. Down a block was the advancing light of torches, their holders not yet visible. In the din of shouts and whistles, she fled hoping that she wouldn't run into any laggard Raggah or another body of soldiers.

Later, she found out that she'd been saved because the soldiers were looking for a prisoner who'd escaped from the dungeon. His name was Badniss, but that's another tale.

4

Masha's two-room apartment was on the third floor of a large adobe building which, with two others, occupied an entire block. She entered it on the side of the Street of the Dry Well, but first she had to wake up old Shmurt, the caretaker, by beating on the thick oaken door. Grumbling at the late hour, he unshot the bolt and let her in. She gave him a *padpool,* a tiny copper coin, for his trouble and to shut him up. He handed her her oil lamp, she lit it, and she went up the three flights of stone steps.

She had to wake up her mother to get in. Wallu, blinking and yawning in the light of an oil lamp in the corner, shot the bolt. Masha entered and at once extinguished her lamp. Oil cost money, and there had been many nights when she had had to do without it.

Wallu, a tall skinny sagging-breasted woman of fifty, with gaunt deeply-lined features, kissed her daughter on the cheek. Her breath was sour with sleep and goat's cheese. But Masha appreciated the peck; her life had little expressions of love in it. And yet she was full of it; she was a bottle close to bursting with pressure.

The light on the rickety table in the corner showed a blank-walled room without rugs. In a far corner the two infants slept on a pile of tattered but clean blankets. Beside them was a small chamberpot of baked clay painted with the black and scarlet rings-within-rings of the Darmek guild.

In another corner was her false-teeth making equipment, wax, molds, tiny chisels, saws, and expensive wire, hardwood, iron, a block of ivory. She had only recently repaid the money she'd borrowed to purchase these. In the opposite corner was another pile of cloth, Wallu's bed, and beside it another thundermug with the same design. An ancient and wobbly spinning wheel was near it; Wallu made some money with it, though not much. Her hands were gnarled with arthritis, one eye had a cataract, and the other was beginning to lose its sight for some unknown reason.

Along the adobe wall was a brass charcoal brazier and above it a wooden vent. A bin held charcoal. A big cabinet beside it held grain and some dried meat and plates and knives. Near it was a baked clay vase for water. Next to it was a pile of cloths.

Wallu pointed at the curtain in the doorway to the other room.

"He came home early. I suppose he couldn't cadge drinks enough from his friends. But he's drunk enough to suit a dozen sailors."

Grimacing, Masha strode to the curtain and pulled it aside.

"Shewaw!" (A combination of "Whew!" "Ugh!", and "Yech!")

The stink was that which greeted her nostrils when she opened the door to The Vulgar Unicorn Tavern. A blend of wine and beer, stale and fresh, sweat, stale and fresh, vomit, urine, frying blood-sausages, *krrf,* and *kleetel.*

Eevroen lay on his back, his mouth open, his arms spread out as if he were being crucified. Once, he had been a tall muscular youth, very broad-shouldered, slim-waisted, and long-legged. Now he was fat, fat, fat, double-chinned, huge-paunched with rings of sagging fat around his waist. The once bright eyes were red and dark-bagged, and the once-sweet breath was a hellpit of stenches. He'd fallen asleep without changing into nightclothes; his tunic was ripped, dirty, and stained with various things, including puke. He wore cast-off sandals, or perhaps he'd stolen them.

Masha was long past weeping over him. She kicked him in the ribs, causing him to grunt and to open one eye. But it closed and he was quickly snoring like a pig again. That, at least, was a blessing. How many nights had she spent in screaming at him while he bellowed at her or in fighting him off when he staggered home and insisted she lie with him? She didn't want to count them.

Masha would have gotten rid of him long ago if she had been able to. But the law of the empire was that only the man could divorce unless the woman could prove her spouse was too diseased to have children or was impotent.

She whirled and walked toward the wash basin. As she passed her mother, a hand stopped her.

Wallu, peering at her with one half-good eye, said, "Child! Something has happened to you! What was it?"

"Tell you in a moment," Masha said, and she washed her face and hands and armpits. Later, she regretted very much that she hadn't told Wallu a lie. But how was she to know that Eevroen had come out of his stupor enough to hear what she said? If only she hadn't been so furious that she'd kicked him . . . but regrets were a waste of time, though there wasn't a human alive who didn't indulge in them.

She had no sooner finished telling her mother what had happened with Benna when she heard a grunt behind her. She turned to see Eevroen swaying in front of the curtains, a stupid grin on his fat face. The face once so beloved.

Eevroen reeled toward her, his hands out as if he intended to grab her. He spoke thickly but intelligibly enough.

"Why'n't you go affer the rat? If you caught it, we coulda been rich?"

"Go back to sleep," Masha said. "This has nothing to do with you."

"Nothin do wi' me?" Eevroen bellowed. "Wha' you mean? I'm your husband! Wha'ss yoursh ish mine. I wan' tha' jewel!"

"You damned fool," Masha said, trying to keep from screaming so that the children wouldn't wake and the neighbors wouldn't hear, "I don't have the jewel. There was no way I could get it—if there ever was any."

Eevroen put a finger alongside his nose and winked the left eye. "If there wa' ever any, heh? Masha, you tryna hol' ou' on me? You go' the jewel, and you lyin' to you' mo . . . mo . . . mama."

"No, I'm not lying!" she screamed, all reason for caution having deserted her quite unreasonably. "You fat stinking pig! I've had a terrible time, I almost got killed, and all you can think about is the jewel! Which probably doesn't exist! Benna was dying! He didn't know what he was talking about! I never saw the jewel! And . . ."

Eevroen snarled, "You tryna keep i' from me!" and he charged her.

She could easily have evaded him, but something swelled up in her and took over, and she seized a baked-clay water jug from a shelf and brought it down hard over his head. The jug didn't break, but Eevroen did. He fell face forward. Blood welled from his scalp; he snored.

By then the children were awake, sitting up, wide-eyed, but silent. Maze children learned at an early age not to cry easily.

Shaking, Masha got down on her knees and examined the wound. Then she rose and went to the rag rack and returned with some dirty ones, no use wasting clean ones on him, and stanched the wound. She felt his pulse; it was beating steadily enough for a drunkard who'd just been knocked out with a severe blow.

Wallu said, "Is he dead?"

She wasn't concerned about him. She was worrying about herself, the children, and Masha. If her daughter should be executed for killing her husband, however justified she was, then she and the girls would be without support.

"He'll have a hell of a headache in the morning," Masha said. With some difficulty, she rolled Eevroen over so that he would be face down, and she turned his head sideways and then put some rags under the side of his head. Now, if he should vomit during the night, he wouldn't choke to death. For a moment she was tempted to put him back as he had fallen. But the judge might think that she was responsible for his death.

"Let him lie there," she said. "I'm not going to break my back dragging him to our bed. Besides, I wouldn't be able to sleep, he snores so loudly and he stinks so badly."

She should have been frightened of what he'd do in the morning. But, strangely, she felt exuberant. She'd done what she'd wanted to do for several years now, and the deed had discharged much of her anger—for the time being, anyway.

She went to her room and tossed and turned for a while, thinking of how much better life would be if she could get rid of Eevroen.

Her last thoughts were of what life could be if she'd gotten the jewel that Benna had thrown to the rat.

5

She awoke an hour or so past dawn, a very late time for her, and smelled bread baking. After she'd sat on the chamberpot, she rose and pushed

the curtain aside. She was curious about the lack
of noise in the next room. Eevroen was gone. So
were the children. Wallu, hearing the little bells
on the curtain, turned.

"I sent the children out to play," she said. "Eevroen woke up about dawn. He pretended he didn't
know what had happened, but I could tell that he
did. He groaned now and then—his head I suppose. He ate some breakfast, and then he got out
fast."

Wallu smiled. "I think he's afraid of you."

"Good!" Masha said. "I hope he keeps on being
afraid."

She sat down while Wallu, hobbling around,
served her a half loaf of bread, a hunk of goat
cheese, and an orange. Masha wondered if her
husband also remembered what she'd said to her
mother about Benna and the jewel.

He had.

When she went to the bazaar, carrying the folding chair in which she put her dental patients, she
was immediately surrounded by hundreds of men
and women. All wanted to know about the jewel.

Masha thought, "The damn fool!"

Eevroen, it seemed, had procured free drinks
with his tale. He'd staggered around everywhere,
the taverns, the bazaar, the farmers' market, the
waterfront, and he'd spread the news. Apparently, he didn't say anything about Masha's knocking him out. That tale would have earned him
only derision, and he still had enough manhood
left not to reveal that.

At first, Masha was going to deny the story. But
it seemed to her that most people would think she
was lying, and they would be sure that she had

kept the jewel. Her life would be miserable from then on. Or ended. There were plenty who wouldn't hesitate to drag her off to some secluded place and torture her until she told where the jewel was.

So she described exactly what had happened, omitting how she had tried to brain Eevroen. There was no sense in pushing him too hard. If he was humiliated publicly, he might get desperate enough to try to beat her up.

She got only one patient that day. As fast as those who'd heard her tale ran off to look for rats, others took their place. And then, inevitably, the governor's soldiers came. She was surprised they hadn't appeared sooner. Surely one of their informants had sped to the palace as soon as he had heard her story, and that would have been shortly after she'd come to the bazaar.

The sergeant of the soldiers questioned her first, and then she was marched to the garrison, where a captain interrogated her. Afterward, a colonel came in, and she had to repeat her tale. And then, after sitting in a room for at least two hours, she was taken to the governor himself. The handsome youth, suprisingly, didn't detain her long. He seemed to have checked out her movements, starting with Doctor Nadeesh. He'd worked out a timetable between the moment she left Shooz's house and the moment she came home. So, her mother had also been questioned.

A soldier had seen two of the Raggah running away; their presence was verified.

"Well, Masha," the governor said. "You've stirred up a rat's nest," and he smiled at his own joke while the soldiers and courtiers laughed.

"There is no evidence that there was any jewel," he said, "aside from the story this Benna told, and he was dying from venom and in great pain. My doctor has examined his body, and he assures me that the swellings were spider bites. Of course, he doesn't know everything. He's been wrong before.

"But people are going to believe that there was indeed a jewel of great value, and nothing anyone says, including myself, will convince them otherwise.

"However, all their frantic activity will result in one great benefit. We'll be rid of the rats for a while."

He paused, frowning, then said, "It would seem, however, that this fellow Benna might have been foolish enough to steal something from the purple mage. I would think that that is the only reason he'd be pursued by the Raggah. But then there might be another reason. In any event, if there is a jewel, then the finder is going to be in great peril. The mage isn't going to let whoever finds it keep it.

"Or at least I believe so. Actually, I know very little about the mage, and from what I've heard about him, I have no desire to meet him."

Masha thought of asking him why he didn't send his soldiers out to the isle and summon the mage. But she kept silent. The reason was obvious. No one, not even the governor, wanted to provoke the wrath of a mage. And as long as the mage did nothing to force the governor into action, he would be left strictly alone to conduct his business—whatever that was.

At the end of the questioning, the governor told

his treasurer to give a gold *sheboozh* to Masha.

"That should more than take care of any business you've lost by being here," the governor said.

Thanking him profusely, Masha bowed as she stepped back, and then walked swiftly homeward.

The following week was the great cat hunt. It was also featured, for Masha anyway, by a break-in into her apartment. While she was off helping deliver a baby at the home of the merchant Ahloo shik-Mhanukhee, three masked men knocked old Shmurt the doorkeeper out and broke down the door to her rooms. While the girls and her mother cowered in a corner, the three ransacked the place, even emptying the chamberpots on the floor to determine that nothing was hidden there.

They didn't find what they were looking for, and one of the frustrated interlopers knocked out two of Wallu's teeth in a rage. Masha was thankful, however, that they did not beat or rape the little girls. That may have been not so much because of their mercifulness as that the doorkeeper regained consciousness sooner than they had expected. He began yelling for help, and the three thugs ran away before the neighbors could gather or the soldiers come.

Eevroen continued to come in drunk late at night. But he spoke very little, just using the place to eat and sleep. He seldom saw Masha when she was awake. In fact, he seemed to be doing his best to avoid her. That was fine with her.

6

Several times, both by day and night, Masha felt someone was following her. She did her best to detect the shadower, but whether she got the feeling by day or night, she failed to do it. She decided that her nervous state was responsible.

Then the great dog hunt began. Masha thought this was the apex of hysteria and silliness. But it worried her. After all the poor dogs were gone, what would next be run down and killed and gutted? To be more precise, who? She hoped that the who wouldn't be she.

In the middle of the week of the dog hunt, little Kheem became sick. Masha had to go to work, but when she came home after sundown, she found that Kheem was suffering from a high fever. According to her mother, Kheem had also had convulsions. Alarmed, Masha set out at once for Doctor Nadeesh's house in the Eastern quarter. He admitted her and listened to her describe Kheem's symptoms. But he refused to accompany her to her house.

"It's too dangerous to go into The Maze at night," he said. "And I wouldn't go there in the day unless I had several bodyguards. Besides, I am having company tonight. You should have brought the child here."

"She's too sick to be moved," Masha said. "I beg you to come."

Nadeesh was adamant, but he did give her some powders which she could use to cool the child's fever.

She thanked him audibly and cursed him silently. On the way back, while only a block from her apartment, she heard a sudden thud of footsteps behind her. She jumped to one side and whirled, drawing her dagger at the same time. There was no moon, and the nearest light was from oil lamps shining through some iron-barred windows in the second story above her.

By its faintness she saw a dark bulk. It was robed and hooded, a man by its tallness. Then she heard a low hoarse curse and knew it was a man. He had thought to grab or strike her from behind, but Masha's unexpected leap had saved her. Momentarily, at least. Now the man rushed her, and she glimpsed something long and dark in his uplifted hand. A club.

Instead of standing there frozen with fear or trying to run away, she crouched low and charged him. That took him by surprise. Before he could recover, he was struck in the throat with her blade.

Still, his body knocked her down, and he fell hard upon her. For a moment, the breath was knocked out of her. She was helpless, and when another bulk loomed above her, she knew that she had no chance.

The second man, also robed and hooded, lifted a club to bring it down on her exposed head.

Writhing, pinned down by the corpse, Masha could do nothing but await the blow. She thought briefly of little Kheem, and then she saw the man drop the club. And he was down on his knees, still gripping whatever it was that had closed off his breath.

A moment later, he was face down in the dry

dirt, dead or unconscious.

The man standing over the second attacker was short and broad and also robed and hooded. He put something in his pocket, probably the cord he'd used to strangle her attacker, and he approached her cautiously. His hands seemed to be empty, however.

"Masha?" he said softly.

By then she'd recovered her wind. She wriggled out from under the dead man, jerked the dagger from the windpipe, and started to get up.

The man said, in a foreign accent, "You can put your knife away, my dear. I didn't save you just to kill you."

"I thank you, stranger," she said, "but keep your distance anyway."

Despite the warning, he took two steps toward her. Then she knew who he was. No one else in Sanctuary stank so of rancid butter.

"Smhee," she said, equally softly.

He chuckled. "I know you can't see my face. So, though it's against my religious convictions, I will have to take a bath and quit smearing my body and hair with butter. I am as silent as a shadow, but what good is that talent when anyone can smell me a block away?"

Keeping her eyes on him, she stopped and cleaned her dagger on the dead man's robe.

"Are you the one who's been following me?" she said. She straightened up.

He hissed with surprise, then said, "You saw me?"

"No. But I knew someone was dogging me."

"Ah! You have a sixth sense. Or a guilty conscience. Come! Let's get away before someone comes along."

"I'd like to know who these men are . . . were."

"They're Raggah," Smhee said. "There are two others fifty yards from here, lookouts, I suppose. They'll be coming soon to find out why these two haven't shown up with you."

That shocked her even more than the attack.

"You mean the purple mage wants *me*? Why?"

"I do not know. Perhaps he thinks as so many others do. That is, that Benna told you more than you have said he did. But come! Quickly!"

"Where?"

"To your place. We can talk there, can't we?"

They walked swiftly toward her building. Smhee kept looking back, but the place where they had killed the two men was no longer visible. When they got to the door, however, she stopped.

"If I knock on the door for the keeper, the Raggah might hear it," she whispered. "But I have to get in. My daughter is very sick. She needs the medicine I got from Dr. Nadeesh."

"So that's why you were at his home," Smhee said. "Very well. You bang on the door. I'll be the rearguard."

He was suddenly gone, moving astonishingly swift and silently for such a fat man. But his aroma lingered.

She did as he suggested, and presently Shmurt came grumbling to the door and unbolted it. Just as she stepped in she smelled the butter more strongly, and Smhee was inside and pushing the door shut before the startled doorkeeper could protest.

"He's all right," Masha said.

Old Shmurt peered with runny eyes at Smhee by the light of his oil lamp. Even with good vision, however, Shmurt couldn't see Smhee's face. It was covered with a green mask.

Shmurt looked disgusted.

"I know your husband isn't much," he croaked. "But taking up with this foreigner, this tub of rotten butter . . . *shewaw!*"

"It's not what you think," she said indignantly.

Smhee said, "I must take a bath. Everyone knows me at once."

"Is Eevroen home?" Masha said.

Shmurt snorted and said, "At this early hour? No, you and your stinking lover will be safe."

"Dammit!" Masha said. "He's here on business!"

"Some business!"

"Mind your tongue, you old fart!" Masha said. "Or I'll cut it out!"

Shmurt slammed the door to his room behind him. He called, "Whore! Slut! Adulteress!"

Masha shrugged, lit her lamp, and went up the steps with Smhee close behind her. Wallu looked very surprised when the fat man came in with her daughter.

"Who is this?"

"Someone *can't* identify me?" Smhee said. "Does she have a dead nose?"

He removed his mask.

"She doesn't get out much," Masha said. She hurried to Kheem, who lay sleeping on her rag pile. Smhee took off his cloak, revealing thin arms and legs and a body like a ball of cheese. His shirt and vest, made of some velvety material speckled

with glittering sequins, clung tightly to his trunk.
A broad leather belt encircled his paunch, and
attached to it were two scabbards containing
knives, a third from which poked the end of a
bamboo pipe, and a leather bag about the size of
Masha's head. Over one shoulder and the side of
his neck was coiled a thin rope.

"Tools of the trade," he said in answer to Masha's look.

Masha wondered what the trade was, but she
didn't have time for him. She felt Kheem's forehead and pulse, then went to the water pitcher on
the ledge in the corner.

After mixing the powder with the water as
Nadeesh had instructed and pouring out some
into a large spoon, she turned. Smhee was on his
knees by the child and reaching into the bag on
his belt.

"I have some talent for doctoring," he said as
she came to his side. "Here. Put that quack's
medicine away and use this."

He stood up and held out a small leather envelope. She just looked at him.

"Yes, I know you don't want to take a chance
with a stranger. But please believe me. This green
powder is a thousand times better than that
placebo Nadeesh gave you. If it doesn't cure the
child, I'll cut my throat. I promise you."

"Much good that'd do the baby," Wallu said.

"Is it a magical potion?" Masha said.

"No. Magic might relieve the symptoms, but
the disease would still be there, and when the
magic wore off, the sickness would return. Here.
Take it! I don't want you two to say a word about
it, ever, but I was once trained in the art of

medicine. And where I come from, a doctor is
twenty times superior to any you'll find in
Sanctuary."

Masha studied his dark shiny face. He looked as
if he might be about forty years old. The high
broad forehead, the long straight nose, the well-
shaped mouth would have made him handsome if
his cheeks weren't so thick and his jowls so baggy.
Despite his fatness, he looked intelligent; the
black eyes below the thick bushy eyebrows were
keen and lively.

"I can't afford to experiment with Kheem," she
said.

He smiled, perhaps an acknowledgment that he
detected the uncertainty in her voice.

"You can't afford not to," he said. "If you don't
use this, your child will die. And the longer you
hesitate, the closer she gets to death. Every second
counts."

Masha took the envelope and returned to the
water pitcher. She set the spoon down without
spilling its contents and began working as Smhee
called out to her his instructions. He stayed with
Kheem, one hand on her forehead, the other on
her chest. Kheem breathed rapidly and shallowly.

Wallu protested. Masha told her to shut up
more harshly than she'd intended. Wallu bit her
lip and glared at Smhee.

Kheem was propped up by Smhee, and Masha
got her to swallow the greenish water. Ten minutes or so later, the fever began to go down. An
hour later, according to the sandglass, she was
given another spoonful. By dawn, she seemed to
be rid of it, and she was sleeping peacefully.

7

Meantime, Masha and Smhee talked in low tones. Wallu had gone to bed, but not to sleep, shortly before sunrise. Eevroen had not appeared. Probably he was sleeping off his liquor in an empty crate on the wharf or in some doorway. Masha was glad. She had been prepared to break another basin over his head if he made a fuss and disturbed Kheem.

Though she had seen the fat little man a number of times, she did not know much about him. Nobody else did either. It was certain that he had first appeared in Sanctuary six weeks (sixty days) ago. A merchant ship of the Banmalts people had brought him, but this indicated little about his origin since the ship ported at many lands and islands.

Smhee had quickly taken a room on the second floor of a building, the first of which was occupied by the Khabeeber or "Diving Bird" Tavern. (The proprietor had jocularly named it thus because he claimed that his customers dived as deeply into alcohol for surcease as the khabeeber did into the ocean for fish.) He did no work nor was he known to thieve or mug. He seemed to have enough money for his purposes, whatever they were, but then he lived frugally. Because he smeared his body and hair with rancid butter, he was called "The Stinking Butterball" or "Old Rotten," though not to his face. He spent time in all the

taverns and also was often seen in the farmers'
market and the bazaar. As far as was known, he
had shown no sexual interest in men or women or
children. Or, as one wag put it, "not even in
goats."

His religion was unknown though it was rumored that he kept an idol in a small wooden case
in his room.

Now, sitting on the floor by Kheem, making the
child drink water every half-hour, Masha questioned Smhee. And he in turn questioned her.

"You've been following me around," Masha
said. "Why?"

"I've also investigated other women."

"You didn't say why."

"One answer at a time. I have something to do
here, and I need a woman to help me. She has to be
quick and strong and very brave and intelligent.
And desperate."

He looked around the room as if anybody who
lived in it had to be desperate indeed.

"I know your history," he said. You came from a
fairly well-to-do family, and as a child you lived
in the Eastern quarter. You were not born and bred
in the Maze, and you want to get out of it. You've
worked hard, but you just are not going to succeed
in your ambition. Not unless something unusual
comes your way and you have the courage to seize
it, no matter what the consequences might be."

"This has to do with Benna and the jewel,
doesn't it?" she said.

He studied her face by the flickering light of the
lamp.

"Yes."

He paused.

"And the purple mage."

Masha sucked in a deep breath. Her heart thudded far more swiftly than her fatigue could account for. A coldness spread from her toes to the top of her head, a not unpleasant coldness.

"I've watched in the shadows near your building," he said. "Many a night. And two nights ago I saw the Raggah steal into other shadows and watch the same window. Fortunately, you did not go out during that time to midwife. But tonight. . . ."

"Why would the Raggah be interested in me?"

He smiled slowly.

"You're smart enough to guess why. The mage thinks you know more than you let on about the jewel. Or perhaps he thinks Benna told you more than you've repeated."

He paused again, then said, "Did he?"

"Why should I tell you if he did?"

"You owe me for your life. If that isn't enough to make you confide in me, consider this. I have a plan whereby you can not only be free of the Maze, you can be richer than any merchant, perhaps richer than the governor himself. You will even be able to leave Sanctuary, to go to the capital city itself. Or anywhere in the world."

She thought, if Benna could do it, we can.

But then Benna had not gotten away.

She said, "Why do you need a woman? Why not another man?"

Smhee was silent for a long time. Evidently, he was wondering just how much he should tell her. Suddenly, he smiled, and something invisible, an unseen weight seemed to fall from him. Somehow, he even looked thinner.

"I've gone this far," he said. "So I must go all the way. No backing out now. The reason I must have a woman is that the mage's sorcery has a weakness. His magical defenses will be set up to repel men. He will not have prepared them against women. It would not occur to him that a woman would try to steal his treasure. Or . . . kill him."

"How do you know that?"

"I don't think it would be wise to tell you that now. You must take my word for it. I do know far more about the purple mage than anyone else in Sanctuary."

"You might, and that still wouldn't be much," she said.

"Let me put it another way. I do know much about him. More than enough to make me a great danger to him."

"Does he know much about you?"

Smhee smiled again. "He doesn't know I'm here. If he did, I'd be dead by now."

They talked until dawn, and by then Masha was deeply committed. If she failed, then her fate would be horrible. And the lives of her daughters and her mother would become even worse. Far worse. But if she continued as she had, she would be dooming them anyway. She might die of a fever or be killed, and then they would have no supporter and defender.

Anyway, as Smhee pointed out, though he didn't need to, the mage was after her. Her only defense was a quick offense. She had no other choice except to wait like a dumb sheep and be slaughtered. Except that, in this situation, the sheep would be tortured before being killed.

Smhee knew what he was saying when he had said that she was desperate.

8

When the wolf's tail, the false dawn, came, she rose stiffly and went through to her room and looked out the window. Not surprisingly, the corpses of the Raggah were gone.

Shortly thereafter, Kheem awoke, bright-eyed, and asked for food. Masha covered her with kisses, and, weeping joyfully, prepared breakfast. Smhee left. He would be back before noon. But he gave her five *shaboozh* and some lesser coin. Masha wakened her mother, gave her the money, and told her that she would be gone for a few days. Wallu wanted to question her, but Masha told her sternly that she would be better off if she knew no more than she did now.

"If Eevroen wants to know where I am, tell him that I have been called to help deliver a rich farmer's baby. If he asks for the man's name, tell him it is Shkeedur sha-Mizl. He lives far out and only comes into town twice a year except on special business. It doesn't matter that it's a lie. By the time I get back—it'll be soon—we'll be leaving at once. Have everything we'll need for a long journey packed into that bag. Just clothes and eating utensils and the medicine. If Kheem has a relapse, give her Smhee's powders."

Wallu wailed then, and Masha had to quiet her down.

"Hide the money. No! Leave one *shaboozh*

where Eevroen will find it when he looks for money. Conceal the rest where he can't find it. He'll take the *shaboozh* and go out to drink, and you won't be bothered with him or his questions."

When the flaming brass bowl of the noon sun had reached its apex, Smhee came. His eyes looked very red, but he didn't act fatigued. He carried a carpet bag from which he produced two dark cloaks, two robes, and the masks which the priests of Shalpa wore in public.

He said, "How did you get rid of your mother and the children?"

"A neighbor is keeping the children until mother gets back from shopping," she said. "Eevroen still hasn't shown up."

"Nor will he for a long time," Smhee said. "I dropped a coin as I passed him staggering this way. He snatched it, of course, and ran off to a tavern.

"The *Sailfish* will be leaving port in three days. I've arranged for passage on her and also to be hidden aboard her if her departure is delayed. I've been very busy all morning."

"Including taking a bath," she said.

"You don't smell too good yourself," he said. "But you can bathe when we get to the river. Put these on."

She went into her room, removed her clothes, and donned the priest's garb. When she came out, Smhee was fully dressed. The bag attached to his belt bulged beneath his cloak.

"Give me your old clothes," he said. "We'll cache them outside the city, though I don't think we'll be needing them."

She did so, and he stuffed them into the belt-
bag.

"Let's go," he said.

She didn't follow him to the door. He turned
and said, "What's the matter? Your liver getting
cold?"

"No," she said. "Only . . . mother's very
short-sighted. I'm afraid she'll be cheated when
she buys the food."

He laughed and said something in a foreign
tongue.

"For the sake of Igil! When we return, we'll
have enough to buy out the farmers' market a
thousand times over!"

"If we get back. . . ." she murmured. She
wanted to go to Looza's room and kiss the children goodbye. But that was not wise. Besides, she
might lose her determination if she saw them
now.

They walked out while old Shmurt stared. He
was the weakest point in their alibi, but they
hoped they wouldn't need any. At the moment, he
was too dumfounded at seeing them to say anything. And he would be afraid to go to the soldiers
about this. He probably was thinking that two
priests had magically entered the house, and it
would be indiscreet to interfere in their business.

Thirty minutes later, they mounted the two
horses which Smhee had arranged to be tied to a
tree outside city limits.

"Weren't you afraid they'd be stolen?" she said.

"There are two stout fellows hidden in the grass
near the river," he said. He waved toward it, and
she saw two men come from it. They waved back

and started to walk back to the city.

There was a rough road along the White Foal River, sometimes coming near the stream, sometimes bending far away. They rode over it for three hours, and then Smhee said, "There's an old adobe building a quarter-mile inland. We'll sleep there for a while. I don't know about you, but I'm weary."

She was glad to rest. After hobbling the horses near a stand of the tall brown desert grass, they lay down in the midst of the ruins. Smhee went to sleep at once. She worried about her family for a while, and suddenly she was being shaken by Smhee. Dawn was coming up.

They ate some dried meat and bread and fruit and then mounted again. After watering the horses and themselves at the river, they rode at a canter for three more hours. And then Smhee pulled up on the reins. He pointed at the trees a quarter-mile inland. Beyond, rearing high, were the towering cliffs on the other side of the river. The trees on this side, however, prevented them from seeing the White Foal.

"The boat's hidden in there," he said. "Unless someone's stolen it. That's not likely, though. Very few people have the courage to go near the Isle of Shugthee."

"What about the hunters who bring down the furs from the north?"

"They hug the eastern shore, and they only go by in daylight. Fast."

They crossed the rocky ground, passing some low-growing purplish bushes and some irontrees with grotesquely twisted branches. A rabbit with long ears dashed by them, causing her horse to

rear up. She controlled it, though she had not
been on a horse since she was eleven. Smhee said
that he was glad that it hadn't been his beast. All
he knew about riding was the few lessons he'd
taken from a farmer after coming to Sanctuary.
He'd be happy if he never had to get on another
one.

The trees were perhaps fifteen or twenty deep
from the river's edge. They dismounted, removed
the saddles, and hobbled the beasts again. Then
they walked through the tall cane-like plants,
brushing away the flies and other pestiferous insects, until they got to the stream itself. Here grew
stands of high reeds, and on a hummock of
spongy earth was Smhee's boat. It was a dugout
which could hold only two.

"Stole it," Smhee said without offering any details.

She looked through the reeds down the river.
About a quarter of a mile away, the river
broadened to become a lake about two and a half
miles across. In its center was the Isle of Shugthee,
a purplish mass of rock. From this distance, she
could not make out its details.

Seeing it, she felt coldness ripple over her.

"I'd like to take a whole day and a night to scout
it," he said. "So you could become familiar with
it, too. But we don't have time. However, I can tell
you everything I know. I wish I knew more."

She doffed her clothes and bathed in the river
while Smhee unhobbled the horses and took them
some distance up to let them drink. When she
came back, she found him just returning with
them.

"Before dusk comes, we'll have to move them

down to a point opposite the isle," he said. "And we'll saddle them, too."

They left the horses to go to a big boulder outside the trees but distant from the road. At its base was a hollow large enough for them to lie down in. Here they slept, waking now and then to talk softly or to eat a bite or to go behind the rock and urinate. The insects weren't so numerous here as in the trees, but they were bad enough.

Not once, as far as they knew, did anyone pass on the road.

When they walked the horses down the road, Smhee said, "You've been very good about not asking questions, but I can see you're about to explode with curiosity. You have no idea who the puple mage really is. Not unless you know more than the other Sancturians."

"All I know," she said, "is that they say that the mage came here about ten years ago. He came with some hired servants, and many boxes, some small, some large. No one knew what his native land was, and he didn't stay long in town. One day he disappeared with the servants and the boxes. It was some time before people found out that he'd moved into the caves of the Isle of Shugthee. Nobody had ever gone there because it was said that it was haunted by the ghosts of the Shugthee. They were a little hairy people who inhabited this land long before the first city of the ancients was built here."

"How do you know he's a mage?" Smhee said.

"I don't, but everybody says he is. Isn't he?"

"He is," Smhee said, looking grim.

"Anyway, he sent his servants in now and then to buy cattle, goats, pigs, chickens, horses, vege-

tables, and animal feed and fruit. These were men
and women from some distant land. Not from his,
though. And then one day they ceased coming in.
Instead, the Raggah came. From that day on, no
one has seen the servants who came with the
mage."

"He probably got rid of them," Smhee said. "He
may have found some reason to distrust them. Or
no reason at all."

"The fur trappers and hunters who've gone by
the isle say they've seen some strange things.
Hairy beast-faced dwarfs. Giant spiders."

She shuddered.

"Benna died of spider bites," Smhee said.

The fat little man reached into his belt-bag and
brought out a metal jar. He said, "Before we leave
in the boat tonight we'll rub the ointment in this
on us. It will repel some of the spiders but not,
unfortunately, all."

"How do you know that?"

"I know."

They walked silently for a while. Then he
sighed, and said, "We'll get bitten. That is certain.
Only . . . all the spiders that will bite us—I hope
so, anyway—won't be real spiders. They'll be
products of the mage's magic. Apparitions. But
apparitions that can kill you just as quickly or as
slowly and usually as painfully as the real spiders."

He paused, then said, "Benna probably died
from their bites."

Masha felt as if she were turning white under
her dark skin. She put her hands on his arm.

"But . . . but . . . !"

"Yes, I know. If the spiders were not real, then

why should they harm him? That is because he thought they were real. His mind did the rest to him."

She didn't like that she couldn't keep her voice from shaking, but she couldn't help it.

"How can you tell which is real and which magical?"

"In the daylight the unreal spiders look a little transparent. By that I mean that if they stand still, you can see dimly through them. But then they don't stand still much. And we'll be in the dark of night. So. . . .

"Look here, Masha. You have to be strong stuff to go there. You have to overcome your fear. A person who lets fear conquer him or her is going to die even if he knows that the spider is unreal. He'll make the sting of the bite himself and the effects of the venom. And he'll kill himself. I've seen it happen in my native land."

"But you say that we might get bitten by a real spider. How can I tell which is which in the dark?"

"It's a problem."

He added after a few seconds, "The ointment should repulse most of the real spiders. Maybe, if we're lucky. You see, we have an advantage that Benna didn't have. I know what faces us because I come from the mage's land. His true name is Kemren, and he brought with him the real spiders and some other equally dangerous creatures. They would have been in some of the boxes. I am prepared for them, and so will you be. Benna wasn't, and any of these Sanctuary thieves will get the same fate."

Masha asked why Kemren had come here.

Smhee chewed on his lower lip for a while before answering.

"You may as well know it all. Kemren was a priest of the goddess Weda Krizhtawn of the island of Sherranpip. That is far east and south of here, though you may have heard of it. We are a people of the water, of lakes, rivers, and the sea. Weda Krizhtawn is the chief goddess of water, and she has a mighty temple with many treasures near the sea.

"Kemren was one of the higher priests, and he served her well for years. In return, he was admitted into the inner circle of mages and taught both black and white magic. Though, actually, there is little difference between the two branches, the main distinction being whether the magician uses his powers for good or evil.

"And it isn't always easy to tell what is good and what is evil. If a mage makes a mistake, and his use turns out to be for evil, even if he sincerely thought it was for good, then there is a . . . backlash. And the mage's character becomes changed for the worse in proportion to the amount of magical energy used."

He stopped walking.

"We're opposite the isle now."

It wasn't visible from the road. The plain sloped upward from the road, becoming a high ridge near the river. The tall spreading blackish *hukharran* bush grew on top of it. They walked the horses up the ridge, where they hobbled them near a pool of rainwater. The beasts began cropping the long brownish grass that grew among the bushes.

The isle was in the center of the lake and seemed to be composed mostly of a purplish rock.

It sloped gently from the shore until near the middle, where a series of peculiar formations formed a spine. The highest prominence was a monolith perforated near its top as if a tunnel had been carved through it.

"The camel's eye Benna spoke of," Smhee said. "Over there is the formation known as the ape's head, and at the other end is that which the natives call the dragon's tail."

On the edge of the isle grew some trees, and in the waters by it were the ubiquitous tall reeds.

There was no sight or sound of life on it. Even the birds seemed to shun it.

"But I floated down past it at night several times," he said, "and I could hear the lowing of some cattle and the braying of a donkey. Also, I heard a weird call, but I don't know if it was from a bird or an animal. And I heard a peculiar grunting sound, but it wasn't from pigs."

"That camel's eye looks like a good place for a sentry," she said. "I got the impression from Benna that that is where he entered the caves. It must've been a very dangerous climb, especially during the dark."

"Benna was a good man," Smhee said. "But he wasn't prepared enough. There are eyes watching now. Probably through holes in the rocks. From what I heard, the mage had his servants buy a number of excavating tools. He would have used them to enlargen the caves and to make tunnels to connect the caves."

She took a final look in the sunlight at the sinister purple mass and turned away.

9

Night had come. The winds had died down. The sky was cloudy, but the covering was thin. The full moon glowed through some of these, and now and then broke through. The nightbirds made crazy startling sounds. The mosquitoes hummed around them in dense masses, and if it hadn't been for Smhee's ointment would have driven them out of the trees within a few minutes. Frogs croaked in vast chorus; things plopped into the water.

They shoved the boat out to the edge of the reeds and climbed in. They wore their cloaks now but would take them off when they got to the isle. Masha's weapons were a dagger and a short thin sword used for thrusting only.

They paddled silently as possible, the current helping their rate of speed, and presently the isle loomed darkly to their right. They landed halfway down the eastern shore and dragged the dugout slowly to the nearest tree.

They put their cloaks in the boat, and Masha placed a coil of rope over her shoulder and neck.

The isle was quiet. Not a sound. Then came a strange grunting cry followed by a half-moaning, half-squalling sound. Her neck iced.

"Whatever that is," Smhee said, "it's no spider."

He chuckled as if he were making a joke.

They'd decided—what else could they do?— that the camel's eye would be too heavily guarded after Benna's entrance through it. But there had to be more accessible places to get in. These would be guarded, too, especially since they must have been made more security-conscious by the young thief.

"What I'd like to find is a secret exit," Smhee said. "Kemren must have one, perhaps more. He knows that there might come a time when he'll be sorely in need of it. He's a crafty bastard."

Before they'd taken the boat, Smhee had revealed that Kemren had fled Sherranpip with many of the temple's treasures. He had also taken along spiders' eggs and some of the temple's animal guardians.

"If he was a high priest," Masha had said, "why would he do that? Didn't he have power and wealth enough?"

"You don't understand our religion," the fat thief had said. "The priests are surrounded by treasures that would pop your eyes out of their sockets if you saw them. But the priests themselves are bound by vows to extreme poverty, to chastity, to a harsh bare life. Their reward is the satisfaction of serving Weda Krizhtawn and her people. It wasn't enough for Kemren. He must have become evil while performing some magic that went wrong. He is the first priest ever to commit such a blasphemy.

"And I, a minor priest, was selected to track him down and to make him pay for his crime. I've been looking for him for thirteen years. During that time, to effect the vengeance of Weda Krizhtawn, I have had to break some of my own vows and to commit crimes which I must pay for when I return to my land."

"Won't she pardon you for these because you have done them in her name?" Masha had said.

"No. She accepts no excuses. She will thank me for completing my mission, but I must still pay. Look at me. When I left Sharranpip, I was as skinny as you. I led a very exemplary life. I ate little, I slept in the cold and rain, I begged for my food, I prayed much. But during the years of my crimes and the crimes of my years, I have eaten too well so that Kemren, hearing of the fat fellow, would not recognize me. I have been reeling drunk, I have gambled—a terrible sin—I have fought with fists and blade, I have taken human lives, I. . . ."

He looked as if he were going to weep.

Masha said, "But you didn't quit smearing yourself with butter?"

"I should have, I should have!" he cried. "But, apart from lying with women, that is the one thing I could not bring myself to do, though it was the first I should have done! And I'll pay for that when I get home, even though that is the hardest thing for a priest to do! Even Kemren, I have heard, though he no longer worships Weda Krizhtawn, still butters himself!

"And the only reason I quit doing that is that I'm sure that he's conditioned his real spiders, and his guardian animals, to attack anyone who's covered with butter. That way he can make sure or thinks he can make sure, that no hunter of him will ever be able to get close. That is why, though it almost killed me with shame and guilt, I bathed this morning!"

Masha would have laughed if she hadn't felt so sorry for him. That was why his eyes had looked so red when he'd shown up at her apartment after bathing. It hadn't been fatigue but tears that had done it.

They drew their weapons, Masha a short sword and Smhee a long dagger. They set out for the base of the ridge of formations that ran down the center of the isle like serrations on a dragon's back. Before they'd gone far, Smhee put a restraining hand on her arm.

"There's a spider's web just ahead. Between those two bushes. Be careful of it. But look out for other dangers, since one will be obvious enough to distract your attention from others. And don't forget that the thorns of these bushes are probably poisonous."

In the dim moonlight she saw the web. It was huge, as wide as the stretch of her arms. She thought, if it's so big, what about its spinner?

It seemed empty, though. She turned to her left and walked slowly, her head turned to watch it.

Then something big scuttled out from under the bush at her. She stifled her scream and leaped toward the thing instead of following her desire to run away from it. Her sword leaped out as the thing sprang, and it spitted itself. Something soft touched the back of her hand. The end of a waving leg.

Smhee came up behind it as she stood there holding the sword out as far as she could to keep the arachnid away. Her arm got heavy with its weight, and slowly the blade sank toward the ground. The fat man slashed the thing's back open with his dagger. A foul odor vented from it. He brought his foot down on a leg and whispered, "Pull your sword out! I'll keep it pinned!"

She did so and then backed away. She was breathing very hard.

He jumped up and came down with both feet on the creature. Its legs waved for a while longer, but it was dying if not already dead.

"That was a real spider," he said, "although I suppose you know that. I suspect that the false spiders will be much smaller.

"Why?" she said. She wished her heart would quit trying to leap up through her throat.

"Because making them requires energy, and it's more effective to make a lot of little spiders and costs less energy than to make a few big ones. There are other reasons which I won't explain just now."

"Look out!" she cried, far louder than she should have. But it had been so sudden and had taken her off guard.

Smhee whirled and slashed out, though he hadn't seen the thing. It bounded over the web, its limbs spread out against the dimness, its great round ears profiled. It came down growling, and it fell upon Smhee's blade. This was no man's-headsized spider but a thing as big as a large dog and furry and stinking of something—monkey?—and much more vital than the arachnid. It bore Smhee backward with his weight; he fell on the earth.

Snarling, it tried to bury its fangs in Smhee's throat. Masha broke from her paralysis and thrust with a fury and strength that only fear could provide. The blade went through its body. She leaped back, drawing it out, and then lunged again. This time the point entered its neck.

Smhee, gasping, rolled it off him and stood up.

He said, "By Wishvu's whiskers! I've got blood all over me. A fine mess! Now the others will smell me!"

"What is it?" Masha said shakily.

"A temple guardian ape. Actually, it's not an ape but a very large tailless monkey. Kemren must have brought some cubs with him."

Masha got close to the dead beast, which was lying on its back. The open mouth showed teeth like a leopard's.

"They eat meat," he said. "Unlike other monkeys, however, they're not gregarious. Our word for them, translated, would be the solitary ape."

Masha wondered if one of Smhee's duties had been teaching. Even under these circumstances, he had to be pedantic.

He looked around. "Solitary or not, there are probably a number on this isle."

After dragging the two carcasses into the river, they proceeded cautiously. Smhee looked mostly ahead; Masha, behind. Both looked to both sides of them. They came to the base of the ridges of rock. Smhee said, "The animal pens are north. That's where I heard them as I went by in the boat. I think we should stay away from them. If they scent us and start an uproar, we'll have the Raggah out and on our asses very quickly."

Smhee stopped suddenly, and said, "Hold it!"

Masha looked around quickly. What had he seen or heard?

The fat man got down on his knees and pushed against the earth just in front of him.

He rose and said, "There's a pit under that firm-looking earth. I felt it give way as I put my foot on it. That's why it pays not to walk swiftly here."

They circled it, Smhee testing each step before taking another. Masha thought that if they had to go this slowly, they would take all night before they got to the ridge. But then he led her to a rocky place, and she breathed easier. However, he said, "They could carve a pit in the stone and put a pivoting lid over it."

She said, "Why are we going this way? You said the entrances are on the north end."

"I said that I only observed people entering on the north end. But I also observed something very interesting near here. I want to check it out. It may be nothing for us, but again. . . ."

Still moving slowly but faster than on the earth, they came to a little pool. It was about ten feet in diameter, a dark sheet of water on which bubbles appeared and popped. Smhee crouched down and stared at its sinister-looking surface.

She started to whisper a question, but he said, "Shh!"

Presently, something scuttled with a clatter across the solid rock from the shore. She jumped but uttered no exclamation. The thing looked like a spider in the dark, an enormous one, larger than the one they'd killed. It paid no attention to them or perhaps it wasn't at all aware of them. It leaped into the pool and disappeared. Smhee said, "Let's get behind that boulder."

When they were in back of it, she said, "What's going on?"

"When I was spying, I saw some things going into and coming out of this hole. It was too far away to see what they were, though I suspected they were giant spiders or perhaps crabs."

"So?"

His hand gripped her wrist.

"Wait!"

The minutes oozed by like snails. Mosquitoes hummed around them, birds across the river called, and once she heard, or thought she heard, that peculiar half-grunt, half-squall. And once she started when something splashed in the river. A fish. She hoped that was all it was.

Smhee said softly, "Ah!"

He pointed at the pool. She strained her eyes and then saw what looked like a swelling of the water in its center. The mound moved toward the edge of the pool, and then it left the water. It clacked as it shot toward the river. Soon another thing came and then another, and all of a sudden at least twenty popped up and clattered across the rocks.

Smhee finally relieved her bursting question.

"They look like the bengil crab of Sharranpip. They live in that hole but they must catch fish in the river."

"What is that to us?"

"I think the pool must be an entrance to a cave. Or caves. The crabs are not water-breathers."

"Are they dangerous?"

"Only when in water. On land they'll either run or, if cornered, try to defend themselves. They aren't poisonous, but their claws are very powerful."

He was silent for a moment, then said, "The mage is using them to defend the entrance to a cave, I'm sure. An entrance which is also an exit.

For him as well as for the crabs. That pool has to be one of his secret escape routes."

Masha thought, "Oh, no!" and she rolled her eyes. Was this fat fool really thinking about trying to get inside through the pool?

"How could the mage get out this way if the crabs would attack him?"

"He would throw poisoned meat to them. He could do any number of things. What matters just now is that he wouldn't have bothered to bring their eggs along from Sharranpip unless he had a use for them. Nor would he have planted them here unless he needed them to guard this pool. Their flesh is poisonous to all living things except the ghoondah fish."

He chuckled. "But the mage has outsmarted himself. If I hadn't noticed the bengil, I would never have considered that pool as an entrance."

While he had been whispering, another group had emerged and run for the river. He counted them, thirty in all.

"Now is the time to go in," he said. "They'll all be feeding. That crab you first saw was their scout. It found a good place for catching fish, determined that there wasn't any enemy around, and returned with the good news. In some ways, they're more ant than crab. Fortunately, their nests aren't as heavily populated as an anthole."

He said, however, that they should wait a few minutes to make sure that all had left. "By all, I mean all but a few. There are always a few who stay behind to guard the eggs."

"Smhee, we'll drown!"

"If other people can get out through the pool, then we can get in."

"You don't know for sure that the pool is an escape route! What if the mage put the crabs there for some other reason?"

"What if? What if? I told you this would be very dangerous. But the rewards are worth the risk."

She stiffened. That strange cry had come again. And it was definitely nearer.

"It may be hunting us," Smhee said. "It could have smelled the blood of the ape."

"What is it?" she said, trying to keep her teeth from chattering.

"I don't know. We're downwind from it, but it sounds as if it'll soon be here. Good! That will put some stiffening in our backbone, heat our livers. Let's go now!"

So, he was scared, too. Somehow, that made her feel a little better.

They stuck their legs down into the chilly water. They found no bottom. Then Smhee ran around to the inland side and bent down. He probed with his hand around the edge.

"The rock goes about a foot down, then curves inward," he said. "I'll wager that this was once a pothole of some sort. When Kemren came here, he carved out tunnels to the cave it led to and then somehow filled it with river water."

He stood up. The low strange cry was definitely closer now. She thought she saw something huge in the darkness to the north, but it could be her imagination.

"Oh, Igil!" she said. "I have to urinate!"

"Do it in the water. If it smells your urine on the land, it'll know a human's been here. And it might call others of its kind. Or make such an uproar the Raggah will come."

He let himself down into the water and clung to the stony edge.

"Get in! It's cold but not as cold as death!"

She let herself down to his side. She had to bite her lip to keep from gasping with shock.

He gave her a few hurried instructions and said, "May Weda Krizhtawn smile upon us!"

And he was gone.

10

She took a deep breath while she was considering getting out of the pool and running like a lizard chased by a fox to the river and swimming across it. But instead she dived, and as Smhee had told her to do, swam close to the ceiling of rock. She was blind here even with her eyes open, and, though she thought mostly about drowning, she had room to think about the crabs.

Presently, when her lungs were about to burst and her head rang and the violent urge to get air was about to make her breathe, her flailing hand was grasped by something. The next instant, she was pulled into air.

There was darkness all about. Her gaspings mingled with Smhee's.

He said, between the wheezings, "There's plenty of airspace between the water and the ceiling. I dived down and came up as fast as I could out of the water, and I couldn't touch the rock above."

After they'd recovered their wind, he said, "You tread water while I go back. I want to see how far back this space goes."

She didn't have to wait long. She heard his swimming—she hoped it was his and not something else—and she called out softly when he was near. He stopped and said, "There's plenty of air until just before the tunnel or cave reaches the pool. Then you have to dive under a downthrust ledge of rock. I didn't go back out, of course, not with that creature out there. But I'm sure my estimate of distance is right."

She followed him in the darkness until he said, "Here's another downthrust."

She felt where he indicated. The stone did not go more than six inches before ceasing.

"Does the rope or your boots bother you any?" he said. "If they're too heavy, get rid of them."

"I'm all right."

"Good. I'll be back soon—if things are as I think they are."

She started to call to him to wait for her, but it was too late. She clung to the rough stone with her fingertips, moving her legs now and then. The silence was oppressive; it rang in her ears. And once she gasped when something touched her thigh.

The rope and boots did drag her down, and she was thinking of at least getting rid of the rope when something struck her belly. She grabbed it with one hand to keep it from biting her and with the other reached for her dagger. She went under water of course, and then she realized that she wasn't being attacked. Smhee, diving back, had run into her.

Their heads cleared the surface. Smhee laughed.

"Were you as frightened as I? I thought sure a bengil had me!"

Gasping, she said, "Never mind. What's over there?"

"More of the same. Another air space for perhaps a hundred feet. Then another downcropping."

He clung to the stone for a moment. Then he said, "Have you noticed how fresh the air is? There's a very slight movement of it, too."

She had noticed but hadn't thought about it. Her experiences with watery caves was nil until now.

"I'm sure that each of these caves is connected to a hole which brings in fresh air from above," he said. "Would the mage have gone to all this trouble unless he meant to use this for escape?"

He did something. She heard him breathing heavily, and then there was a splash.

"I pulled myself up the rock and felt around," he said. "There is a hole up there to let air from the next cave into this one. And I'll wager that there is a hole in the ceiling. But it must curve so that light doesn't come in. Or maybe it doesn't curve. If it were day above, we might see the hole."

He dived; Masha followed him. They swam ahead then, putting their right hands out from side to side to feel the wall. When they came to the next downcropping, they went through beneath it at once.

At the end of this cave they felt a rock ledge that sloped gently upward. They crawled out onto it. She heard him fumbling around and then he said, "Don't cry out. I'm lighting a torch."

The light nevertheless startled her. It came from

the tip of a slender stick of wood in his hand. By its illumination she saw him apply it to the end of a small pine torch. This caught fire, giving them more area of vision. The fire on the stick went out. He put the stick back into the opened belt-bag.

"We don't want to leave any evidence we've been here," he said softly. "I didn't mention that this bag contains many things, including another waterproof bag. But we must hurry. The torch won't last long, and I've got just one more."

They stood up and moved ahead. A few feet beyond the original area first illuminated by the torch were some dark bulks. Boats. Twelve of them, with light wood frameworks and skin-coverings. Each could hold three people. By them were paddles.

Smhee took out a dagger and began ripping the skins. Masha helped him until only one boat was left undamaged.

He said, "There must be entrances cut into the stone sections dividing the caves we just came through. I'll wager they're on the left-hand side as you come in. Anyone swimming in would naturally keep to the right wall and so wouldn't see the archways. The ledges where the crabs nest must also be on the left. Remember that when we come back. But I'd better find out for sure. We want to know exactly how to get out when the time comes."

He set his torch in a socket in the front of the boat and pushed the boat down the slope and into the water. While Masha held the narrow craft steady, he got into it. She stood on the shore, feeling lonely with all that darkness behind her while she watched him by the light of the brand. Within a few minutes he came back, grinning.

"I was right! There's an opening cut into the stone division. It's just high enough for a boat to pass through if you duck down."

They dragged the boat back up onto the ledge. The cave ended about a hundred feet from the water. To the right was a U-shaped entrance. By its side were piles of torches and flint and steel and punk boxes. Smhee lit two, gave one to Masha, and then returned to the edge of the ledge to extinguish his little one.

"I think the mage has put all his magic spiders inside the caves," he said. "They'd require too much energy to maintain on the outside. The further away they are from him, the more energy he has to use to maintain them. The energy required increases according to the square of the distance."

Masha didn't ask him what he meant by "square."

"Stick close to me. Not just for your sake. For mine also. As I said, the mage will not have considered women trying to get into his place, so his powers are directed against men only. At least, I hope they are. That way he doesn't have to use as much energy on his magic."

"Do you want me to lead?" she said, hoping he wouldn't say yes.

"If you had as much experience as I, I wouldn't hesitate a moment. But you're still an apprentice. If we get out of here alive, you will be on your way to being a master."

They went up the steps cut out of the stone. At

the top was another archway. Smhee stopped before it and held his torch high to look within it. But he kept his head outside it.

"Ha!"

11

He motioned her to come to his side. She saw that the interior of the deep doorway was grooved. Above the grooves was the bottom of a slab of stone.

"If the mechanism is triggered, that slab will crash down and block off anyone chasing the mage," he said. "And it'd crush anyone in the portal. Maybe. . . ."

He looked at the wall surrounding the archway but could find nothing.

"The release mechanism must be in the other room. A time-delay device."

He got as near to the entrance as he could without going into it, and he stuck his torch through the opening.

"I can't see it. It must be just around the corner. But I do see what looks like webs."

Masha breathed deeply.

"If they're real spiders, they'll be intimidated by the torches," he said. "Unless the mage has conditioned them not to be or uses magic to overcome their natural fear. The magic spiders won't pay any attention to the flame."

She thought that it was all very uncertain, but she did not comment.

He bent down and peered at the stone floor just

beyond the doorway. He turned. "Here. Your young eyes are better than my old ones. Can you see a thread or anything like it raised above the floor just beyond the door?"

She said, "No, I can't."

"Nevertheless."

He threw his torch through the doorway. At his order, she got down with her cheek against the stone and looked against the flame.

She rose, saying, "I can see a very thin line about an inch above the floor. It could be a cord."

"Just as I thought. An old Sharranpip trick."

He stepped back after asking her to get out of the way. And he leaped through the doorway and came down past the cord. She followed. As they picked up their torches, he said pointing, "There are the mechanisms. One is the time-delay. The other releases the door so it'll fall behind the first who enters and trap him. Anyone following will be crushed by the slab."

After telling her to keep an eye on the rest of the room, he examined the array of wheels, gears, and counterweights and the rope that ran from one device through a hole in the ceiling.

"The rope is probably attached to an alarm system above," he said. "Very well. I know how to actuate both of these. If you should by any foul chance come back alone, all you have to do is to jump through and then throw a torch or something on that cord. The door will come down and block off your pursuers. But get outside as fast as you can because. . . ."

Masha said, "I know why."

"Good woman. Now, the spiders."

The things came before the webs were clearly

visible in the light. She had expected to see the light reflected redly in their eyes, but they weren't. Their many eyes were huge and purplish and cold. They scuttled forward, waving the foremost pair of legs, then backed away as Smhee waved his torch at them. Masha walked half-turned away from him so that she could use the brand to scare away any attack from the rear or side.

Suddenly, something leaped from the edge of the darkness and soared toward her. She thrust the brand at it. But the creature seemed to go through the torch.

It landed on her arm and seized the hand that held the torch. She had clenched her teeth to keep from screaming if something like this happened. But she didn't even think of voicing her terror and disgust. She closed her hand on the body of the thing to crush it, and the fingers felt nothing.

The next moment, the spider disappeared.

She told Smhee what had happened.

"Thanks be to Klooshna!" he said. "You are invulnerable to them. If you weren't, you'd be swelling up now!"

"But what if it'd been a real spider?" she said as she kept waving her torch at the monsters that circled them. "I didn't know until my hand closed on it that it was not real."

"Then you'd be dying. But the fact that it ignored the brand showed you what it really was. You realized that even if you didn't think consciously about it."

They came to another archway. While she threw her torch through it and got down to look for another thread, Smhee held off the spiders.

"There doesn't seem to be any," she said.

"Seem isn't good enough," he said. "Hah, back, you creatures of evil! Look closely! Can you see any thin lines in the floor itself? Minute cracks?"

After a few seconds, she said, "Yes. They form a square."

"A trapdoor to drop us into a pit," he said. "You jump past it. And let's hope there isn't another trap just beyond it."

She said that she'd need a little run to clear the line. He charged the spiders, waving his torch furiously, and they backed away. When she called to him that she was safe, he turned and ran and leaped. A hairy, many-legged thing dashed through the entrance after him. Masha stepped up to the line and thrust her brand at it. It stopped. Behind it were masses that moved, shadows of solidity.

Smhee leaped toward the foremost one and jammed the burning red of his brand into the head. The stink of charred flesh assailed their nostrils. It ran backward but was stopped by those behind it. Then they retreated, and the thing, its eyes burned out, began running around and around, finally disappearing into the darkness. The others were now just beyond the doorway in the other cave. Smhee threw his torch into it.

"That'll keep them from coming through!" he said, panting. "I should have brought some extra torches, but even the greatest mind sometimes slips. Notice how the weight of those spiders didn't make the trapdoor drop? It must have a minimum limit. You only weigh eighty-five pounds. Maybe . . . ?"

"Forget it," she said.

"Right you are," he said, grinning. "But Masha, if you are to be a master thief, you must think of everything."

She thought of reminding him about the extra torches he'd forgotten but decided not to. They went on ahead through an enormous cavern and came to a tunnel. From its dark mouth streamed a stink like a newly opened tomb. And they heard the cry that was half-grunt, half-squall.

Smhee halted. "I hate to go into that tunnel. But we must. You look upward for holes in the ceiling, and I'll look everwhere else."

The stone, however, looked solid. When they were halfway down the bore, they were blasted with a tremendous growling and roaring.

"Lions?" Masha said.

"No. Bears."

12

At the opposite end were two gigantic animals, their eyes gleaming redly in the light, their fangs a dull white.

The two intruders advanced after waiting for the bears to charge. But these stayed by the doorway, though they did not cease their thunderous roaring nor their slashes at the air with their paws.

"The bears were making the strange cry," she said. "I've seen dancing bears in the bazaars, but I never heard them make a noise like that. Nor were they near as large."

He said, "They've got chains around their necks. Come on."

When they were within a few feet of the beasts, they stopped. The stench was almost overpowering now, and they were deafened by the uproar in the narrowness of the tunnel.

Smhee told her to hold her torch steady. He opened his belt-bag and pulled out two lengths of bamboo pipe and joined them. Then, from a small wooden case, he cautiously extracted a feathered dart. He inserted it in one and raised the blowpipe almost to his lips.

"There's enough poison on the tip of the dart to kill a dozen men," he said. "However, I doubt that it would do much harm, if any, if the dart sticks in their thick fat. So. . . ."

He waited a long time, the pipe now at his lips. Then, his cheeks swelled, and the dart shot out. The bear to the right, roaring even louder, grabbed at the missile stuck in its left eye. Smhee fitted another dart into the pipe and took a step closer. The monster on the left lunged against the restraining collar and chain. Smhee shot the second dart into its tongue.

The first beast struck fell to one side, its paws waving, and its roars subsided. The other took longer to become quiet, but presently both were snoring away.

"Let's hope they die," Smhee said. "I doubt we'll have time to shoot them again when we come back."

Masha thought that a more immediate concern was that the roaring might have alarmed the mage's servants.

They went through a large cavern, the floor of which was littered with human, cattle, and goat skeletons and bear dung. They breathed through their mouths until they got to an exit. This was a doorway which led to a flight of steps. At the top of the steps was another entrance with a closed massive wooden door. Affixed to one side was a great wooden bar.

"Another hindrance to pursuers," Smhee said. "Which will, in our case, be the Raggah."

After a careful inspection of the door, he gripped its handle and slowly opened it. Freshly oiled, it swung noiselessly. They went out into a very large room illuminated by six great torches at one end. Here streams of water ran out from holes in the ceiling and down wooden troughs and onto many wooden wheels set between metal uprights.

Against the right-hand side of the far wall was another closed door as massive as the first. It, too, could be barred shut.

Unlike the bare walls of the other caves, these were painted with many strange symbols.

"There's magic here," Smhee said. "I smell it."

He strode to the pool in which were set the wheels. The wheels went around and around impelled by the downpouring water. Masha counted aloud. Twelve.

"A magical number," Smhee said.

They were set in rows of threes. At one end of the axle of each were attached some gears which in turn were fixed to a shaft that ran into a box under the wheel. Smhee reached out to the nearest wheel from the pool edge and stopped it. Then he released it and opened the lid of the box beneath the wheel. Masha looked past him into the interior of the box. She saw a bewildering array of tiny gears and shafts. The shafts were connected to more gears at the axle end of tiny wheels on uprights.

Smhee stopped the wheel again and spun it against the force of the waterfall. The mechanism inside started working backward.

Smhee smiled. He closed the box and went to the door and barred it. He walked swiftly to the other side of the pool. There was a large box on the floor by it. He opened it and removed some metal pliers and wrenches.

"Help me get those wheels off their stands," he said.

"Why?"

"I'll explain while we work." He looked around. "Kemren would have done better to have set human guards here. But I suppose he thought that no one would ever get this far. Or, if they did, they'd not have the slightest idea what the wheels are for."

He told her what she was to do with the wheels, and they waded into the pool. The water only came to their ankles; a wide drain in the center ensured against overflow.

Masha didn't like being drenched, but she was sure that it would be worthwhile.

"These boxes contain devices which convert the mechanical power of the water-driven wheels to magical power," he said. "There are said to be some in the temple of Weda Krizhtawn, but I was too lowly to be allowed near them. However, I heard the high priests talking about them. They sometimes got careless in the presence of us lowly ones. Anyway, we were bound by vows to keep silent.

"I don't know exactly what these particular wheels are for. But they must be providing energy for whatever magic he's using. Part of the energy, anyway."

She didn't really understand what he was talking about, though she had an inkling. She worked steadily, ignoring the wetting and removed a wheel. Then she turned it around and reattached it.

The wheel bore symbols on each of the paddles set along its rims. There were also symbols painted on its side.

Each wheel seemed to have the same symbols but in a different sequence.

When their work was done, Smhee said, "I don't know what their reversal will do. But I'll wager that it won't be for Kemren's good. We must hurry now. If he's sensitive to the inflow-outflow of his magic, he'll know something's wrong."

She thought that it would be better not to have aroused the mage. However, Smhee was the master; she, the apprentice.

Smhee started to turn away from the wheels but stopped.

"Look!"

His finger pointed at the wheels.

"Well?"

"Don't you see something strange?"

It was a moment before she saw what had made her uneasy without realizing why. No water was spilling from the paddles down to the pool. The water just seemed to disappear after striking them.

She looked wonderingly from them to him. "I see what you mean."

He spread out his hands. "I don't know what's happening. I'm not a mage or a sorcerer. But . . . that water has to be going some place."

They put their boots back on, and he unshot the bar of the door. It led to another flight of steps, ending in another door. They went down a corridor the walls of which were bare stone. But there were also lit torches set in brackets on them.

At the end of the corridor they came to a round room. Light came down from torches; the room was actually a tall shaft. Looking up from the bottom, they could see a black square outlined narrowly by bright light at its top.

13

Voices came from above.

"It has to be a lift," Smhee whispered. He said something in his native tongue that sounded like a curse.

"We're stuck here until the lift comes down."

He'd no sooner spoken than they heard a squeal as of metal, and the square began descending slowly.

"We're in luck!" Smhee said. "Unless they're sending down men to see what's happened to the wheels."

They retreated through the door at the other end. Here they waited with their blades ready. Smhee kept the door open a crack.

"There are only two. Both are carrying bags and one has a haunch of meat. They're going to feed the bears and the spiders!"

Masha wondered how the men intended to get past the bears to the arachnids. But maybe the bears attacked only strangers.

"One man has a torch," he said.

The door swung open, and a Raggah wearing a red-and-black striped robe stepped through. Smhee drove his dagger into the man's throat. Masha came out from behind the door and thrust her sword through the other man's neck.

After dragging the bodies into the room, they took off the robes and put them on.

"It's too big for me," she said. "I look ridiculous."

"Cut off the bottom," he said, but she had already started doing that.

"What about the blood on the robes?"

"We could wash it out, but then we'd look strange with dripping robes. We'll just have to take a chance."

They left the bodies lying on the floor and went back to the lift. This was an open-sided cage built of light (and expensive) imported bamboo. The top was closed, but it had a trap door. A rope descended through it.

They looked up but could see no one looking down.

Smhee pulled on the rope, and a bell clanged. No one was summoned by it, though.

"Whoever pulls this up is gone. No doubt he, or they, are not expecting the two to return so early. Well, we must climb up the pull-ropes. I hope you're up to it."

"Better than you, fat one," Masha said.

He smiled. "We'll see."

Masha, however, pulled herself up faster than he. She had to climb up onto the beam to which the wheel was attached and then crawl along it and swing herself down into the entrance. Smhee caught her as she landed on the edge, though she didn't need his help.

They were in a hallway the walls of which were hung with costly rugs and along which was expensive furniture. Oil lamps gave an adequte illumination.

"Now comes the hard part," he said between deep breaths. "There is a staircase at each end of this hall. Which leads to the mage?"

"I'd take that one," she said, pointing.

"Why?"

"I don't exactly know why. I just feel that it's the right one."

He smiled, saying, "That's as good a reason as any for me. Let's go."

Their hands against each other inside their voluminous sleeves, but holding daggers, the hoods pulled out to shadow their faces, they walked up the stairs. These curved to end in another hall, even more luxuriously furnished. There were closed doors along it, but Smhee wouldn't open them.

"You can wager that the mage will have a guard or guards outside his apartment."

They went up another flight of steps in time to see the back of a Raggah going down the hall. At the corner, Masha looked around it. No one in sight. She stepped out, and just then a Raggah came around the corner at the right-hand end of the hall. She slowed, imperceptibly, she hoped, then resumed her stride. She heard Smhee behind her saying, "When you get close, within ten feet of her, move quickly to one side."

She did so just as the Raggah, a woman, noticed the blood on the front of her robe. The woman opened her mouth, and Smhee's thrown knife plunged into her belly. She fell forward with a thump. The fat man withdrew his knife, wiped it on the robe, and they dragged her through a doorway. The room was unlit. They dropped her near the door and went out, closing it behind them.

They went down to the end of the hall from which the woman had come and looked around the corner. There was a very wide and high-ceilinged corridor there, and from a great doorway halfway down it came much light, many voices, and the odor of cooking. Masha hadn't realized until then how hungry she was; saliva ran in her mouth.

"The other way," Smhee said, and he trotted toward the staircase. At its top, Masha looked around the corner. Halfway down the length of this hall a man holding a spear stood before a door. By his side crouched a huge black wolfish dog on a leash.

She told Smhee what she'd seen.

As excited as she'd ever seen him, he said, "He must be guarding the mage's rooms!"

Then, in a calmer tone, "He isn't aware of what we've done. He must be with a woman or a man. Sexual intercourse, you know, drains more out of a person than just physical energy. Kemren won't be sensitive to the wheels just now."

Masha didn't see any reason to comment on

that. She said, "The dog didn't notice me, but we can't get close before he alerts the guard."

Masha looked behind her. The hall was still empty. But what if the mage had ordered a meal to be delivered soon?

She told Smhee what she'd just thought. After a brief consultation, they went back down the stairs to the hall. There they got an exquisitely silver-chased tray and put some small painted dishes and gold pitchers on it. These they covered with a golden cloth, the worth of which was a thousand times more than Masha could make if she worked as dentist and midwife until she was a hundred years old.

With this assemblage, which they hoped would look like a late supper tray, they went to the hall. Masha had said that if the mage was with a sexual partner, it would look more authentic if they carried two trays. But even before Smhee voiced his objections, she had thought that he had to have his hands free. Besides, one tray clattering on the floor was bad enough, though its impact would be softened by the thick rug.

The guard seemed half-asleep, but the dog, rising to its feet and growling, fully awakened him. He turned toward them, though not without a glance at the other end of the hall first. Masha, in front of Smhee, walked as if she had a right to be there. The guard held the spear pointing at them in one hand and said something in his harsh back-of-the-throat speech.

Smhee uttered a string of nonsense syllables in a low but equally harsh voice. The guard said something. And then Masha stepped to one side, dropping the tray. She bent over, muttering something guttural, as if she were apologizing for her clumsiness.

She couldn't see Smhee, but she knew that he was snatching the blowpipe from his sleeve and applying it to his lips. She came up from her bent position, her sword leaping out of her scabbard, and she ran toward the dog. It bounded toward her, the guard having released the leash. She got the blade out from the leather just in time and rammed it into the dog's open mouth as it sprang soundlessly toward her throat. The blade drove deep into its throat, but she went backward from its weight and fell onto the floor.

The sword had been torn from her grip, but the dog was heavy and unmoving on her chest. She pushed him off though he must have weighed as much as she. She rolled over and got quickly, but trembling, to her feet. The guard was sitting down, his back against the wall. One hand clutched the dart stuck in his cheek. His eyes were open but glazing. In a few seconds the hand fell away. He slumped to one side, and his bowels moved noisily.

The dog lay with the upper length of the sword sticking from its mouth. His tongue extended from the jaws, bloody, seeming almost an independent entity, a stricken worm.

Smhee grabbed the bronze handle of the door.

"Pray for us, Masha! If he's barred the door on the inside . . . !"

The door swung open.

Smhee bounded in, the dead man's spear in his hands. Masha, following, saw a large room the air of which was green and reeking of incense. The walls were covered with tapestries, and the heavy dark furniture was ornately carved with demon's heads. They paused to listen and heard nothing except a faint burbling noise.

"Get the bodies in quickly!" Smhee said, and they dragged the corpses inside. They expected the dreaded mage to walk in at any time, but he still had not appeared when they shut the door.

Smhee whispered, "Anyone coming by will notice that there is no guard."

They entered the next room cautiously. This was even larger and was obviously the bedroom. The bed was huge and round and on a platform with three steps. It was covered with a rich scarlet material brocaded in gold.

"He must be working in his laboratory," Smhee whispered.

They slowly opened the door to the next room.

The burbling became louder then. Masha saw that it proceeded from a great glass vessel shaped like an upside-down cone. A black-green liquid simmered in it, and large bubbles rose from it and passed out the open end. Beneath it was a brazier filled with glowing coals. From the ceiling above a metal vent admitted the fumes.

The floor was mosaic marble in which were set pentagrams and nonagrams. From the center of one rose a wisp of evil-smelling smoke. A few seconds later, the smoke ceased.

There were many tables holding other mysterious equipment and racks holding long thick rolls of parchment and papyrus. In the middle of the room was a very large desk of some shiny reddish wood. Before it was a chair of the same wood, its arms and back carved with human-headed dragons.

The mage, clad in a purple silk robe which was embroidered with golden centaurs and gryphons, was in the chair. His face was on the desk, and his arms were spread out on it. He stank of rancid butter.

Smhee approached him slowly, then grabbed the thin curly hair of the mage's topknot and raised the head.

There was water on the desk, and water ran from the dead man's nose and mouth.

"What happened to him?" she whispered.

Smhee did not reply at once. He lifted the body from the chair and placed it on the floor. Then he knelt and thumped the mage's chest.

The fat man rose smiling.

"What happened is that the reversal of the wheels' motion caused the water which should have fallen off the paddles to go instead to the mage. The conversion of physical energy to magical energy was reversed."

He paused.

"The water went into the mage's body. He drowned!"

He raised his eyes and said, "Blessed is Weda Krizhtawn, the goddess of water! She has her revenge through her faithful servant, Rhandhee Ghee!"

He looked at Masha. "That is my true name, Rhandhee Ghee. And I have revenged the goddess and her worshippers. The defiler and thief is dead, and I can go home now. Perhaps she will forgive some of my sins because I have fulfilled her intent. I won't go to hell, surely. I will suffer in a purgatory for a while and then, cleansed with pain, will go to the lowest heaven. And then, perhaps. . . ."

"You forget that I am to be paid," she said.

"No, I didn't. Look. He wears golden rings set with jewels of immense value. Take them, and let's be off."

She shuddered and said, "No. They would bring misfortune."

"Very well. The next room should be his treasure chamber."

It was. There were chests and boxes filled with emeralds, diamonds, turquoises, rubies, and many other jewels. There were golden and silver idols and statuettes. There was enough wealth to purchase a dozen of the lesser cities of the empire and all their citizens.

But she could only take what she could carry and not be hampered in the leaving.

Exclaiming ecstatics, she reached toward a coffer sparkling with diamonds.

At her touch, the jewels faded and were gone.

14

She cried out in anguish.

"They're products of his magic!" Smhee said. "Set here to fool thieves. Benna must have taken one of these, though how he got here and then away I've no idea! The jewel did not disappear because the mage was alive and his powers were strong. But I'll wager that not long after the rat carried the jewel off, it disappeared. That's why

the searchers found no jewel though they turned
the city upside down and inside out!"

"There's plenty of other stuff to take!" she said.

"No, too heavy. But he must have put his real
jewels somewhere. The next room!"

But there were no other rooms.

"Don't you believe it," Smhee said. He tore
down the tapestries and began tapping on the
walls, which were of a dense-grained purplish
wood erected over the stone. Presently, he said,
"Ah!" and he moved his hands swiftly over the
area. "Here's a hole in the wood just big enough to
admit my little finger. I put my finger in thus, and
I pull thus, and thus . . . !"

A section of the wood swung out. Masha got a
burning lamp and thrust it into the room beyond.
The light fell on ten open chests and twenty open
coffers. Jewels sparkled.

They entered.

"Take two handsful," Smhee said. "That's all.
We aren't out of here yet."

Masha untied the little bag attached to her belt,
hesitated, then scooped out enough to fill the bag.
It almost tore her heart apart to leave the rest, but
she knew that Smhee's advice was wisdom.
Perhaps, some day, she could come back for more.
No. That would be stupid. She had far more than
enough.

On the way out, Smhee stopped. He opened the
mage's robe and revealed a smooth-shaven chest
on which was tatooed a representation of a fearful
six-armed four-legged being with a glaring long-
tusked face. He cut around this and peeled the
skin off and put it rolled and folded into a small jar
of ointment. Replacing the jar in his bag, he rose,

saying, "The goddess knows that I would not lie about his death. But this will be the proof if any is demanded."

"Maybe we should look for the mage's secret exit," she said. "That way, we won't run into the Raggah."

"No. At any moment someone may see that the guard is missing. Besides, the mage will have put traps in his escape route, and we might not elude those."

They made their way back to the corridor of the lift shaft without being observed. But two men stood in front of the entrance to the lift. They were talking excitedly and looking down the shaft. Then one ran down the corridor, away from the corner behind which the two intruders watched.

"Going to get help before they venture down to find out why the two feeders haven't come back," Smhee muttered.

The man who'd stayed was looking down the shaft. Masha and Smhee took him from behind, one cutting the throat, the other stabbing him in the back. They let themselves down on the ropes and then cut them before going down through the open trap door. But as they left the cage, a spear shot through the trap door and thudded point-first into the floor. Men shouted above.

"They'll bring ropes and come down on those," Smhee said. "And they'll send others outside to catch us when we come out of the pool. Run, but remember the traps!"

And the spiders, she thought. And the crabs. I hope the bears are dead.

They were. The spiders, all real now that the mage was dead, were alive. These were driven back by the torches the two had paused to light, and they got to the skin-boat. They pushed this out and began paddling with desperation. The craft went through the first arch and then through the second. To their right now were some ledges on which were masses of pale-white things with stalked eyes and clacking pincers. The crabs. The two directed their boat away from these, but the writhing masses suddenly became individual figures leaping outward and splashing into the dark water. Very quickly, the ledges were bare. There was no sign of the monsters, but the two knew that these were swimming toward them.

They paddled even faster, though it had not seemed possible until then. And then the prow of the boat bumped into the wall.

"Swim for it!" Smhee bellowed, his voice rebounding from the far walls and high ceilings of the cave.

Masha feared entering the water; she expected to be seized by those huge claws. But she went over, the boat tipping, and dived.

Something did touch her leg as she went under the stone downcropping. Then her head was above the surface of the pool and Smhee's was beside her.

They scrambled out onto the hard stone. Behind them came the clacking, but none of the crabs tried to leave the pool.

The sky was black; thunder bellowed in the north; lightning traced white veins. A wind blew, chilling them in their wet clothes.

They ran toward the dugout but not in a straight line since they had to avoid the bushes with the poisonous thorns. Before they reached it, rain fell.

They dragged the craft into the river and got aboard. Above them lightning cracked across the sky. Another bolt struck shortly thereafter, revealing two bears and a number of men behind them.

"They can't catch us now!" Smhee yelled. "But they'll be going back to put their horses on rafts. They'll go all the way into Sanctuary itself to get us!"

Save your breath, Masha thought. I know all that.

The wind-struck river was rough now, but they got through the waves to the opposite shore. They climbed panting up the ridge and found their horses, whinnying from fear of the lightning. When they got to the bottom of the ridge, they sped away, their passage fitfully lit by the dreadful whiteness that seemed to smash all around them. They kept their horses at a gallop for a mile, then eased them up.

"There's no way they can catch us!" Smhee shouted through the thunder. "We've got too much of a head-start!"

Dawn came. The rain stopped. The clouds cleared away; the hot winter sun of the desert rose. They stopped at the hut where they had slept, and the horses rested, and they ate bread and cheese.

"Three more hours will bring us within sight of Sanctuary," the fat man said. "We'll get your family aboard the *Swordfish*, and the Raggah can search for us in vain."

He paused, then said, "What do you intend to do about Eevroen?"

"Nothing," she said. "If he gets in my way I'll brain him again."

He laughed so much he choked on his bread. When he'd cleared his throat, he said, "You are some woman! Brave as the goddess makes them! And supple in mind, too! If I were not vowed to chastity, I would woo you! I may be forty-five and fat, but. . . ."

He stopped to stare down at his hand. His face froze into an expression of horror.

Masha became equally paralyzed.

A small purple spider was on Smhee's hand.

"Move slowly," he said softly through rigid lips. "I dare not move. Slap it when you've got your hand within a few inches of it."

She got up and took a step toward him. Where had the creature come from? There were no webs in the hut. Had it come from outside and crawled upon him?

She took another step, leaned over, and brought her hand slowly down at an angle toward the thing. Its eyes were black and motionless, seemingly unaware of her presence.

Maybe it's not poisonous, she thought.

Suddenly, Smhee screamed, and he crushed the spider with his other hand. He leaped up then, brushing off the tiny body.

"It bit me! It bit me!"

The dark swelling had started.

"It's not one of the mage's creatures," she said. "Its venom may not be deadly."

"It's the mage's," he said. His face was white under the heavy pigment.

"It must have crawled into my bag. It couldn't have done it when we were on the way to the mage's rooms. It must have gotten in when I opened the bag to skin off the tattoo."

He howled. "The mage has gotten *his* revenge!"

"You don't know that," she said, but she was certain that it was as Smhee had said. She removed her small belt-bag and carefully poured out the jewels. But that was all it contained.

"It's beginning to hurt," Smhee said. "I can make it back to the city. Benna did, and he was bitten many times. But I know these spiders. I will die as surely as he did, though I will take longer. There is no antidote."

He sat down, and for a while he rocked back and forth, eyes closed, moaning. Then he said, "Masha, there is no sense in my going on with you. But, since I have made it possible for you to be as wealthy as a queen, I beg you to do one favor for me. If it is not too much to ask."

"What is that?" she said.

"Take the jar containing the tattooed skin to Sharranpip. And there tell our story to the highest priest of Weda Krizhtawn. He will pray for me to her, and a great tombstone will be erected for me in the courtyard of the peacocks, and pilgrims will come from all over Sharranpip and the islands around and will pray for me. But if you don't want . . ."

Masha knelt and kissed him on the mouth. He felt cold.

She stood up and said, "I promise you that I will do that. That, as you said, is the least I can do."

He smiled, though it cost him to do it.

"Good. Then I can die in peace. Go. May Weda Krizhtawn bless you."

"But the Raggah . . . they will torture you!"

"No. This bag contains a small vial of poison.

They will find only a corpse. If they find me at all."

Masha burst into tears, but she took the jar, and after kissing Smhee again, she rode off, his horse trotting behind hers.

At the top of the hill she stopped to look behind at the hut.

Far off, coming swiftly, was a dark mass. The Raggah.

She turned away and urged her horse into a gallop.

GODDESS

David Drake

"By Savankala and the Son!" Regli swore, "why can't she bear and be done with it? And why does she demand to see her brother but won't see me?" The young lord's sweat-stained tunic looked as if it had been slept in. Indeed, Regli would have slept in it if he had slept any during the two days he had paced outside the bedroom, now couching room, of his wife. Regli's hands repeatedly flexed the shank of his riding crop. There were those—and not all of them women— who would have said that agitation heightened Regli's already notably good looks, but he had no mind for such nonsense now. Not with his heir at risk!

"Now, now," said Doctor Mernorad, patting the silver-worked lapels of his robe. The older man prided himself as much on his ability to see both sides of a question as he did on his skill at physic—though neither ability seemed much valued today in Regli's townhouse. "One can't hurry the gods, you know. The child will be born when Sabellia says it should be. Any attempt to hasten matters would be sacrilege as well as foolishness. Why, you know there are some . . . I don't know what word to use, *practitioners,* who use forceps in a delivery? Forceps of *metal!* It's disgusting. I tell you, Prince Kadakithis makes a great noise about smugglers and thieves; but if he wanted to clean up a *real* evil in Sanctuary, he'd start with the so-called doctors who don't have proper connections with established temples."

"Well, damn it," Regli snapped, "you've got a 'proper connection' to the Temple of Sabellia in Ranke itself, and you can't tell me why my wife's been two days in labor. And if any of those bitch-midwives who've stood shift in there know"—he gestured toward the closed door— "they sure aren't telling anybody." Regli knuckled the fringe of blond whiskers sprouting on his jawbone. His wealth and breeding had made him a person of some importance even in Ranke. Here in Sanctuary, where he served as Master of the Scrolls for the royal governor, he was even less accustomed to being balked. The fact that Fate, in the form of his wife's abnormally-prolonged labor, was balking him infuriated Regli to the point that he needed to lash out at something. "I can't imagine why Samlane insists on seeing no one but midwives from the Temple of Heqt," he continued, snapping his riding crop at specks on the mosaic walls. "That place has no very good reputation, I'm told. Not at all."

"Well, you have to remember that your wife is from Cirdon," said Mernorad reasonably, keeping a wary eye on his patron's lash. "Though they've been forty years under the Empire, worship of the Trinity hasn't really caught on there. I've investigated the matter, and these women do have proper midwives' licenses. There's altogether too much loose talk among laymen about 'this priest-hood' or 'that particular healer' not being compe-tent. I assure you that the medical profession keeps very close watch on itself. The worst to be said on the record—the only place it counts—about the Temple of Heqt here in Sanctuary is that thirty years ago the chief priest disappeared. Un-fortunate, of course, but nothing to discredit the temple."

The doctor paused, absently puffing out one cheek, then the other, so that his curly white side-burns flared. "Though I do think," he added, "that since you have engaged me anyway, that their midwives might consult with one of my, well, stature."

The door between the morning room and the hall was ajar. A page in Regli's livery of red and gold tapped the jamb deferentially. The two Ran-kans looked up, past the servant to the heavier man beyond in the hall. "My lord," said the page bowing, "Samlor hil Samt."

Samlor reached past the servant to swing the door fully open before Regli nodded entry. He had unpinned his dull travelling cloak and draped it over his left arm, close to his body where it almost hid the sheathed fighting knife. Northern fashion, Samlor wore boots and breeches with a long-sleeved over-tunic gathered at the wrists. The garments were plain and would have been a nondescript brown had they not been covered with white road dust. His sole jewelry was a neck-thonged silver medallion stamped with the toad face of the goddess Heqt. Samlor's broad face was deep red, the complexion of a man who will never tan but who is rarely out of the sun. He cleared his throat, rubbed his mouth with the back of his big fist, and said, "My sister sent for me. She's in there, the servant says?" He gestured.

"Why yes," said Regli, looking a little puzzled to find the quirt in his hands. The doctor was getting up from his chair. "Why, you're much older, aren't you?" the lord continued inanely.

"Fourteen years," Samlor agreed sourly, stepping past the two Rankans to the bedroom door. He tossed his cloak over one of the ivory-inlaid tables along the wall. "You'd have thought the folks would have guessed something when the five between us were still-born, but no, Hell, no. . . . And much luck the bitch ever brought them."

"I say!" Regli gasped at the stocky man's back. "You're speaking of my wife!"

Samlor turned, his knuckles already poised to rap on the door panel. "You had a choice," he said. "I'm the one who was running caravans through the mountains, trying to keep the Noble House of Kodrix afloat long enough to marry its daughter well—and her slutting about so that the folks had to go to Ranke to get offers from anybody but a brothel keeper. No wonder they drink." He hammered on the door.

Mernorad tugged the white-faced Regli back. "Master Samlor," the physician said sharply.

"It's Samlor, dammit!" the Cirdonian was shouting in response to a question from within the bedroom. "I didn't ride 500 miles to stand at a damned doorway, either." He turned to Mernorad. "Yes?" he asked.

The physician pointed. "Your weapon," he said. "The lady Samlane has been distraught. Not an uncommon thing for women in her condition, of course. She, ah, attempted to have her condition, ah, terminated some months ago. . . . Fortunately, we got word before. . . . And even though she has since been watched at all times, she, ah, with a spoon. . . . Well. I'd simply rather that—things like your knife—not be where the Lady could snatch them, lest something untoward occur. . . ."

Within the bedroom, a bronze bar creaked as it was lifted from the door slots. Samlor drew his long dagger and laid it on an intaglio table. Only the edge of the steel winked. The hilt was of a hard, pale wood, smooth but wrapped with a webbing of silver wire for a sure grip. The morning room had been decorated by a former occupant. In its mosaic battle scenes and the weapons crossed on its walls, the room suited Samlor's appearance far better than it did that of the young Rankan lord who now owned it.

The door was opened inward by a sour, greyhaired woman in temple garb. The air that puffed from the bedroom was warm and cloying like the smell of an overripe peach. Two branches of the sextuple oil lamp within had been lighted, adding to the sunlight seeping through the stained glass separating the room from the inner court.

If the midwife looked harsh, then Samlane herself on the bed looked like Death. All the flesh of her face and her long, white hands seemed to have been drawn into the belly that now mounded her linen wrapper. A silk coverlet lay rumpled at the foot of the bed. "Come in, brother dear." A spasm rippled the wrapper. Samlane's face froze, her mouth half open. The spasm passed. "I won't keep you long, Samlor," she added through a false smile. "Leah, wait outside."

Midwife, husband, and doctor all began to protest. "Heqt's face, get out, get *out!*" Samlane shrieked, her voice rising even higher as a new series of contractions racked her. Her piercing fury cut through all objection. Samlor closed the door behind the midwife. Those in the morning room heard the door latched but not barred. Regli's house had been built for room-by-room defense in the days when bandits or a mob would burst into a dwelling and strip it, in despite of anything the government might attempt.

The midwife stood, stiff and dour, with her back to the door. Regli ignored her and slashed at the wall again. "In the year I've known her, Samlane hasn't mentioned her brother a dozen times—and each of those was a curse!" he said.

"You must remember, this is a trying time for the lady, too," Mernorad said. "With her parents, ah, unable to travel, it's natural that she wants her brother—"

"Natural?" Regli shouted. "It's my child she's bearing! My son, perhaps. What am I doing out here?"

"What would you be doing in there?" the doctor observed, tart himself in response to his patron's anger.

Before either could say more, the door swung open, bumping the midwife. Samlor gestured with his thumb. "She wants you to fix her pillows," he said curtly. He picked up his knife and began walking across the morning room toward the hall. The midwife eeled back into the bedroom, hiding all but a glimpse of Samlane's face.

The lampstand beside the bed gave her flesh a yellow cast. The bar thudded back in place almost as soon as the door closed.

Regli grabbed Samlor's arm. "But what did she want?" he demanded.

Samlor shook his arm free. "Ask her, if you think it's any of your business," he said. "I'm in no humor to chatter." Then he was out of the room and already past the servant who should have escorted him down the staircase to the front door.

Mernorad blinked. "Certainly a surly brute," he said. "Not at all fit for polite company."

For once it was Regli who was reasonable. "Oh, that's to be expected," he said. "In Cirdon, the nobility always prided itself on being useless— which is why Cirdon is part of the Rankan Empire and not the reverse. It must have bothered him very much when he had to go into trade himself or starve with the rest of his family." Regli cleared his throat, then patted his left palm with the quirt. "That of course explains his hostility toward Samlane and the absurd—"

"Yes, quite absurd," Mernorad agreed hastily.

"—absurd charges he leveled at her," the young noble continued. "Just bitterness, even though he himself had preserved her from the, oh, as he saw it, lowering to which he had been subjected. Actually, I have considerable mining and trading interests myself, besides my—very real—duties here to the State."

The diversion had settled Regli's mind only briefly. He resumed his pacing, the shuffle of his slippers and his occasional snappish comments being almost the only sounds in the morning room for an hour. "Do you hear something?"

Mernorad said suddenly.

Regli froze, then ran to the bedroom door. "Samlane!" he shouted. "*Samlane!*" He gripped the bronze latch and screamed as his palm seared.

Acting with dreadful realization and more strength than was to be expected of a man of his age, Mernorad ripped a battle-axe from the staples holding it to the wall. He swung it against the door panel. The oak had charred to wafer thinness. The heavy blade splintered through, emitting a jet of oxygen into the superheated bedroom.

The room exploded, blasting the door away in a gout of fire and splinters. The flames hurled Mernorad against the far wall as a blazing husk before they curled up to shatter the plastered ceiling.

The flame sucked back, giving Regli a momentary glimpse into the fully-involved room. The midwife had crawled from the bed almost back to the door before she died. The fire had arched her back so that the knife wound in her throat gaped huge and red.

Samlane may have cut her own jugular as well, but too little remained of her to tell. She had apparently soaked the bedding in lamp oil and then clutched the open flame to her. All Regli really had to see, however, to drive him screaming from his house, was the boot knife. The wooden hilt was burned off, and the bare tang poked upright from Samlane's distended belly.

Samlor had asked a street-boy where the Temple of Heqt was. The child had blinked, then brightened and said, "Oh—the Black Spire!" Sitting on a bench outside a tavern across from the temple, Samlor thought he understood why. The

temple had been built of gray limestone, its walls
set in a square but roofed with the usual hemi-
spherical dome. The obelisk crowning the dome
had originally commemorated the victories of
Alar hil Aspar, a mercenary general of Cirdonian
birth. Alar had done very well by his adopted
city—and well enough for himself in the process
to be able to endow public buildings as one form
of conspicuous consumption. None of Alar's
boasts remained visible through the coating three
decades of wood and dung smoke had deposited
on the spire. Still, to look at it, the worst that could
be said about the Temple of Heqt was that it was
ugly, filthy, and in a bad district—all of which
were true of most other buildings in Sanctuary, so
far as Samlor could tell.

As the caravan-master swigged his mug of blue
john, an acolyte emerged from the main doorway
of the temple. She waved her censer three times
and chanted an evening prayer to the disin-
terested street before retreating back inside.

The tavern's doorway brightened as the tapster
stepped out carrying a lantern. "Move, buddy,
these're for customers," he said to the classically
handsome young man sitting on the other bench.
The youth stood but did not leave. The tapster
tugged the bench a foot into the doorway, stepped
onto it, and hung the lantern from a hook beneath
the tavern's sign. The angle of the lantern limned
in shadow a rampant unicorn, its penis engorged
and as large as the horn on its head.

Instead of returning to the bench on which he
had been sitting, the young man sat down beside
Samlor. "Not much to look at, is it?" he said to the
Cirdonian, nodding toward the temple.

"Nor popular, it seems," Samlor agreed. He eyed the local man carefully, wondering how much information he could get from him. "Nobody's gone in there for an hour."

"Not surprising," the other man said with a nod. "They come mostly after dark, you know. And you wouldn't be able to see them from here anyway."

"No?" said Samlor, sipping a little more of his clabbered milk. "There's a back entrance?"

"Not just that," said the local man. "There's a network of tunnels beneath the whole area. They—the worshippers—enter from inns or shops or tenements from blocks away. In Sanctuary, those who come to Heqt come secretly."

Samlor's left hand toyed with his religious medallion. "I'd heard that before," he said, "and I don't figure it. Heqt brings the Spring rains . . . she's the genetrix, not only in Cirdon but everywhere she's worshipped at all—except Sanctuary. What happened here?"

"You're devout, I suppose?" asked the younger man, eying the disk with the face of Heqt.

"Devout, devout," said Samlor with a grimace. "I run caravans, I'm not a priest. Sure, maybe I spill a little drink to Heqt at meals . . . without her, there'd be no world but desert, and I see enough desert already."

The stranger's skin was so pale that it looked yellow now that most of the light was from the lamp above. "Well, they say there was a shrine to Dyareela here before Alar tore it down to build his temple. There wouldn't be anything left, of course, except perhaps the tunnels, and they may have been old when the city was built on top of them. Have you heard there's supposed to be a demon kept in the lower crypts?"

Samlor nodded curtly. "I heard that."

"A hairy, long-tailed, fang-snapping demon," said the younger man with a bright smile. "Pretty much of a joke nowadays, of course. People don't really believe in that sort of thing. Still, the first priest of Heqt here disappeared. . . . And last year Alciros Foin went into the temple with ten hired bravos to find his wife. Nobody saw the bullies again, but Foin was out on the street the next morning. He was alive, even though every inch of skin had been flayed off him."

Samlor finished his mug of blue john. "Men could have done that," he said.

"Would you prefer to meet men like that rather than . . . a demon?" asked the local, smiling.

The two men stared in silence at the temple. "Do you want a drink?" Samlor asked abruptly.

"Not I," said the other.

"You say that fellow was looking for his wife?" the Cirdonian pressed, his eyes on the shadow-hidden temple and not on his companion.

"That's right. Women often go through the tunnels, they say. Fertility rites. Some say the priests themselves have more to do with any increase in conceptions than the rites do—but what man can say what women are about?"

"And the demon?"

"Aiding the conceptions?" said the local. Samlor had kept his face turned from the other so that he would not have to see his smile, but the smile freighted the words themselves stickily. "Perhaps, but some people will say anything.

That would be a night for the . . . suppliant, wouldn't it?"

Samlor turned and smiled back, baring his teeth like a cat eying a throat vein. "Quite a night indeed," he said. "Are there any places known to have entrances to—that?" He gestured across the dark street. "Or is it just rumor? Perhaps this inn itself?"

"There's a hostel west of here a furlong," said the youth. "Near the Beef Market—The Man In Motley. They say there's a network beneath like worm tunnels, not really connected to each other. A man could enter one and walk for days without ever seeing another soul."

Samlor shrugged. He stood and whistled for attention, then tossed his empty mug to the tapster behind the bar. "Just curiosity," he said to his companion. "I've never been in Sanctuary before." Samlor stepped into the street, over a drain which held something long dead. When he glanced back, he saw the local man still seated empty-handed on the bench. In profile against the light, his face had the perfection of an ancient cameo.

Samlor wore boots and he was long familiar with dark nights and bad footing, so he did not bother to hire a linkman. When he passed a detachment of the Watch, the Imperial officer in command stared at the dagger the Cirdonian now carried bare in his hand. Still, Samlor looked to be no more than he was, a sturdy man who would rather warn off robbers than kill them, but who was willing and able to do either. I'll have to buy another boot knife, Samlor thought; but for the time he'd make do, make do. . . .

The Man In Motley was a floor lower than the four-story tenements around it. The ground level was well lighted. Across the street behind a row of palings, a slave gang worked under lamps scraping dung from the cobbles of the Beef Market. Tomorrow their load would be dried in the sun for fuel. The public room of the inn was occupied by a score of men, mostly drovers in leather and homespun. A barmaid in her fifties was serving a corner booth. As Samlor entered, the host thrust through the hangings behind the bar with a cask on his shoulder.

Samlor had sheathed his knife. He nodded to the brawny innkeeper and ducked beneath the bar himself. "Hey!" cried the host.

"It's all right," Samlor muttered. He slipped behind the hangings.

A stone staircase, lighted halfway by an oil lamp, led down into the cellars. Samlor followed it, taking the lamp with him. The floor beneath the public room was of dirt. A large trap, now closed and bolted, gave access to deliveries from the street fronting the inn. The walls were lined with racked bottles, small casks, and great forty-gallon fooders set on end. One of the fooders was of wood so time-blackened as to look charred. Samlor rapped it with his knife hilt, then compared the sound to the duller note of the tun beside it.

The stairs creaked as the host descended. He held a bung-starter in one heavy fist. "Didn't they tell you to go by the side?" he rasped. "D'ye think I want the name of running a devil's brothel?" He took another step. "By Ils and his sisters, you'll remember the next time!"

Samlor's fingers moved on his knife hilt. He still held the point away from the innkeeper. "We don't have a quarrel," he said. "Let's leave it at that."

The host spat as he reached the bottom of the stairs. "Sure, I know you hot-pants folderols. Well, when I'm done with you, you take my greetings to your pandering psalm-singers and tell them there'll be no more customers through here!"

"The priests share their privileges for a price?" Samlor said in sudden enlightenment. "But I don't come for sex, friend."

Whatever the tavern-keeper thought he understood, it frightened him as sight of the dagger had not. He paused with the bung-starter half raised. First he swallowed. Then, with a guttural sound of pure terror he flung the mallet into the shadows and fled back up the stairs. Samlor frowned, shrugged, and turned again to the fooder.

There was a catch disguised as a knot, obvious enough if one knew something of the sort had to be there. Pressed, the side of the cask swung out to reveal a dry, dark tunnel sloping gently downward. Samlor's tongue touched his lips. It was, after all, what he had been looking for. He picked up the lamp, now burned well down. He stepped into the tunnel, closing the door behind him.

The passage twisted but did not branch. It was carven through dense, yellow clay, shored at intervals with timbers too blackened for Samlor to identify the wood. There were tiny skitterings which seemed to come from just beyond the light.

Samlor walked slowly enough not to lose the lampflame, steadily enough not to lose his nerve. Despite the disgrace of his vocation, Samlor was a noble of Cirdon; and there was no one else in his family to whom he could entrust this responsibility.

There was a sound behind him. Without turning, Samlor lashed out with a boot. His hobnails ground into something warm and squealing where his eyes saw nothing at all. He paused for a moment to finger his medallion of Heqt, then continued. The skittering preceded him at a greater distance.

When the tunnel entered a shelf of rock it broadened suddenly into a low-ceilinged, circular room. Samlor paused. He held his lamp out at arm's length and a little back of his line of sight so that the glare would not blind him. The room was huge and empty, pierced by a score of doorways. Each but the one at which Samlor stood and one other was closed by an iron grate.

Samlor touched but did not draw his double-edged dagger. "I'll play your silly game," he whispered. Taking short steps, he walked around the circumference of the room and out the other open door. Another empty passage stretched beyond it. Licking his lips again, Samlor followed the new tunnel.

The double clang of gratings behind him was not really unexpected. Samlor waited, poised behind his knife point, but no one came down the stone boring from either direction. No one and no thing. Samlor resumed walking, the tunnel curving and perhaps descending slightly with each step. The stone was beginning to vibrate, a tremor that was too faint to be music.

The passage broadened again. This time the room so formed was not empty. Samlor spun to face what first seemed a man standing beside the doorway. The figure's only movement was the flicker of the lampflame over its metallic luster. The Cirdonian moved closer and prodded the empty torso. It was a racked suit of mail, topped by a slot-fronted helmet.

Samlor scratched at a link of the armor, urged by a suspicion that he did not consciously credit even as he attempted to prove it. The tightly-woven rings appeared to be of verdigrised copper, but the edge of Samlor's knife could not even mar the apparent corrosion. "Blood and balls," the caravan-master swore under his breath.

He was touching one of the two famed suits of armor forged by the sorcerer Hast-ra-kodi in the fire of a burning diamond. Forged with the help of two demons, legend had it; and if that was open to doubt by a modern rationalist, there could be no doubt at all that the indestructible armor had clothed heroes for three of the five ages of the world.

Then, twelve hundred years ago, the twin brothers Harash and Hakkad had donned the mail and marched against the wizard-prince Sterl. A storm overtook the expedition in the mountains; and in the clear light of dawn, all had disappeared—armor, brothers, and the three thousand men of their armament. Some said the earth had gaped; others, that everything had been swallowed by the still-wider jaws of airy monsters whose teeth flashed in the lightning and whose backs arched high as the thunderheads. Whatever the cause, the armor had vanished in that night. The reappearance of one of the suits in this underground room gave Samlor his first tangible proof of the power that slunk through the skittering passages.

From the opening across the room came the sound of metal scraping stone, scraping and jingling. Samlor backed against the wall, sucking his cheeks hollow.

Into the chamber of living rock stepped the other suit of Hast-ra-kodi's armor. This one fitted snugly about a man whom it utterly covered, creating a figure which had nothing human in it but its shape. The unknown metal glowed green, and the sword the figure bore free in one gauntleted hand blazed like a green torch.

"Do you come to worship Dyareela?" the figure asked in a voice rusty with disuse.

Samlor set his lamp carefully on the flooring and sidled a pace away from it. "I worship Heqt," he said, fingering his medallion with his left hand. "And some others, perhaps. But not Dyareela."

The figure laughed as it took a step forward. "I worshipped Heqt, too. I was her priest—until I came down into the tunnels to purge them of the evil they held." The tittering laughter richochetted about the stone walls like the sound caged weasels make. "Dyareela put a penance on me in return for my life, my life, my life. . . . I wear this armor. That will be your penance too, Cirdonian: put on the other suit."

"Let me pass, priest," Samlor said. His hands were trembling. He clutched them together on his bosom. His fighting knife was sheathed.

"No priest," the figure rasped, advancing.

"Man! Let me pass!"

"No man, not man," said the thing, its blade rising and a flame that dimmed the oil lamp. "They say you keep your knife sharp, *suppliant*—but did gods forge it? Can it shear the mesh of Hast-ra-kodi?"

Samlor palmed the bodkin-pointed push dagger from his wrist sheath and lunged, his left foot thrusting against the wall of the chamber. Armor or no armor, the priest was not a man of war. Samlor's left hand blocked the sword arm while his right slammed the edgeless dagger into the figure's chest. The bodkin slipped through the rings like thread through a needle's eye. The figure's mailed fist caught the Cirdonian and tore the skin over his cheek. Samlor had already twisted his steel clear. He punched it home again through armor, ribs, and the spongy lungs within.

The figure staggered back. The sword clanged to the stone flooring. "What—?" it began. Something slopped and gurgled within the indestructible helmet. The dagger hilt was a dark tumor against the glowing mail. The figure groped vainly at the knob hilt with both hands. "What are you?" it asked in a whisper. "You're not a man, not. . . ." Muscles and sinews loosened as the brain controlling them starved for lack of oxygen. One knee buckled and the figure sprawled headlong on the stone. The green glow seeped out of it like blood from a rag, staining the flooring and dripping through it in turn.

"If you'd been a man in your time," Samlor said harshly, "I wouldn't have had to be here now."

He rolled the figure over to retrieve his bodkin

from the bone in which it had lodged. Hemorrhages from mouth and nose had smeared the front of the helmet. To Samlor's surprise, the suit of mail now gaped open down the front. It was ready to be stripped off and worn by another. The body within was shrivelled, its skin as white as that of the grubs which burrow beneath tree bark.

Samlor wiped his edgeless blade with thumb and forefinger. A tiny streak of blood was the only sign that it had slipped between metal lines to do murder. The Cirdonian left both suits of armor in the room. They had not preserved other wearers. Wizard mail and its tricks were for those who could control it, and Samlor was all too conscious of his own humanity.

The passageway bent, then formed a tee with a narrow corridor a hundred paces long. The corridor was closed at either end by living rock. Its far wall was, by contrast, artificial—basalt hexagons a little more than a foot in diameter across the flats. There was no sign of a doorway. Samlor remembered the iron grates clanging behind him what seemed a lifetime ago. He wiped his right palm absently on his thigh.

The caravan-master walked slowly down and back the length of the corridor, from end to end. The basalt plaques were indistinguishable one from another. They rose ten feet to a bare ceiling which still bore the tool-marks of its cutting. Samlor stared at the basalt from the head of the tee, aware that the oil in his lamp was low and that he had no way of replenishing it.

After a moment he looked down at the floor. Struck by a sudden notion, he opened his fly and urinated at the base of the wall. The stream splashed, then rolled steadily to the right down the invisible trench worn by decades of footsteps. Thirty feet down the corridor the liquid stopped and pooled, slimed with patches of dust that broke up the reflected lamplight.

Samlor examined with particular care the plaques just beyond the pool of urine. The seeming music was louder here. He set his knife-point against one of the hexagons and touched his forehead to the butt-cap. Clearly and triumphantly rolled the notes of a hydraulic organ, played somewhere in the complex of tunnels. Samlor sheathed the knife again and sighted along the stones themselves, holding the light above his head. The polished surface of one waist-high plaque had been dulled by sweat and wear. Samlor pressed it and the next hexagon over hinged out of the wall.

The plaque which had lifted was only a hand's breadth thick, but what the lamp showed beyond it was a tunnel rather than a room: the remainder of the wall was of natural basalt columns, twenty feet long and lying on their sides. To go further, Samlor would have to crawl along a hole barely wide enough to pass his shoulders; and the other end was capped as well.

Samlor had spent his working life under an open sky. He had thus far borne the realization of the tons of rock above his head only by resolutely not thinking about it. This rat-hole left him no choice . . . but he would go through it anyway. A man had to be able to control his mind, or he wasn't a man. . . .

The Cirdonian set the lamp on the floor. It would gutter out in a few minutes anyway. If he

had tried to take it into the tunnel with him, it
would almost immediately have sucked all the
life from the narrow column of air among the
hexagons. He drew his fighting knife and, holding both arms out in front of him, wormed
through the opening. His body blocked all but the
least glimmer of the light behind him, and the
black basalt drank even that.

Progress was a matter of groping with boot toes
and left palm, fighting the friction of his shoulders and pelvis scraping the rock. Samlor took
shallow breaths, but even so before he had
crawled his own length the air became stale. It
hugged him like a flabby blanket as he inched
forward in the darkness. The music of the water
organ was all about him.

The knife-point clinked on the far capstone.
Samlor squirmed a little nearer, prayed to Heqt,
and thrust outward with his left hand. The stone
swung aside. Breathable air flooded the Cirdonian with the rush of organ music.

Too relieved to be concerned at what besides air
might wait beyond the opening, Samlor struggled
out. He caught himself on his knuckles and left
palm, then scrabbled to get his legs back under
him. He had crawled through the straight side of a
semicircular room. Panels in the arched ceiling
fifty feet above his head lighted the room ochre. It
was surely not dawn yet. Samlor realized he had
no idea of what might be the ultimate source of the
clear, rich light.

The hydraulic organ must still be at a distance
from this vaulted chamber, but the music made
the walls vibrate with its intensity. There was
erotic love in the higher notes, and from the lower

register came fear as deep and black as that which had settled in Samlor's belly hours before. Lust and mindless hatred lilted, rippling and bubbling through the sanctuary. Samlor's fist squeezed his dagger hilt in frustration. He was only the thickness of the edge short of running amok in this empty room. Then he caught himself, breathed deeply, and sheathed the weapon until he had a use for it.

An archway in the far wall suggested a door. Samlor began walking toward it, aware of the scrapes the basalt had given him and the groin muscle he had pulled while wrestling with the figure in armor. I'm not as young as I was, he thought. Then he smiled in a way that meshed all too well with the pattern of the music: after all, he was likely through with the problems of aging very soon.

The sanctuary was strewn with pillows and thick brocades. There was more substantial furniture also. Its patterns were unusual but their function was obvious in context. Samlor had crossed enough of the world to have seen most things, but his personal tastes remained simple. He thought of Samlane; fury lashed him again. This time instead of gripping the knife, he touched the medallion of Heqt. He kicked at a rack of switches. They clattered into a construct of ebony with silken tie-downs. Its three hollow levels could be adjusted toward one another by the pulleys and levers at one end of it.

Well, it wasn't for her, Samlor thought savagely. It was for the house, the honor of the Lords Kodrix of Cirdon. And perhaps—perhaps for Heqt. He'd never been a religious man, always figured it'd be best if the gods settled things among themselves . . . but there were some things that *any* man—

Well, that was a lie. Not any man, just Samlor hil Samt for sure and probably no other fool so damned on the whole continent. Well, so be it then; he was a fool and a fanatic, and before the night finished he'd have spilled the blood of a so-called demon or died trying.

Because the illumination was from above, Samlor had noticed the bas reliefs only as patterns of shadows along the walls. The detail struck him as he approached the archway. He stopped and looked carefully.

The carvings formed a series of panels running in bands across the polished stone. The faces in each tableau were modeled with a precise detail that made it likely they were portraits, though none of the personages were recognizable to Samlor. He peered up the curving walls and saw the bands continuing to the roof vaults. How and when they had been carved was beyond estimation; the caravan-master was not even sure he could identify the stone, creamy and mottled but seemingly much harder than marble.

Time was of indeterminable importance. Knowing that he might have only minutes to live, Samlor began following some of the series of reliefs. One group of carvings made clear the unguessed unity between the 'sorcerer' Hast-ra-kodi and the 'goddess' Dyareela. Samlor stared at the conclusion of the pattern, swallowing hard but not speaking. He was unutterably glad he had not donned either suit of mail when he might have done so.

The panels reeked of bloodshed and repression. Kings and priests had stamped out the worship of Dyareela a hundred times in a hundred places. The rites had festered in the darkness, then burst out again—cancers metastasizing from the black lump here in the vaults beneath Sanctuary. A shrine in the wasteland before it was a city; and even as a city, a brawling, stinking, leaderless hive where no one looked too hard for Evil's heart since Evil's limbs enveloped all.

Alar hil Aspar—a brash outsider, a reformer flushed with his triumph over brigandage—had at last razed the fane of Dyareela here. Instead of salt, he had sown the ruins with a temple to Heqt, the goddess of his upbringing. Fool that he was, Alar had thought that ended it.

Just above the archway, set off from the courses around it by a border of ivy leaves, was a cameo that caught Samlor's eye as he returned sick and exhausted by what he had been looking at. A file of women led by a piper cavorted through the halls of a palace. The women carried small animals and icons of obviously more than symbolic significance, but it was to the piper's features that Samlor's gaze was drawn. The Cirdonian swore mildly and reached up to touch the stone. It was smooth and cold to his fingertips.

So much fit. Enough, perhaps.

Samlor stepped through the double-hung doors closing the archway. The crossbowman waiting beyond with his eyes on the staircase screamed and spun around. The patterned screen that would have concealed the ambush from someone descending the stairs was open to the archway—but judging from the bowman's panic, the mere sight of something approaching from the sanctuary would probably have flushed him anyway.

Samlor had survived too many attacks ever to be wholly unprepared for another. He lunged forward, shouting to further disconcert the bowman. The screen was toppling as the bowman jerked back from the fingers of Samlor's left hand thrusting for his eyes. The bowstring slapped and the quarrel spalled chips from the archway before ricochetting sideways through a swinging doorpanel. Samlor, sprawled across his attacker's lower legs, slashed at the other's face with the knife he had finally cleared. The bowman cried out again and parried with the stock of his own weapon. Samlor's edge thudded into the wood like an axe in a firelog. Three of the bowman's fingers flew out into the room.

Unaware of his maiming, the bowman tried to club Samlor with his weapon. It slipped away from him. He saw the blood-spouting stumps of his left hand, the index finger itself half severed. Fright had made the bowman scream; mutilation now choked his voice with a rush of vomit.

Samlor squirmed forward, pinning his attacker's torso with his own. He wrestled the crossbow out of the unresisting right hand. There was a pouch of iron quarrels at the bowman's belt, but Samlor ignored them: they were on the left side and no longer a threat. The gagging man wore the scarlet and gold livery of Regli's household.

The Cirdonian glanced quickly around the room, seeing nothing but a helical staircase reaching toward more lighted panels a hundred feet above. He waggled his knife a foot from his captive's eyes, then brought the point of it down on the other's nose. "You tried to kill me," he said softly. "Tell me why or you're missing more than some fingers only."

"Sabellia, Sabellia," the maimed retainer moaned. "You've ruined me now, you bastard."

Samlor flicked his blade sideways, knowing that the droplet of blood that sprang out would force the other's eyes to cross on it. They would fill with its red proximity. "Talk to me, little man," the caravan-master said. "Why are you here?"

The injured man swallowed bile. "My lord Regli," he said, closing his eyes to avoid the blood and the dagger point. "He said you'd killed his wife. He sent us all after you."

Samlor laid the dagger point on the other's left eyesocket. "How many?" he demanded.

"A dozen," gabbled the other. "All the guards and us coachmen besides."

"The Watch?"

"Oh, gods, get that away from my eye," the retainer moaned. "I almost shook—" Samlor raised the blade an inch. "Not the Watch," the other went on. "My lord wants to handle this himself for the, the scandal."

"And where are the others?" the point dipped, brushed an eyelash, and rose again harmlessly.

The wounded man was rigid. He breathed through his mouth, quick gasps as if a lungful of air would preserve him in the moment the knife-edge sawed through his windpipe. "They all thought you'd run for Cirdon," he whispered. "You'd left your cloak behind. I slipped it away, took it to a S'danzo I know. She's a liar like all of

them, but sometimes not. . . . I told her I'd pay
her for the truth of where I'd find you, and I'd pay
her for nothing; but I'd take a lie out of her hide if
six of my friends had to hold down her blacksmith
buddy. She, she described where I'd meet you. I
recognized it, I'd taken the Lady Samlane—"

"Here?" Samlor's voice and his knife both
trembled. Death slid closer to the room than it had
been since the first slash and scramble of the fight.

"Lord, lord," the captive pleaded. "Only this
far. I swear by my mother's bones!"

"Go on, then." The knife did not move.

The other man swallowed. "That's all. I waited
here—I didn't tell anybody, Lord Regli put a
thousand royals on your head . . . and . . . and
the S'danzo said I'd live through the meeting. Oh
gods, the slut, the slut. . . ."

Samlor smiled. "She hasn't lied to you yet," he
said. The smile was gone, replaced with a bleak-
ness as cruel as the face of a glacier. "Listen," he
went on, rising to one knee and pinning his prisoner by psychological dominance in the stead of
his body weight. "My sister asked me for a knife. I
told her I'd leave her one if she gave me a reason
to."

A spasm wracked the Cirdonian's face. His
prisoner winced at the trembling of the dagger
point. "She said the child wasn't Regli's," Samlor
went on. "Well, who ever thought it would be, the
way she sniffed around? But she said a demon had
got it on her . . . and that bothered even her at the
last. Being used, she said. Being used. She'd tried
to have it aborted after she thought about things
for a while, but a priest of Heqt was waiting with
Regli in the shop where she'd gone to buy the

drugs. After that, she wasn't without somebody watching her, asleep or awake. The Temple of Heqt wanted the child born. Samlane said she'd use the knife to end the child when they pulled it from her . . . and I believed that, though I knew she'd be in no shape for knifings just after she'd whelped.

"Seems she knew that too, but she was more determined than even I'd have given her credit for being. She could give a lot of folks points for stubborn, my sister."

Samlor shook himself, then gripped a handful of the captive's tunic. He ripped the garment with his knife. "What are you doing?" the retainer asked in concern.

"Tying you up. Somebody'll find you here in time. I'm going to do what I came here for, and when it's done I'll leave Sanctuary. If I've got that option still."

Sweat was washing streaks in the blood-flecks on the captive's face. "Sweet goddess, don't do that," he begged. "Not tied, not—that. You haven't been here when . . . others were here. You—" the injured man wiped his lips with his tongue. He closed his eyes. "Kill me yourself, if you must," he said so softly it was almost a matter for lip-reading to understand him. "Don't leave me here."

Samlor stood. His left hand was clenched, his right holding the dagger pointed down at a slight angle. "Stand up," he ordered. Regli's man obeyed, wide-eyed. He braced his back against the wall, holding his left hand at shoulder height but refusing to look at its ruin. The severed arteries had pinched off. Movement had dislodged some of the scabs, but the blood only oozed instead of spurting as it had initially. "Tell Regli that I'm mending my family's honor in my way, as my sister seems to have done in hers," Samlor said. "But don't tell him where you found me—or how. If you want to leave here now, you'll swear that."

"I swear!" the other babbled. "By anything you please!"

The caravan-master's smile flickered again. "Did you ever kill anyone, boy?" he asked conversationally.

"I was a coachman," the other said with a nervous frown. "I—I mean . . . no."

"Once I pulled a man apart with hot pincers," Samlor continued quietly. "He was headman of a tribe that had taken our toll payment but still tried to cut out a couple horses from the back of our train. I slipped into the village that night, jerked the chief out of his bed, and brought him back to the laager. In the morning I fixed him as a display for the rest." The Cirdonian reached forward and wiped his dagger clean on the sleeve of the other man's tunic. "Don't go back on your word to me, friend," he said.

Regli's man edged to the helical staircase. As he mounted each of the first dozen steps, he looked back over his shoulder at the Cirdonian. When the pursuit or thrown knife did not come as he had feared or expected, the retainer ran up the next twenty steps without pausing. He looked down from that elevation and said, "One thing, master."

"Say it," responded Samlor.

"They opened the Lady Samlane to give the child separate burial."

"Yes?"

"And it didn't look to be demon spawn, as you say," Regli's man called. "It was a perfect little boy. Except that your knife was through its skull."

Samlor began to climb the steps, ignoring the scrabbling slippers of the man above him on the twisting staircase. The door at the top thudded, leaving nothing of the hapless ambusher but splotches of his blood on the railing. Should have stuck to his horses, Samlor thought. He laughed aloud, well aware that the epitaph probably applied to himself as well. Still, he had a better notion than that poor fool of a coachman of what he was getting into . . . though the gods all knew how slight were his chances of getting out of it alive. If the fellow he was looking for was a real magician, rather than someone like Samlor himself who had learned a few spells while knocking around the world, it was over for sure.

The door at the top of the stairs pivoted outward. Samlor tested it with a fingertip, then paused to steady his heart and breathing. As he stood there, his left hand sought the toad-faced medallion. The dagger in his right hand pointed down, threatening nothing at the moment but—ready.

He pushed the door open.

On the other side, the secret opening was only a wall panel. Its frescoes were geometric and in no way different from those of the rest of the temple hallway. To the left, the hall led to an outside door heavily banded with iron. From his livery and the mutilation of his outflung left hand, the coachman could be recognized where he lay. The rest of the retainer appeared to have been razored into gobbets of flesh and bone, no other one of them as large as what remained of the left hand. Under the circumstances, Samlor had no sympathy to waste on the corpse.

The Cirdonian sighed and turned to the right, stepping through the hangings of brass beads into the sanctuary of Heqt. The figure he expected was waiting for him.

Soft, gray dawnlight crept through hidden slits in the dome. Mirrors had been designed to light the grinning, gilded toad-face of Heqt at the top of the dome beneath the spire. Instead, the light was directed downward onto the figure on the floral mosaic in the center of the great room. The hair of the waiting man glowed like burning wire. "Did the night keep you well, friend?" Samlor called as he stepped forward.

"Well," agreed the other with a nod. There was no sign of the regular priests and acolytes of Heqt. The room brightened as if the light fed on the beauty of the waiting man. "As I see she kept you, Champion of Heqt."

"No champion," Samlor said, taking another step as casual as the long knife dangling from his right hand. "Just a man looking for the demon who caused his sister's death. I didn't have to look any farther than the bench across the street last night, did I?"

The other's voice was a rich tenor. It had a vibrancy that had been missing when he and Samlor had talked of Heqt and Dyareela the night before. "Heqt keeps sending her champions, and I . . . I deal with them. You met the first of them, the priest?"

"I came looking for a demon," the Cirdonian said, walking very slowly, "and all it was was a poor madman who had convinced himself that he was a god."

"I am Dyareela."

"You're a man who saw an old carving down below that looked like him," Samlor said. "That worked on your mind, and you worked on other people's minds. . . . My sister, now, she was convinced her child would look like a man but be a demon. She killed it in her womb. The only way that she'd have been able to kill it, because they'd never have let her near it, Regli's heir, and her having tried abortion. But such a waste, because it was just a child, only a madman's child."

The sun-crowned man gripped the throat of his white tunic and ripped downward with unexpected strength. "I am Dyareela," it said. Its right breast was pendulous, noticeably larger than the left. The male genitals were of normal size, flaccid, hiding the vulva that must lie behind them. "The one there," it said, gesturing toward the wall beyond which the coachman lay, "came to my fane to shed blood *without my leave.*" The naked figure giggled. "Perhaps I'll have you wash in his blood, Champion," it said. "Perhaps that will be the start of your penance."

"A mad little hermaphrodite who knows a spell or two," Samlor said. "But there'll be no penance for any again from you, little one. You're fey, and I know a spell for your sort. She wasn't much, but I'll have your heart for what you led my sister to."

"Will you conjure me by Heqt, then, Champion?" asked the other with its arms spread in welcome and laughter in its liquid voice. "Her temple is my temple, her servants are my servants

. . . the blood of her champions is mine for a sacrifice!"

Samlor was twenty feet away, a full turn and half a turn. He clutched his medallion left-handed, hoping it would give him enough time to complete his spell. "Do I look like a priest to talk about gods?" he said. "Watch my dagger, madman."

The other smiled, waiting as Samlor cocked the heavy blade. It caught a stray beam of sunlight. The double edge flashed black dawn.

"By the Earth that bore this," Samlor cried, "and the Mind that gave it shape;

"By the rown of this hilt and the silver wire that laps it;

"By the cold iron of this blade and by the white-hot flames it flowed from;

"By the blood it has drunk and the souls it has eaten—

know thy hour!"

Samlor hurled the dagger. It glinted as it rotated. The blade was point-first and a hand's breadth from the smiling face when it exploded in a flash and a thunderclap that shook the city. The concussion hurled Samlor backward, bleeding from the nose and ears. The air was dense with flecks of paint and plaster from the frescoed ceiling.

Dyareela stood with the same smile, arms lifting in triumph, lips opening further in throaty laughter. *"Mine for a sacrifice!"*

A webbing of tiny cracks was spreading from the center of the dome high above. Samlor staggered to his feet, choking on dust and knowing that if he was lucky he was about to die.

Heqt's gilded bronze head, backed by the lime-stone spire, plunged down from the ceiling. It struck Dyareela's upturned face like a two-hundred ton crossbow bolt. The floor beneath dis-integrated. The limestone column scarcely slowed, hurtling out of sight as the earth itself shuddered to the impact.

Samlor lost his footing in the remains of Regli's coachman. An earth-shock pitched him forward against the door panel. It was unlocked. The Cir-donian lunged out into the street as the shattered dome followed its pinnacle into a cavern that gaped with a sound like the lowest note of an organ played by gods.

Samlor sprawled in the muddy street. All around him men were shouting and pointing. The Cirdonian rolled onto his back and looked at the collapsing temple.

Above the ruins rose a pall of shining dust. More than imagination shaped the cloud into the head of a toad.

THE FRUIT OF ENLIBAR

Lynn Abbey

The hillside groves of orange trees were all that
remained of the legendary glory of Enlibar. Hum-
bled descendants of the rulers of an empire dwarf-
ing Ilsig or Ranke eked out their livings among the
gnarled, ancient trees. They wrapped each unripe
fruit in leaves for the long caravan journey and
wrapped each harvest in a fresh retelling of their
legends. By shrewd storytelling these once
proud families survived, second only to the
S'danzo in their ability to create mystery, but like
the S'danzo crones they flavored their legends
with truth and kept the skeptics at bay.

The oranges of Enlibar made their way to
Sanctuary once a year. When the fist-sized fruits
were nearly ripe Haakon, the sweetmeat vendor of
the bazaar, would fill his cart and hawk oranges in
the town as well as in the stalls of the bazaar.
During those few days he would make enough
money to buy expensive trinkets for his wife and
children, another year's lodgings for his mistress,
and have enough gold left to take to Gonfred, the
only honest goldsmith in town.

The value of each orange was such that Haakon
would ignore the unwritten code of the bazaar

and reserve the best of his limited supply for his patrons at the Governor's Palace. It had happened, however, that two of the precious fruits had been bruised. Haakon decided not to sell that pair at all but to share them with his friends the bazaar-smith, Dubro, and his young wife, the half-S'danzo Illyra.

He scored the peel deftly with an inlaid silver tool meant especially for this one purpose. When his fingers moved away the pebbly rind fell back from the deep-colored pulp and Illyra gasped with delight. She took one of the pulp sections and drizzled the juice onto the back of her hand, then lapped it up with the tip of her tongue: the mannerly way to savor the delicate flavor of the blood-red juice.

"These are the best; better than last year's," she exclaimed with a smile.

"You say that every year, Illyra. Time dulls your memory; the taste brings it back." Haakon sucked the juice off his hand with less delicacy: his lips showed the Stain of Enlibar. "And, speaking of time dulling your memory—Dubro, do you recall, about fifteen years back, a death-pale boy with straw hair and wild eyes running about the town?"

Haakon watched as Dubro closed his eyes and sank back in thought. The smith would have been a raw youth then himself, but he had always been slow, deliberate, and utterly reliable in his judgments. Illyra would have been a skirt-clinging toddler that long ago so Haakon did not think to ask her, nor to glance her way while he awaited Dubro's reply. Had he done so he would have seen her tremble and a blood-red drop of juice disappear into the fine dust beneath her chair.

"Yes," Dubro said without opening his eyes, "I remember one as that: quiet, pale . . . nasty. Lived a few years with the garrison, then disappeared."

"Would you know him again after all this time?"

"Nay. He was that sort of lad who looks childish until he becomes a man, then one never sees the child in his face again."

"Would you reckon 'Walegrin' to be his name?"

Ignored, beside them, Illyra bit down on her tongue and stifled sudden panic before it became apparent.

"It might be . . . nay, I could not be sure. I doubt as I ever spoke to the lad by name."

Haakon shrugged as if the questions had been idle conversation. Illyra ate her remaining share of the oranges, then went into the ramshackle stall where she lit three cones of incense before returning to the men with a ewer of water.

"Illyra, I've just asked your husband if he'd come with me to the Palace. I've got two sacks of oranges to deliver for the Prince and another set of arms would make the work easier. But he says he won't leave you here alone."

Illyra hesitated. The memories Haakon had aroused were still fresh in her mind, but all that had been fifteen years ago, as he had said. She stared at the clouded-over sky.

"No, there'll be no problem. It may rain today and, anyway, you've taken everyone's money this week with your oranges," she said with forced brightness.

"Well then, you see Dubro—there's no problem. Bank the fires and we'll be off. I'll have you back sweating again before the first raindrops fall."

Illyra watched them leave. Fear filled the forge, fear left over from a dimly remembered childhood. Visions she had shared with no one, not even Dubro. Visions not even the S'danzo gifts could resolve into truth or illusion. She caught up her curly black hair with a set of combs and went back inside.

When the bed was concealed under layers of gaudy, bright cloth and her youth under layers of kohl, Illyra was ready to greet the townsfolk. She had not exaggerated her complaints about the oranges. It was just as well that Haakon's supply was diminishing. For two days now she had had no querents until late in the day. Lonely and bored she watched the incense smoke curl into the darkness of the room, losing herself in its endless variations.

"Illyra?"

A man drew back the heavy cloth curtain. Illyra did not recognize his voice. His silhouette revealed only that he was as tall as Dubro, though not as broad.

"Illyra? I was told I'd find Illyra, the crone, here."

She froze. Any querent might have cause to resent a S'danzo prophecy, regardless of its truth, and plot revenge against the seeress. Only recently she had been threatened by a man in the red-and-gold livery of the Palace. Her hand slid under the folds of the tablecloth and eased a tiny dagger loose from a sheath nailed to the table leg.

"What do you want?" She held her voice

steady; greeting a paying querent rather than a thug.

"To talk with you. May I come in?" He paused, waiting for a reply and when there was none continued, "you seem unduly suspicious, S'danzo. Do you have many enemies here, Little Sister?"

He stepped into the room and let the cloth fall behind him. Illyra's dagger slid silently from her hand into the folds of her skirts.

"Walegrin."

"You remember so quickly? Then you did inherit *her* gift?"

"Yes, I inherited it, but this morning I learned that you had returned to Sanctuary."

"Three weeks past. It has not changed at all except, perhaps, for the worse. I had hoped to complete my business without disturbing you but I have encountered complications, and I doubt any of the other S'danzo would help me."

"The S'danzo will never forget."

Walegrin eased his bulk into one of Dubro's chairs. Light from the candelabra fell on his face. He endured the exposure, though as Dubro had guessed, there was no trace of youth left in his features. He was tall and pale, lean in the way of powerful men whose gentler tissues have boiled away. His hair was sun-bleached to brittle straw, confined by four thick braids and a bronze circlet. Even for Sanctuary he cut an exotic, barbarian figure.

"Are you satisfied?" he asked when her gaze returned to the velvet in front of her.

"You have become very much like him," she answered slowly.

"I think not, 'Lyra. My tastes, anyway, do not

run as our father's did—so put aside your fears on that account. I've come for your help. True S'danzo help, as your mother could have given me. I could pay you in gold, but I have other items which might tempt you more."

He reached under his bronze-studded leather kilt to produce a suede pouch of some weight which he set, unopened, on the table. She began to open it when he leaned forward and grasped her wrist tightly.

"It wasn't me, 'Lyra. I wasn't there that night. I ran away, just like you did."

His voice carried Illyra back those fifteen years sweeping the doubts from her memories. "I was a child then, Walegrin. A little child, no more than four. Where could I have run to?"

He released her wrist and sat back in the chair. Illyra emptied the pouch onto her table. She recognized only a few of the beads and bracelets, but enough to realize that she gazed upon all of her mother's jewelry. She picked up a string of blue glass beads strung on a creamy braided silk.

"These have been restrung," she said simply.

Walegrin nodded. "Blood rots the silk and stinks to the gods. I had no choice. All the others are as they were."

Illyra let the beads fall back into the pile. He had known how to tempt her. The entire heap was not worth a single gold piece, but no storehouse of gold could have been more valuable to her.

"Well, then, what do you want from me?"

He pushed the trinkets aside and from another pouch produced a palm-sized pottery shard which he placed gently on the velvet.

"Tell me everything about that: where the rest

of the tablet is; how it came to be broken; what the symbols mean—everything!"

There was nothing in the jagged fragment that justified the change that came over Walegrin as he spoke of it. Illyra saw a piece of common orange pottery with a crowded black design set under the glaze; the sort of ware that could be found in any household of the Empire. Even with her S'danzo gifts focused on the shard it remained stubbornly common. Illyra looked at Walegrin's icy green eyes, his thought-protruded brows, the set of his chin atop the studded grieve on his forearm, and thought better of telling him what she actually saw.

"Its secrets are locked deeply within it. To a casual glance its disguises are perfect. Only prolonged examination will draw its secrets out." She placed the shard back on the table.

"How long?"

"It would be hard to say. The gift is strengthened by symbolic cycles. It may take until the cycle of the shard coincides. . . ."

"I know the S'danzo! I was there with you and your mother—don't play bazaar-games with me, Little Sister. I know too much."

Illyra sat back on her bench. The dagger in her skirts clunked to the floor. Walegrin bent over to pick it up. He turned it over in his hands and without warning thrust it through the velvet into the table. Then, with his palm against the smooth of the blade, he bent it back until the hilt touched the table. When he removed his hand the knife remained bent.

"Cheap steel. Modern stuff; death to the one who relies on it," he explained, drawing a sleek knife from within the grieve. He placed the dark-steel blade with the beads and bracelets. "Now, tell me about my pottery."

"No bazaar-games. If I didn't know from looking at you, I'd say it was a broken piece of 'cotta. You've had it a long time. It shows nothing but its associations with you. I believe it is more than that, or you wouldn't be here. You know about the S'danzo and what you call 'bazaar-games,' but it's true—right now I see nothing; later I might. There are ways to strengthen the vision—I'll try them."

He flipped a gold coin onto the table. "Get what you'll need."

"Only my cards," she answered, flustered by his gesture.

"Get them!" he ordered without picking up the coin.

She removed the worn deck from the depths of her blouse and set the shard atop them while she lit more candles and incense. She allowed Walegrin to cut the pack into three piles, then turned over the topmost card of each pile.

Three of Flames: a tunnel running from light to darkness with three candle sconces along the way.

The Forest: primeval, gnarled trunks; green canopy; living twilight.

Seven of Ore: red clay; the potter with his wheel and kiln.

Illyra stared at the images, losing herself in them without finding harmony or direction. The Flame card was pivotal, but the array would not yield its perspective to her; the Forest, symbolic of the wisdom of the ages, seemed unlikely as either her brother's goal or origin; and the Seven must

mean more than was obvious. But, was the Ore-
card appearing in its creativity aspect? Or was red
clay the omen of bloodletting, as was so often true
when the card appeared in a Sanctuary-cast array?

"I still do not see enough. Bazaar-games or not,
this is not the time to scry this thing."

"I'll come again after sundown—that would be
a better time, wouldn't it? I've no garrison duties
until after sunrise tomorrow."

"For the cards, yes, of course, but Dubro will
have banked the forge for the night by then, and I
do not want to involve him in this."

Walegrin nodded without argument. "I understand. I'll come by at midnight. He should be long
asleep by then, unless you keep him awake."

Illyra sensed it would be useless to argue. She
watched silently as he swept the pile of baubles,
the knife, and the shard into one pouch, wincing
slightly as he dribbled the last beads from her
sight.

"As is your custom, payment will not be made
until the question is answered."

Illyra nodded. Walegrin had spent many years
around her mother learning many of the S'danzo
disciplines and rousing his father's explosive
jealousy. The leather webbing of his kilt creaked
as he stood up. The moment for farewell came and
passed. He left the stall in silence.

A path cleared when Walegrin strode through a
crowd. He noticed it here, in this bazaar where his
memories were of scrambling through the aisles,
taunted, cursed, fighting, and thieving. In any
other place he accepted the deference except here,

which had once been his home for a while.

One of the few men in the throng who could match his height, a dark man in a smith's apron, blocked his way a moment. Walegrin studied him obliquely and guessed he was Dubro. He had seen the smith's short aquiline companion several times in other roles about the town without learning the man's true name or calling; they each glanced to one side to avoid a chance meeting.

At the entrance to the bazaar, a tumble-down set of columns still showing traces of the Ilsig kings who had them built, a man crept out of the shadows and fell in step beside Walegrin. Though this second had the manner and dress of the city-born, his face was like Walegrin's: lean, hard, and parched.

"What have you learned, Thrusher?" Walegrin began, without looking down.

"That man Downwind who claimed to read such things. . . ."

"Yes?"

"Runo went down to meet with him, as you were told. When he did not return for duty this morning Malm and I went to look for him. We found them both . . . and these." He handed his captain two small copper coins.

Walegrin turned them over in his palm, then threw them far into the harbor. "I'll take care of this myself. Tell the others we will have a visitor at the garrison this evening—a woman."

"Yes, captain," Thrusher responded, a surprised grin making its way across his jaw. "Shall I send the men away?"

"No, set them as guards. Nothing is going well. Each time we have set a rendezvous something has gone wrong. At first it was petty nuisance, now Runo is dead. I will not take chances in this city above all others. And, Thrusher . . ." Walegrin caught his man by the elbow, "Thrusher, this woman is S'danzo, my half-sister. See that the men understand this."

"They will understand, we all have families somewhere."

Walegrin grimaced and Thrusher understood that his commander had not suddenly weakened to admit family concerns.

"We have need of the S'danzo? Surely there are more reliable seers in Sanctuary than scrounging the aisles of the bazaar. Our gold is good and nearly limitless." Thrusher, like many men in the Ranken Empire, considered the S'danzo best suited to resolving love triangles among house-servants.

"We have need of this one."

Thrusher nodded and oozed back into the shadows as deftly as he had emerged. Walegrin waited until he was alone on the filthy streets before changing direction and striding, shoulders set and fists balled, into the tangled streets of the Maze.

The whores of the Maze were a special breed unwelcomed in the great pleasure houses beyond the city walls. Their embrace included a poison dagger and their nightly fee was all the wealth that could be removed from a man's person. A knot of these women clung to the doorway of the Vulgar Unicorn, the Maze's approximation to Town Hall, but they stepped aside meekly when Walegrin approached. Survival in the Maze depended upon careful selection of the target.

An aura of dark foul air enveloped Walegrin as he stepped down into the sunken room. A moment's quiet passed over the other guests, as it always did when someone entered. A Hell Hound, personal puritan of the prince, could shut down conversation for the duration of his visit, but a garrison officer, even Walegrin, was assumed to have legitimate business and was ignored with the same slit-eyed wariness the regulars accorded each other.

The itinerant story-teller, Hakiem, occupied the bench Walegrin preferred. The heavy-lidded little man was wilier than most suspected. Clutching his leather mug of small ale tenderly, he had selected one of the few locations in the room that provided a good view of all the exits, public and private. Walegrin stepped forward, intending to intimidate the weasel from his perch, but thought better of the move. His affairs in the Maze demanded discretion, not reckless bullying.

From a lesser location he signalled the bartender. No honest wench would work the Unicorn so Buboe himself brought the foaming mug, then returned a moment later with one of the Enlibar oranges he had arranged behind the counter. Walegrin broke the peel with his thumbnail; the red juice ran through the ridges of the peel forming patterns not unlike those on his pottery shard.

A one-armed beggar with a scarred face and a pendulant, cloudy eye sidled into the Unicorn, careful to avoid the disapproving glance of Buboe. As the ragged creature moved from table to table collecting copper pittance from the disturbed patrons, Walegrin noted the tightly wound tunic under his rags and knew the left arm was as good as the one that was snapping up the coins. Likewise, the scar was a self-induced disfigurement and the yellow rheum running down his cheek the result of seeds placed under his eyelids. The beggar announced his arrival at Walegrin's table with a tortured wheeze. Without looking up Walegrin tossed him a silver coin. He had run with the beggars himself and seen their cunning deceit become crippling reality many times too often.

Buboe split the last accessible louse in his copious beard between his grimy fingernails, looked up, and noticed the beggar, whom he threw into the street. He shuffled a few more mugs of beer to his patrons, then returned to the never-ending task of chasing lice.

The door opened again, admitting another who, like Walegrin, was in the Maze on business. Walegrin drew a small circle in the air with a finger and the newcomer hastened to his table.

"My man was slain last night by following your suggestions." Walegrin stared directly into the newcomer's eyes as he spoke.

"So I've heard, and the Enlibrite potter as well. I've rushed over here to assure you that it was not *my* doing (though I knew you would suspect me). Why, Walegrin, even if I did want to double-cross you (and I doubly assure you that such thoughts never go through my mind) I'd hardly have killed the Enlibrite as well, would I?"

Walegrin grunted. Who was to say what a man of Sanctuary might do to achieve his goals? But the information broker was likely to be telling the truth. He had an air of distracted indignation about him that a liar would not think to affect.

And if he were truthful then, like as not, Runo had been the victim of coincidental outrage. The coins showed that robbery was not the motive. Perhaps the potter had enemies. Walegrin reminded himself to enter the double slaying in the garrison roster where, in due course, it might be investigated when the dozens preceding it had been disposed of.

"Still, once again, I have received no information. I will still make no payment." Walegrin casually spun the beer mug from one hand to the other as he spoke, concealing the import of his conversation from prying eyes.

"There're others who can bait your bear: Markmor, Enas Yorl, even Lythande, if the price is right. Think of this only as a delay, my friend, not failure."

"No! The omens here grow bad. Three times you've tried and failed to get me what I require. I conclude my business with you."

The information broker survived by knowing when to cut his losses. Nodding politely, he left Walegrin without a word and left the Unicorn before Buboe had thought to get his order.

Walegrin leaned back on his stool, hands clenched behind his head, his eyes alert for movement but his thoughts wandering. The death of Runo had affected him deeply, not because the man was a good soldier and long-time companion, though he had been both, but because the death had demonstrated the enduring power of the S'danzo curse on his family. Fifteen years before, the S'danzo community had decreed that all things meaningful to his father should be taken away or destroyed while the man looked helplessly on. For good measure the crones had extended the curse for five generations. Walegrin was the first. He dreaded that day when his path crossed with some forgotten child of his own who would bear him no better will than he bore his own ignominious sire.

It had been sheer madness to return to Sanctuary, to the origin of the curse, despite the assurances of the Purple Mage's protection. Madness! The S'danzo felt him coming. The Purple Mage, the one person Walegrin trusted to unravel the spell, had disappeared long before he and his men arrived in town. And now the Enlibrite potter and Runo were dead by some unknown hand. How much longer could he afford to stay? True, there were many magicians here, and any could be bought, but they all had their petty loyalties. If they could reconstruct the shard's inscription, they certainly could not be trusted to keep quiet about it. If Illyra did not provide the answers at midnight, Walegrin resolved to take his men somewhere far from this accursed town.

He would have continued his litany of dislike had he not been brought to alertness by the distress call of a mountain hawk: a bird never seen or heard within the walls of Sanctuary. The call was the alarm signal amongst his men. He left a few coins on the table and departed the Unicorn without undue notice.

A second call led him down a passageway too narrow to be called an alley, much less a street. Moving with stealth and caution, Walegrin eased around forgotten doorways suspecting ambush with every step. Only a third call and the appearance of a familiar face in the shadows quickened his pace.

"Malm, what is it?" he asked, stepping over some soft, stinking mass without looking down.

"See for yourself."

A weak shaft of light made its way through the jutting roofs of a half dozen buildings to illuminate a pair of corpses. One was the information broker who had just left Walegrin's company, a makeshift knife still protruding from his neck. The other was the beggar to whom he'd given the silver coin. The latter bore the cleaner mark of the accomplished killer.

"I see," Walegrin replied dully.

"The ragged one, he followed the other away from the Unicorn. I'd been following the broker since we found out about Runo, so I began to follow them both. When the broker caught on that he was being followed, he lit up this cul-de-sac —by mistake, I'd guess—and the beggar followed him. I found the broker like this and killed the beggar myself."

Two more deaths for the curse. Walegrin stared at the bodies, then praised Malm's diligence and sent him back to the garrison barracks to prepare for Illyra's visit. He left the corpses in the cul-de-sac where they might never be found. This pair he would not enter into the garrison roster.

Walegrin paced the length of the town, providing the inhibiting impression of a garrison officer actually on duty, though if a murder had occurred at his feet he would not have noticed. Twice he passed the entrance of the bazaar, twice hesitated, and twice continued on his way. Sunset found

him by the Promise of Heaven as the priests withdrew into their temples and the Red Lanterns
women made their first promenade. By full darkness he was on the Wideway, hungry and close in
spirit to the fifteen-year-old who had swum the
harbor and stowed away in the hold of an out-
bound ship one horrible night many years ago.

In the moonless night that memory returned to
him with palpable force. In the grip of his de-
pravities and obsessed by the imagined infidelity
of his mistress, his father had tortured and killed
her. Walegrin could recall that much. After the
murder he had run from the barracks to the harbor. He knew the end of the story from campfire
tales after he'd joined the army himself. Unsatis-
fied with murder, his father had dismembered her
body, throwing the head and organs into the
palace sewer-stream and the rest into the garrison
stewpot.

Sanctuary boasted no criers to shout out the
hours of the night. When there was a moon its
progress gave approximate time, but in its absence night was an eternity, and midnight that
moment when your joints grew stiff from sitting
on the damp stone pilings of the Wideway and
dark memories threatened the periphery of your
vision. Walegrin bought a torch from the cadaver-
ous watchman at the charnel house and entered
the quiet bazaar.

Illyra emerged from the blacksmith's stall the
second time Walegrin used the mountain hawk
cry. She had concealed herself in a dark cloak
which she held tightly around herself. Her
movements betrayed her fears. Walegrin led the
way in hurried silence. He took her arm at the

elbow when they came into sight of the barracks. She hesitated, then continued without his urging.

Walegrin's men were nowhere to be seen in the common room that separated the men's and officer's quarters. Illyra paced the room like a caged animal, remembering.

"You'll need a table, candles, and what else?" he asked, eager to be on with the night's activity and suddenly mindful that he had brought her back to this place.

"It's so much smaller than I remember it," she said, then added, "just the table and candles, I've brought the rest myself."

Walegrin pulled a table closer to the hearth. While he gathered up candles she unfastened her cloak and placed it over the table. She wore somber woolens appropriate for a modest woman from the better part of town instead of the gaudy layers of the S'danzo costume. Walegrin wondered from whom she had borrowed them and if she had told her husband after all. It mattered little so long as she could pierce the spell over his shard.

"Shall I leave you alone?" Walegrin asked after removing the pottery fragment from the pouch and placing it on the table.

"No, I don't want to be alone in here." Illyra shuffled her fortune cards, dropping several in her nervousness, then set the deck back on the table and asked, "Is it too much to ask for some wine and information about what I'm supposed to be looking for?" A trace of the bazaar scrappiness returned to her voice and she was less lost within the room.

"My man Thrusher wanted to lay in an orgy

feast when I told him I'd require the common room tonight. Then I told him I only wanted the men out—but it's a poor barracks without a flask in it, poorer than Sanctuary." He found a half-filled wineskin behind a sideboard, squirted some into his mouth, and swallowed with a rare smile. "Not the best vintage, but passable. You'll have to drink from the skin. . . ." He handed it to her.

"I drank from a skin before I'd seen a cup. It's a trick you never forget." Illyra took the wineskin from him and caught a mouthful of wine without splattering a drop. "Now, Walegrin," she began, emboldened by the musty wine, "Walegrin, I can't get either your pottery nor Haakon's oranges out of my mind. What is the connection?"

"If this Haakon peddles Enlibar oranges, then it's simple. I got the shard in Enlibar, in the ruins of the armory there. We searched three days and found only this. But, if anyone's got a greater piece he knows not what he has, else there'd be an army massing somewhere that'd have the Empire quaking."

Illyra's eyes widened. "All from a piece of cheap red clay?"

"Not the pottery, my dear sister. The armorer put the formula for Enlibar steel on a clay tablet and had a wizard spell the glaze to conceal it. I sensed the spell, but I cannot break it."

"But this might only be a small piece." Illyra ran her finger along the fragment's worn edges. "Maybe not even a vital part."

"Your S'danzo gifts are heedless of time, are they not?"

"Well, yes—the past and future are clear to us."

"Then you should be able to scry back to when

the glaze was applied and glimpse the entire tablet."

Illyra shifted uneasily. "Yes, perhaps, I could glimpse it but, Walegrin, I don't 'read,' " she shrugged and grinned with the wine.

Walegrin frowned, considering the near-perfect irony of the curse's functioning. No doubt Illyra could, would, see the complete tablet and be unable to tell him what was on it.

"Your cards, they have writing on them." He pointed at the runic verses hoping that she could read runes but not ordinary script.

She shrugged again. "I use the pictures and my gifts. My cards are not S'danzo work." She seemed to apologize for the deck's origin, turning the pile face down to hide the offensive ink trails. "S'danzo are artists. We paint pictures in fate." She squirted herself another mouthful of wine.

"Pictures?" Walegrin asked. "Would you see a clear enough image of the tablet to draw its double here on the table?"

"I could try. I've never done anything like that before."

"Then try now," Walegrin suggested, taking the wineskin away from her.

Illyra placed the shard atop the deck, then brought both to her forehead. Exhaling until she felt the world grow dim, the wine-euphoria left her and she became S'danzo exercising that capricious gift the primordial gods had settled upon her kind. She exhaled again and forgot that she was in her mother's death chamber. Eyes closed, she lowered the deck and pottery to the table and drew three cards, face up.

Seven of Ore: again, red clay; the potter with his wheel and kiln.

Quicksilver: a molten waterfall; the alchemic ancestor of all ores: the ace-card of the suit of Ores.

Two of Ore: steel; war-card; death-card with masked men fighting. She spread her fingers to touch each card and lost herself in search of the Enlibrite forge.

The armorer was old, his hand shook as he moved the brush over the unfired tablet. An equally ancient wizard fretted beside him, glancing fearfully over her shoulder beyond the limits of Illyra's S'danzo gifts. Their clothing was like nothing Illyra had seen in Sanctuary. The vision wavered when she thought of the present and she dutifully returned to the armory. Illyra mimicked the armorer's motions as he covered the tablet with rows of dense, incomprehensible symbols. The wizard took the tablet and sprinkled fine sand over it. He chanted a sing-song language as meaningless as the ink marks. Illyra sensed the beginnings of the spell and withdrew across time to the barracks in Sanctuary.

Walegrin had removed the cloth from the table and placed a charcoal stylus in her hand without her sensing it. For a fleeting moment she compared her copying to the images still in her mind. Then the image was gone and she was fully back in the room, quietly watching Walegrin as he stared at the table.

"Is it what you wanted?" she asked softly.

Walegrin did not answer, but threw back his head in cynical laughter. "Ah, my sister! Your mother's people are clever. Their curse reaches back to the dawn of time. Look at this!"

He pointed at the copied lines and obediently Illyra examined them closely.

"They are not what you wanted?"

Walegrin took the card of Quicksilver and pointed to the lines of script that delineated the waterfall. "These are the runes that have been used since Ilsig attained her height, but this—" he traced a squiggle on the table, "this is older than Ilsig. By Calisard, Vortheld, and a thousand gods of long dead soldiers, how foolish I've been! For years I've chared the secret of Enlibar steel and never realized that the formula would be as old as the ruins we found it in."

Illyra reached across the table and held his clenched fists between her palms. "Surely there are those who can read this? How different can one sort of writing be from another?" she asked with an illiterate's innocence.

"As different as the speech of the Raggah is from yours."

Illyra nodded. It was not the time to tell him that when the Raggah came to trade they bargained with hand signals so none could hear their speech. "You could go to a scriptorium along Governor's Walk. They sell letters like Blind Jakob sells fruit—it won't matter what the letter says as long as you pay the price," she suggested.

"You don't understand, 'Lyra. If the formula becomes known again, ambition will seek it out. Rulers will arm their men with Enlibar steel and set out to conquer their neighbors. Wars will ruin the land and the men who live on it." Walegrin had calmed himself and begun to trace the charcoal scratches onto a piece of translucent parchment.

"But, you wish to have it." Illyra's tone became accusing.

"For ten years I've campaigned for Ranke. I've taken my men far north, beyond the plains. In those lands there're nomads with no cause to fear us. Swift and outnumbering us by thousands they cut through our ranks like a knife through soft cheese. We fell back and the Emperor had our commanders hung as cowards. We went forward again, with new officers, and were thrown back again with the same results. I was commissioned myself and feared we'd be sent forward a third time, but Ranke has discovered easier gold to conquer in the east and the army left its dead in the field to chase some other Imperial ambition.

"I remembered the stories of Enlibar. I hid there when I first escaped this town. With Enlibar steel my men's swords would reap nomad blood and I would not be deemed a coward.

"I found men in the capitol who listened to my plans. They knew the army and knew the battlefield. They're no friends of a hidebound Emperor who sees no more of war than a parade ground, but they became my friends. They gave me leave to search the ruins with my men and arranged for the garrison posts here when all omens said the answer lay in Sanctuary. If I can return to them with the formula the army won't be the whipping-boy of lazy Emperors. Someday men who understand steel and blood would rule . . . but, I've failed them. The damned S'danzo curse has preceded me! The mage was gone when I got here and my dreams have receded further with each step I decided to take."

"Walegrin," Illyra began, "the S'danzo are not

that powerful. Look at the cards. I cannot read
your writing, but I can read them and there are no
curses in your fate. You've found what you came
for. Red clay yields steel through the Ore-ruler,
Quicksilver. True, Quicksilver is a deceiver, but
only because its depths are concealed.
Quicksilver will let you change this cribbling into
something more to your liking." She was S'danzo
again, dispensing wisdom amid her candles, but
without the bright colors and heavy kohl her
words had a new urgent sincerity.

"You are touched by the same curse! You lie
with your husband yet have no children."

Illyra shrank back ashamed. "I . . . I use the
S'danzo gifts; I must believe in their powers. But
you seek the power of steel and war. You need not
believe in S'danzo; you need not fear them. You
ran away—you escaped! The only curse upon you
is that of your own guilt."

She averted her eyes from his face and collected
her cards carefully lest her trembling fingers send
the deck flying across the rough-hewn floors. She
shook out her cloak, getting relief from her anger
in the whip-like snap of the heavy material.

"I've answered your questions. I'll take my
payment, if you please." She extended her hand,
still not looking at his face.

Walegrin unfastened the suede pouch from his
belt and placed it on the table. "I'll get the torch
and we can leave for the bazaar."

"No, I'll take the torch and go alone."

"The streets are no place for a woman after
dark."

"I'll get by—I did before."

"I'll have one of my men accompany you."

"All right," Illyra agreed, inwardly relieved by the compromise.

From the speed with which the soldier appeared Illyra guessed he had been right outside all along and party to everything that had passed. Regardless, the man took the torch and walked slightly ahead of her, attentive to duty but without any attempt at conversation until they reached the bazaar gates where Illyra had to step forward to guide them both through the maze of stalls.

She took her leave of the man without farewell and slipped into the darkness of her home. Familiarity obviated need for light. She moved quickly and quietly, folding the clothes into a neat bundles and storing the precious pouch with her few other valuables before easing into the warm bed.

"You've returned safely. I was ready to pull on my trousers and come looking for you. Did he give you all that he promised?" Dubro whispered, settling his arms around her.

"Yes, and I answered all his questions. He has the formula now for Enlibar steel, whatever that is, and if his purposes are true he'll make much of it." Her body released its tension in a series of small spasms and Dubro held her tighter.

"Enlibar steel," he mused softly. "The swords of legend were of Enlibar steel. The man who possesses such steel now would be a man to be reckoned with . . . even if he were a blacksmith."

Illyra pulled the linen over her ears and pretended not to hear.

"Sweetmeats! Sweetmeats! Always the best in the bazaar! Always the best in Sanctuary!"

Mornings were normal again with Haakon

wheeling his cart past the blacksmith's stall before the crowds disrupted the community. Illyra, one eye ringed with kohl and the other still pristine, raced out to purchase their breakfast treats.

"There's news in the town," the vendor said as he dropped three of the pastries onto Illyra's plate. "Twice news in fact. All of last night's watch from the garrison took its leave of the town during the night and the crippled scribe who lived in the Street of Armorer's was carried off amid much screaming and commotion. Of course, there was no watch to answer the call. The Hell Hounds consider it beneath them to patrol the law-abiding parts of town." Haakon's ire was explained, in part, by his own residence in the upper floors of a house on the Street of Armorers.

Illyra looked at Dubro, who nodded slowly in return.

"Might they be connected?" she asked.

"Pah! What would fleeing garrison troops want with a man who reads fifteen dead languages but can't pass water without someone to guide his hands?"

What indeed?

Dubro went back to his forge and Illyra stared over the bazaar walls to the palace which marked the northern extent of the town. Haakon, who had expected a less mysterious reaction to his news, muttered farewell and wheeled his cart to another stall for a more sympathetic audience.

The first of the day's townsfolk could be heard arguing with other vendors. Illyra hurried back into the shelter of the stall to complete her daily transformation into a S'danzo crone. She pulled

Walegrin's three Ore cards from her deck and placed them in the pouch with her mother's jewelry, lit the incense of gentle-forgetting, and greeted the first querent of the day.

THE DREAM OF THE SORCERESS

A. E. van Vogt

The scream brought Stulwig awake in pitch darkness. He lay for a long moment stiff with fear. Like any resident of old, decadent Sanctuary his first fleeting thought was that the ancient city, with its night prowlers, had produced another victim's cry of terror. This one was almost as close to his second-floor, greenhouse residence as—

His mind paused. Realization came, then, in a flickering self-condemnation.

Did it again!

His special nightmare. It had come out of that shaded part of his brain where he kept his one dark memory. Never a clear recall. Perhaps not even real. But it was all he had from the night three years and four moons ago when his father's death cry had come to him in his sleep.

He was sitting up, now, balancing himself on the side of the couch. And thinking once more, guiltily: if only that first time I had gone to his room to find out.

Instead, it was morning before he had discovered the dead body with its slit throat and its horrifying grimace. Yet there was no sign of a struggle. Which was odd. Because his father at

151

fifty was physically a good example of the healer's art he and Alten both practiced. Lying there in the light of day after his death, his sprawled body looked as powerful and strong as that of his son at thirty.

The vivid images of that past disaster faded. Stulwig sank back and down onto the sheep fur. Covered himself. Listened in the continuing dark to the sound of wind against a corner of his greenhouse. It was a strong wind; he could feel the bedroom tremble. Moments later, he was still awake when he heard a faraway muffled cry— someone being murdered out there in the Maze?

Oddly, that was the final steadying thought. It brought his inner world into balance with the outer reality. After all, this was Sanctuary where, every hour of each night, a life ended violently like a candle snuffed out.

At this time of early, early morning he could think of no purpose that he could have about anything. Not with those dark, dirty, dusty, windblown streets. Nor in relation to the sad dream that had brought him to shocked awareness. Nothing for him to do, actually, but turn over, and—

He woke with a start. It was daylight. And someone was knocking at his outer door two rooms away.

"One moment!" he called out.

Naturally, it required several moments. A few to tumble out of his night robe. And even more to slip into the tunic, healer's gown, and slippers. Then he was hurrying through the bright sunlight of the greenhouse. And on into the dimness of the hallway beyond, with its solid door. Solid, that was, except for the vent at mouth level.

Stulwig placed his lips at his end of the slanted vent, and asked, "Who is it?"

The answering voice was that of a woman. "It's me. Illyra. Alone."

The seeress! Stulwig's heart quickened. His instant hope: another chance for her favors. And alone—that was a strange admission this early in the morning.

Hastily, he unblocked the door. Swung it open, past his own gaunt form. And there she stood in the dimness, at the top of his stairway. She was arrayed as he remembered her, in her numerous skirts and S'danza scarfs. But the beautiful face above all those cloth frills was already shaded with creams and powders.

She said, "Alten, I dreamed of you."

There was something in her tone: an implication of darkness. Stulwig felt an instant chill. She was giving him a sorceress' signal.

Her presence, alone, began to make sense. What she had to offer him transcended a man's itching for a woman. And she expected him to realize it.

Standing there, just inside his door, Stulwig grew aware that he was trembling. A dream. The dream of a sorceress.

He swallowed. And found his voice. It was located deep in his throat, for when he spoke it was a husky sound: "What do you want?"

"I need three of your herbs." She named them: Stypia, gernay, dalin.

This was the bargaining moment. And in the world of Sanctuary there were few victims at such a time. From his already long experience, Stulwig made his offer: "The stypia and the gernay for the dream. For the dalin one hour in my bed tonight for an assignation."

Silence. The bright eyes seemed to shrink.

"What's this?" asked Stulwig. "Is it possible that with your seeress' sight you believe that this time there will be no evasion?"

Twice before, she had made reluctant assignation agreements. On each occasion, a series of happenings brought about a circumstance whereby he needed her assistance. And for that, release from the assignation was her price.

Stulwig's voice softened to a gentler tone: "Surely, it's time, my beautiful, that you discover how much greater pleasure it is for a woman to have lying on her the weight of a normal man rather than that monstrous mass of blacksmith's muscles, the possessor of which by some mysterious power captured you when you were still too young to know any better. Is it a bargain?"

She hesitated a moment longer. And then, as he had expected after hearing the name of the third drug, she nodded.

A business transaction. And that required the goods to be on hand. Stulwig didn't argue. "Wait!" he admonished.

Himself, he did not wait. Instead, he backed quickly out of the hallway and into the greenhouse. He presumed that, with her seeress' sight, she knew that he knew about the very special person who wanted the dalin. He felt tolerant. That prince—he thought. In spite of all the advice the women receive as to when they are, and are not, capable of accepting the male seed, the

youthful governor evidently possesses his concubines so often that they are unable to divert his
favors away from the one who—by sorceress's
wisdom—is most likely in the time of pregnancy
capability.

And so—a miscarriage was needed. An herb to
bring it on.

Suppressing excitement, the dream almost forgotten in his state of overstimulation, the healer
located all three herbs, in turn. The stypia came
from a flowering plant that spread itself over one
entire end of his big, bright room. Someone would
be using it soon for a persistent headache. The
gernay was a mixture of two roots, a flower, and a
leaf, all ground together, to be made into a tea
with boiling water, steeped, and drunk throughout the day. It was for constipation.

While he worked swiftly, deftly, putting each
separately into a small pouch, Stulwig pictured
Illyra leaving her little stall. At the opportune
moment she had pushed aside the black curtains
that blocked her away from the sight of curious
passersby. His mental image was of a one-room
dwelling place in a dreary part of the Maze. Coming out of that flimsy shelter at this hour of the
morning was not the wisest act even for a seeress.
But, of course, she would have some knowing to
guide her. So that she could dart from one concealment to another at exactly the right moments, avoiding danger. And then, naturally,
once she got to the narrow stairway leading up to
his roof abode, there would be only the need to
verify that no one was lurking on the staircase
itself.

He brought the three bags back to the hallway,

and placed two of them into her slender hands. And with that, there it was again, the reason for her visit. The special dream. For him.

He waited, not daring to say anything for, suddenly, there was that tenseness again.

She seemed not to need prompting. She said simply, "In my dream, Ils came to me in the form of an angry young man and spoke to me about you. His manner was ferocious throughout; and my impression is that he is displeased with you." She finished, "In his human form he had jet black hair that came down to his shoulders."

There was silence. Inside Stulwig, a blankness spread from some inner center of fear. A numbness seemed to be in all locations.

Finally: "Ils!" he croaked.

The impossible!

There were tales that reported the chief god of old Ilsig occasionally interfering directly in human affairs. But that he had done so in connection with Alten Stulwig brought a sense of imminent disaster.

Illyra seemed to know what he was feeling. "Something about your father," she said, softly, "is the problem."

Her hand and arm reached out. Gently, she took hold of the third pouch; tugged at it. Stulwig let go. He watched numbly, then as she turned and went rapidly down the stairway. Moments later there was a flare of light as the bottom door opened—and shut. Just before it closed he had a glimpse of the alley that was there, and of her turning to go left.

Ils!

All that morning, after the sick people started to

arrive, Stulwig tried to put the thought of the god out of his mind. There were several persons who talked excessively about their ailments; and for a change he let them ramble on. The sound of each person's voice, in turn, distracted him for a precious time from his inner feeling of imminent disaster. He was accustomed to pay attention, to compare, and decide. And, somehow, through all the numbness he managed to hold onto that ability.

A persistent stomach ache—"What have you been eating?" The flower of the agris plant was exchanged for a silver coin.

A pain in the chest. "How long? Where, exactly?" The root of the dark melles was eaten and swallowed while he watched, in exchange for one small Rankan gold piece.

Persistently bleeding gums. The flower and seeds of a rose, and the light brown grindings from the husk of grain were handed over, with the instruction: "Take a spoonful of each morning and night."

There were a dozen like that. All were anxious and disturbed. And they took up his time until the morning was almost over. Suddenly, the visitors ceased to come. At once, there was the awful thought of Ils the Mighty, angry with him.

"What could he want of me?"

That was the persistent question. Not, what purpose could Alten Stulwig have in this awful predicament? But what intention did the superbeing have in relation to him? Or what did he require of him?

It was almost the noon hour before the second possibility finally penetrated the madness of merely waiting for further signals. And the more personal thought took form.

"It's up to me. I should ask certain people for advice, or even—" sudden hope—"information."

Just like that he had something he could do.

At that moment there was one more patient. And then, as the rather stocky woman departed with her little leather bag clutched in one greasy hand, Stulwig hastily put on his street boots. Grabbed his stave. And, moments later, was heading down the stairs two at a time.

Arrived at the bottom; naturally, he paused. And peered forth cautiously. The narrow street, as he now saw it, pointed both left and right. The nearest crossing was an alleyway to the left. And Stulwig presumed, as his gaze flicked back and forth, Illyra, on her leave-taking that morning, had turned up that alley.

—Though it was still not clear why she had gone left when her stall was to the right. Going by the alley was, for her, a long, devious route home. . . .

His own destination, already decided, required Stulwig to pass her stall. And so, his stave at the ready, he walked rightward. A few dozen steps brought him to a crowded thoroughfare. Again, a pause. And, once more, his gaze flicking back and forth. Not that he felt in danger here, at this hour. What he saw was a typical throng. There were the short people who wore the sheeny satinish cloth of west Caronne. They mingled casually with the taller folk in dark tunics from the far south of the Empire. Equally at ease were red-garbed sailors on shore leave from a Cleean vessel. Here and there a S'danza woman in her rich attire reminded him of Illyra. There were other races, and other dress, of course. But these were more of a kind. The shabby poor. The thieves. The beggars. All too similar, one to the other, to be readily identified.

For a few moments, as he stood there, Stulwig's own problem faded from the forefront of his mind. In its place came a feeling he had had before: a sense of wonder.

Me! Here in this fantastic world.

All these people. This street, with its ancient buildings, its towers, and its minarets. And the meaning of it all going back and back into the dim reaches of a fabulous history.

Almost—standing there—Stulwig forgot where he was heading. And when the memory came again it seemed to have a different form.

A more practical form. As if what he had in mind was a first step of several that would presently lead him to—what?

Mental pause.

It was, he realized, the first dim notion of having a goal beyond mere information. First, of course, the facts; those he had to have.

Somehow, everything was suddenly clearer. As he started forward it was almost as if he had a purpose with a solution implicit in it.

Illyra's stall he passed a short time later. Vague disappointment, then, as he saw that the black curtains were drawn.

Stulwig stalked on, heading west out of town across the bridge which spanned the White Foal River. He ignored the hollow-eyed stares of the Downwinders as he passed their hovels, and only slowed his pace when he reached his destination, a large estate lorded over by a walled mansion. A sell-sword stood guard just inside the large, spreading yard. Theirs was a language Stulwig understood. He took out two coppers and held them forth.

"Tell Jubal that Alten Stulwig wishes to see him."

The coppers were skillfully palmed, and transferred to a slitted pocket in the tight-fitting toga. In a baritone voice the sell-sword called out the message—

Stulwig entered the throne room, and saw that gleaming-skinned black man sitting on the throne chair. He bowed courteously toward the throne. Whereupon Jubal waved one large arm, beckoning his visitor. And then he sat scowling as Stulwig told his story.

Despite the scowl, there was no resistance, or antagonism, in the bright, wicked eyes; only interest. Finally, as Stulwig fell silent, the merchant said, "You believe, as I understand you, that one or another of my numerous paid informants may have heard something at the time of your father's death that would provide a clue: information, in short, that is not even available from a sorceress."

"I so believe," acknowledged Stulwig.

"And how much will you pay if I can correctly recall something that was said to me in passing more than three long years ago?"

Stulwig hesitated; and hoped that his desperation did not show on that sunburned face of his; it was the one thing the chapped skin was good for: sometimes it enabled him to conceal his feelings. What he sensed now was a high cost; and the best outward show for that was to act as if this was a matter about which he was merely curious.

"Perhaps," he said, in his best practical tone, "your next two visits for healing free—"

"For what I remember," said the big black, "the price is the medium Rankan gold piece *and* the two visits."

Long, unhappy pause. All this trouble and cost for an innocent man who, himself, had done nothing. It seemed unfair. "Perhaps," ventured Stulwig, "if you were to give me the information I could decide if the price is merited."

He was slightly surprised when Jubal nodded. "That seems reasonable. We're both men of our word." The big man twisted his lips, as if he were considering. Then: "The morning after your father died, a night prowler who watches the dark hours for me saw Vashanka come through your door—not out of it, through it. He was briefly a figure of dazzling light as he moved down the street. Then he vanished in a blinding puff of brightness akin to lightning. The flareup, since it lit up the entire street, was seen by several other persons, who did not know its origin."

Jubal continued, "I should tell you that there is an old story that a god can go through a wall or a door only if a second god is nearby on the other side. So we may reason that for Vashanka to be able to emerge in the fashion described there was another god outside. However, my informants did not see this second mighty being."

"Bu-u-t-t!" Stulwig heard a stuttering voice. And only when the mad sound collapsed into silence did he realize that it was his own mouth that had tried to speak.

What he wanted to say, what was trying to form in his mind and in his tongue was that, for Vashanka to have penetrated into the barricaded greenhouse in the first place, then there must already have been a god inside; who had somehow inveigled his way past his father's cautious resistance to nighttime visitors.

The words, the meaning, wouldn't come. The logic of it was too improbable for Stulwig to pursue the matter.

Gulping, he fumbled in his pocket. Identified the desired coin with his fingers. Brought it out. And laid it into the outstretched palm. The price was cheap—it was as if a voice inside him spoke his acceptance of that truth.

For a while after Stulwig left Jubal's grounds, his feeling was that he had now done what there was to do. He had the information he had craved. So what else was there? Go home and—and—

Back to normalcy.

It was an unfortunate way of describing the reality to himself. It brought a mental picture of a return to his daily routine as if no warning had been given. His deep, awful feeling was that something more was expected of him. What could it be?

It was noon. The glowing orb in the sky burned down upon Stulwig. His already miserably sunburned face itched abominably, and he kept scratching at the scabs; and hating himself because his sun-sensitive skin was his one disaster that no herb or ointment seemed to help. And here he was stumbling in the direct rays, making it worse.

He was walking unsteadily, half-blinded by his own inner turmoil and physical discomfort, essentially not heeding the crowds around him when . . . the part of him that was guiding him, holding him away from collisions, helping him find a pathway through an everchanging river of people—*that* part, still somehow observant, saw a familiar man's face.

Stulwig stopped short. But already the man was gone by; his feet scraping at the same dusty street as were the feet of a dozen other passers of the moment; scraping dust and breathing it in.

Normally, Stulwig would have let him go. But this was not a normal time. He spun around. He jammed his stave against the ground as a brace. And took four, long, swift steps. He reached.

Almost gently, then, his fingers touched the sleeve and, through it, the arm of the man. "Cappen Varra," Stulwig said.

The young man with the long black hair that rested on his shoulders, turned his head. The tone of Stulwig's voice was evidently not threatening; for Cappen merely paused without tensing. Nor did he make a quick reach of the hand toward the blade at his side.

But it took several moments before he seemed to realize who his interceptor was. Then: "Oh! the healer?" He spoke questioningly.

Stulwig was apologetic. "I would like to speak to you, sir. Though, as I recall it you only sought my services on one occasion. And I think somebody told me that you had recently departed from Sanctuary for a visit to your distant home."

The minstrel did not reply immediately. He was backing off, away from the main stream of that endlessly moving crowd; backing towards a small space between a fruit stand and a table on which stood a dozen small crates, each containing a half dozen or so small, live, edible, noisy birds.

Since Stulwig had shuffled after him, Cappen was able to say in a low voice, "It was a very decisive time for me. The herbs you gave me produced a series of regurgitations which probably saved my life. I still believe I was served poisoned food."

"I need advice," said Alten Stulwig.

"We can talk here," said Cappen.

It was not an easy story to tell. There was a rise and fall of street sounds. Several times he coughed from an intake of dust thrown at him by the heel of a passerby. But in the end he had completed his account. And it was then, suddenly, that the other man's eyes widened, as if a startling thought had come to him.

"Are you telling me that you are seriously pursuing the murderer of your father, despite that you have now discovered that the killer may well be the second most powerful Rankan god?"

It was the first time that meaning had been spoken so exactly. Stulwig found himself suddenly as startled as his questioner. Before he could say anything, the lean-faced, good-looking wandering singer spoke again: "What—what happens if he ever lets you catch up with him?"

The way the question was worded somehow steadied the healer. He said, "As we know, Vashanka can come to me any time he wishes. My problem is that I do not know why he came to my father, nor why he would come to me? If I could find that out, then perhaps I could go to the temple of Ils and ask the priests for help."

Cappen frowned, and said, "Since you seem to

have these powerful purposes, perhaps I should remind you of the myth." He went on: "You know the story. Vashanka is the god of warriors and weapons, the wielder of lightning, and other powerful forces. You know of this?"

"What I don't understand," Stulwig replied helplessly, "is why would such a being kill my father?"

"Perhaps—" a shrug—"they were rivals for the affection of the same woman." He went on, "It is well known that the gods frequently assume human form in order to have concourse with human females." The beautiful male face twisted. The bright eyes gazed into Stulwig's. "I have heard stories," Cappen said, "that you, as your father before you, often accept a woman's favors in exchange for your services as a healer; the woman having nothing else to give pays the price in the time-honored way of male-female. As a consequence you actually have many half-brothers out there in the streets, and you yourself—so it has been said—have sired a dozen sons and daughters, unacknowledged because of course no one can ever be sure who is the father of these numerous waifs, unless there is unmistakable facial resemblance."

Another shrug. "I'm not blaming you. These are the truths of our world. But—"

He stopped. His hand extended gingerly, and touched Stulwig's stave. "It's tough wood."

Stulwig was uneasy. "Awkward to handle in close quarters, and scarcely a weapon to ward off the god of lightning."

"Nevertheless," said Cappen, "it's your best defense. Use it firmly. Keep it between you and any attacker. Yield ground and flee only when there's a good moment."

"But," protested Stulwig, "suppose Vashanka seeks me out? Shall I pit my staff against the Rankan god of war?" When Cappen merely stood there, looking indifferent now, the healer continued in a desperate tone, "There are stories of how Ils helped individuals in battle in the old days. But I grew up after the Rankan conquest and—" he was gloomy—"somehow the powers of the defeated god of old Ilsig didn't seem worth inquiring about. So I'm ignorant of what he did, or how."

Abruptly, Cappen Varra was impatient. "You asked for my advice," he said curtly. "I have given it to you. Goodbye."

He walked off into the crowd.

. . . They brought Stulwig before the prince, who recognized him. "Why, it's the healer," he said. Whereupon, he glanced questioningly at Molin Torchbearer.

The hall of justice was all too brightly lit by the mid-afternoon sunlight. The sun was at that location in the sky whereby its rays shone directly through the slanting vents that were designed to catch, and siphon off, rain water . . . as the high priest said accusingly, "Your most gracious excellency, we found this follower of Ils in the temple of Vashanka."

With the brilliant light pouring down upon him, Stulwig started toward the dais—and the two Hell Hounds, who had been holding him, let him go.

He stopped only when he came to the long

wooden barrier that separated the accused crimi-
nals from the high seat, where the prince sat in
judgment. From that fence, Stulwig spoke his protest. "I did no harm, your highness. And I meant
no harm. Tell his excellency—" he addressed
Torchbearer—"that your assistants found me on
my knees before the—" he hesitated; he had been
about to say "the idol". Uneasily, his mind moved
over to the word, "statue". But he rejected that
also, shuddering. After a long moment he
finished lamely—"before Vashanka himself,
praying for his assistance."

"Yes, but a follower of Ils praying to a son of
Savankala—" Torchbearer was grim—"absolutely forbidden by the doctrines of our religion."

There seemed to be no answer that he could
make. Feeling helpless, Stulwig waited. It was a
year since he had last seen the youthful governor,
who would now decide his fate. Standing there,
Stulwig couldn't help but notice that there were
changes in the young ruler's appearance—for the
better, it seemed to him.

The prince, as all knew, was at this time 20
years old. He had been representative in
Sanctuary for his older half-brother, the emperor,
for only one of those years, but that year had
brought a certain maturity where once there had
been softness. It was still a boyish face, but a year
of power had marked it with an appearance of
confidence.

The young governor seemed undecided, as he
said, "Well—it does not look like a serious crime.
I should think we would encourage converts
rather than punishing them." He hesitated, then
followed the amenities. "What penalty do you

recommend?" He addressed the high priest of Rankan deities courteously.

There was a surprisingly long pause. Almost, it was as if the older man was having second thoughts. Torchbearer said finally, "Perhaps, we should inquire what he was praying for. And then decide."

"An excellent idea," the prince agreed heartily.

Once more, then, Stulwig told his story, ending in a humble tone, "Therefore, sir, as soon as I discovered that, apparently, the great gods themselves were involved in some disagreement, I decided to pray to Vashanka to ask what he wanted me to do; asked him what amends I could make for whatever my sin might be."

He was surprised as he completed his account to see that the prince was frowning. And, in fact, moments later, the young governor bent down towards one of the men at a table below him to one side, and said something in a low voice. The aide's reply was equally inaudible.

The youngest ruler Sanctuary had ever had thereupon faced forward. His gaze fixed on Stulwig's face. "There are several people in these parts," he said in an alarmingly severe voice, "of whose whereabouts we maintain a continuing awareness. Cappen Varra, for several reasons, is one of these. And so, Mr. Healer, I have to inform you that Cappen left Sanctuary half a moon ago, and is not expected back for at least two more moons."

"B-b-bu-ut—" Stulwig began. And stopped. Then in a high pitched voice: "That man in the seeress' dream!" he stuttered. "Long black hair to the shoulders. Ils in human form!"

There was silence after he had spoken there in
that great hall of justice, where a youthful Rankan
prince sat in judgment, looking down from his
high bench. Other offenders were waiting in the
back of the room. They were guarded by slaves,
with the two Hell Hounds that had brought Stulwig acting as overseers.

So there would be witnesses to this judgment.
The wisdom of it, whatever course it might take,
would be debated when the news of it got out.

Standing there, Stulwig suppressed an impulse
to remind his highness of a certain night thirteen
moons ago. In the wee hours he had been called
out of his bed, and escorted to the palace.

On that occasion he had been taken directly
into the prince's bedroom. There he found a
frightened young man, who had awakened in the
darkness with an extremely fast heartbeat—more
than double normal, Stulwig discovered when he
counted the pulse. The attending court healer had
not been able, by his arts, to slow the madly beating organ. Stulwig had braced himself, and had
taken the time to ask the usual questions, which
produced the information that his highness had
imbibed excessively all evening.

A minor heart condition was thus revealed. The
cure: primarily time for the body to dispose of the
alcohol through normal channels. But Stulwig
asked, and was given, permission to return to his
greenhouse. He raced there accompanied by a
Hell Hound. Arrived at his quarters, he procured
the mixture of roots, nettles, and a large red flower
which, when steeped in boiling water, and swallowed in mouthfuls every few minutes, within an
hour had the heartbeat down, not to normal, but

sufficiently to be reassuring.

He thereupon informed the young man that according to his father persons that he had attended when they were young, who had the same reaction, were still alive two decades later. The prince was greatly relieved, and promised to limit himself to no more than one drink of an evening.

Remained, then, the task of saving face for the court healer. Which Stulwig did by thanking that disgraced individual for calling him for consultation; and, within the hearing of the prince, adding that it took many individuals to accumulate experience of all the ills that men were heir to. "And one of these days I shall be asking your help."

. . . Would the youthful governor remember that night, and decide—hopeful thought—that Alten Stulwig was too valuable to penalize?

What the prince did, first, was ask one more question. He said, "During the time you were with the person who seemed to be Cappen Varra, did he break into song, or recite a verse?"

The significance of the question was instantly apparent. The minstrel was known for his gaiety, and his free and easy renditions under all circumstances. Stulwig made haste to say, "No, highness, not a sound, or a poetic phrase. Contrariwise, he seemed very serious."

A few moments later, the prince rendered his judgment. He said, "Since mighty Vashanka himself seems to be acting directly in this matter, it would be presumptious of us to interfere."

The lean-faced young man glanced at Molin. The high priest hesitated, then nodded. Whereupon the prince turned once more to Stulwig.

"Most worthy healer," he said, "you are released to whatever the future holds for you. May the gods dispense justice upon you, balancing your virtues against your sins."

"—So he does remember!" thought Stulwig, gratefully.

Surprisingly, after he had been escorted outside, Stulwig knew at once which was the proper place for him to go. Many times he had been confronted by grief or guilt, or the hopelessness of a slighted lover, or a betrayed wife. For none of these had his herbs ever accomplished more than a passing moment of sleep or unconsciousness.

So now, as he entered the Vulgar Unicorn, he muttered under his breath the bitter advice he had given on those special occasions for what his father had called ailments of the spirit. The words, heard only by himself, were: "What you need, Alten, is a good stiff drink."

It was the ancient prescription for calming the overwrought or the overemotional. In its fashion, however, liquor in fact was a concoction of brewed herbs, and so within his purview.

The smell of the inn was already in his nostrils. The dimly lit interior blanked his vision. But Stulwig could see sufficiently well so that he was aware of vague figures sitting at tables, and of the gleam of polished wood. He sniffed of the mingling odors of hot food cooking. And already felt better.

And he knew this interior sufficiently well. So he strode forward confidently toward the dividing barrier where the brew was normally dispensed. And he had his lips parted to give his order when his eyes, more accustomed to the light, saw who it was that was taking the orders.

"One-Thumb!" The name was almost torn out of his lips; so great was his surprise and delight.

Eagerly, he reached forward and grasped the other's thick hand. "My friend, you had us all worried. You have been absent—" He stopped, confused. Because the time involved even for a long journey was long. Much more than a year. He finished his greeting with a gulp, "You are right welcome, sir."

The owner of the Vulgar Unicorn had become more visible with each passing moment. So that when he gestured with one of his big hands at a helper, Stulwig perceived the entire action; even saw the youth turn and come over.

The rolypoly but rugged One-Thumb indicated a table in one corner. "Bring two cups of brew thither for my friend and myself," he said. To Alten he added, "I would have words with you, sir."

So there they sat presently. And, after several sips, One-Thumb said, "I shall say quickly what need be said. Alten, I must confess that I am not the real One-Thumb. I came because, with my sorcerer's seeing, when this past noon hour my body took on the form at which you are gazing, I had a visitor who informed me that the transformation to a known person related to you."

It was a long explanation. Long enough for Stulwig to have a variety of reactions. First, amazement. Then, progressively, various puzzlements. And, finally, tentative comprehension, and acceptance.

And since he held a drink in his hand, he raised it, and said, "To the real One-Thumb, wherever he may be."

With that, still thinking hard as to what he could gain from this meeting, he sipped from his cup, took a goodly quaff from it, and set it down. All the while noticing that the other did not drink to the toast.

The false One-Thumb said unhappily, "My seeing tells me that the real One-Thumb is in some strange location. It is not quite clear that he is still dead; but he was killed."

Up came Stulwig's glass. "Very well, then, to Enas Yorl, the sorcerer, who in whatever shape seems to be willing to be my friend."

This time the other man's cup came up slowly. He sipped. "I suppose," he said, "no one can refuse to drink to himself; since my motives are worthy I shall do so."

Stulwig's mind was flickering again with the meanings of what had been said in that long explanation. So, now, he asked the basic question: "Enas," he mumbled, "in what way does your being in One-Thumb's body shape relate to me?"

The fleshy head nodded. "Pay careful heed," said the voice of One-Thumb. "The goddess Azyuna appeared to me as I was experiencing the anguish of changing form, and ask me to give you this message. You must go home before dark. But do not this night admit to your quarters any person who has the outward appearance of a man. Do this no matter how pitifully he begs for a healer's assistance, or how many pieces of gold he is prepared to pay. Tonight, direct all male visitors to other healers."

It took a while to drink to that, and to wonder about it aloud. And, of course, as Sanctuarites, they discussed once more the story of Azyuna.

How Vashanka had discovered that she (his sister) and his ten brothers had plotted to murder the father-god of Ranke, Savakala. Whereupon, Vashanka in his rage slew all ten of the brothers; but his sister he reserved for a worse fate. She became his unwilling mistress. And at time when the winds moaned and sobbed, it was said that Azyuna was again being forced to pay the price of her intended betrayal of her parents.

And now she had come down from heaven to warn a mere human being against the brother who exacted that shame from her.

"How," asked Stulwig, after he had quaffed most of a second cup and had accordingly reached a philosophical state of mind, "would you, old wise Enas Yorl, explain why a goddess would take the trouble to warn a human being against some scheme of her god-brother-lover?"

"Because," was the reply, "she may be a goddess but she is also a woman. And as all men know, women get even in strange ways."

At that, Stulwig, remembering certain experiences of his own, shuddered a little, nodded agreement, and said, "I estimate that we have been imbibing for a goodly time, and so perhaps I had better take heed of your warning, and depart. Perhaps, there is something I can do for you. A fee, perhaps."

"Make it one free visit when one of my changing shapes becometh ill."

"But not this night." Stulwig stood up, somewhat lightheaded, and was even able to smile at his small jest.

"No, not this night," agreed One-Thumb, also standing up. The big man added quickly, "I shall appear to accompany you to the door as if to bid you goodbye. But in fact I shall go out with you. And so One-Thumb will vanish once more, perhaps this time forever."

"He has done nobly this day," said Stulwig. Whereupon he raised the almost empty third cup, and said, "To the spirit of One-Thumb, wherever it may be, my good wishes."

As it developed, Enas Yorl's plan of escape was made easy. Because as they emerged from the inn there, coming up, was a small company of Rankan military led by a Hell Hound. The latter, a man named Quag, middle-aged, but with a prideful bearing, said to Stulwig, "Word came to his highness that you were imbibing heavily; and so he has sent me and this company to escort you to your residence."

Stulwig turned to bid farewell to the false One-Thumb. And at once observed that no such person was in sight. Quag seemed to feel that he was surprised. "He went around that corner." He indicated with his thumb. "Shall we pursue him?"

"No, no."

It was no problem at all for a man with three cups of brew in him to step forward, and walk beside a Hell Hound like an equal.

And to say, "I'm somewhat surprised at his highness taking all this trouble for a person not of Ranke birth, or—" daringly—"religion."

Quag was calm, seemingly unoffended. "These are not matters about which I am qualified to have an opinion."

"Of course," Stulwig continued with a frown, "getting me back to my quarters could place me in a location where the mighty Vashanka could most easily find me."

They were walking along a side street in the Maze. But a goodly crowd pressed by at that moment. So if Quag were contemplating a reply it was interrupted by the passing of so great a number of individuals.

When they had wended through the mob, Stulwig continued, "After all, we have to remember that it is Ils that is the god of a thousand eyes. Which, presumably, means that he can see simultaneously where everybody in the world of Ilsig is at any one moment. No such claim—of many eyes—is made for either Savankala or his son, Vashanka. And so we may guess that Vashanka does not know that—"

He stopped, appalled. He had almost let slip that the goddess Azyuna had come to Enas Yorl with a warning. And, of course, her brother-lover, with his limited vision, would not know that she had done so.

"These are all fine points," Stulwig finished lamely, "and of concern only to an individual like myself who seems to have earned the displeasure of one of these mighty beings."

Quag was calm. "Having lived many years," he said, "it could be that I have some clarifying information for you, whereby you may judge the seriousness of your situation." He continued, after a moment of silence, "In Sanctuary, the reason for the gods interfering in human affairs can have only one underlying motive. Someone has got above himself. What would be above a healer? A woman of noble family taken advantage of. An insult to a priest or god. Was your father guilty of either sin?"

"Hmmm!" Stulwig did not resist the analysis. He nodded thoughtfully in the Sanctuary way of agreement, shaking his head from side to side. "No question," he said, "it was not a chance killing. The assassin by some means penetrated a barricaded residence, committed the murder, and departed without stealing any valuables. In a city where people are daily killed most casually for their possessions, when—as in this instance of my father's assassination—the possessions are untouched, we are entitled to guess a more personal motive."

He added unhappily, "I have to confess that the reason I did not run to his rescue when I heard his cry, was that he had established an agreement with me that neither of us would intrude upon the other during the night hours. So it could have been a lady of quality being avenged."

For a small time they walked silently. Then: "I advise you to abandon this search." Quag spoke earnestly. "Go back to your healing profession, and leave murderers to the authorities."

This time Stulwig did the up and down headshake, meaning no. He said unhappily, "When Ils himself manifests in a dream, which unmistakably commands me to track down the killer, I have no choice."

The Hell Hound's craggy face was visibly unimpressed. "After all," he said dismissingly, "Your Ils failed all his people in Sanctuary when he allowed the city to be overrun by armies that worshiped another god."

"The city is being punished for its sinfulness."
Stulwig automatically spoke the standard explanation given by the priests of Ils. "When we have
learned our lesson, and paid our penalty, the in-
vader will be impelled to depart."

"When I left the palace," said Quag, "there was
no sign of the prince's slaves packing his goods."
Shrugging. "Such a departure for such a reason is
difficult for me to envision, and I suggest you
build no hopes on it."

He broke off. "Ah, here we are. As soon as you
are safely inside—and of course we'll search the
place and make sure there is no one lurking in a
dark corner—"

It was a few periods later. "Thank you," said a
grateful Stulwig. He watched them, then, go
down the stairs. When Quag paused at the bottom,
and looked back questioningly, Stulwig dutifully
closed and barricaded the door.

And there he was.

It was a quiet evening. Two men patients and
one woman patient knocked on the door. Each,
through the vent, requested healing service.
Stulwig sent the men down the street to Kurd; and
they departed in their considerably separated
times, silently accepting.

Stulwig hesitated when he heard the woman's
voice. She was a long-time patient, and would pay
in gold. Nevertheless, he finally directed her to a
healer named Nemis. When the woman objected,
he gave as his excuse that he had eaten bad food,
and was not well. She seemed to accept that; for
she went off, also.

Shortly after midnight there was a fourth hesi-
tant knock. It was Illyra. As he heard her whisper,

something inside Stulwig leaped with excitement. She had come, she said, as they had agreed upon that morning.

An exultant Stulwig unlocked the door. Admitted her. Motioned her towards his bedroom. And, as she went with a heavy rustling of her numerous skirts, he barricaded the door again.

Moments later, he was snuffing out the candles, and flinging off his clothes. And then in pitch darkness he joined her in the bed. As he located her naked body, he had no sense of guilt; no feeling of being wrong.

In Sanctuary everybody knew the game. There were no prissies. Every woman was someone's mistress whether she liked it or not. Every man was out for himself, and took advantage where he could. There were, true, codes of honor and religion. But they did not apply to love, liquor, or making a living. You drove the hardest bargain right now.

The opportunity seen. Instantly, the mind wildly scanned the possibilities. Then came the initial outrageous demand, thereupon negotiated downward by the equally determined defenses of the second party to the transaction.

And that was what had brought the beautiful Illyra into his embrace. Her own agreement that, unless something happened to interfere, she would be available for him in the man-woman relation.

Apparently, once she realized that the bargain was binding, she did not resist its meaning. In the darkness Stulwig found her naked body fully acceptant of him. Complete with many small motions and excitements. Most of the women who paid in kind for his services lay like frozen statues, occasionally vibrating a little in the final moments of the act. After which they hastily slipped out of bed. Dressed. And raced off down the stairs and out into the Maze.

With Illyra so different, even to the point of sliding her palms over his skin, Stulwig found himself thinking once more of the huge blacksmith who was her established lover. It was hard to visualize this female, even though she seemed somewhat larger than he would have guessed, with such a massive male on top of her. Although—

A sudden realization: there were surprisingly strong muscles that lay under him. . . . This woman is no weakling. In fact—

Presently, as he proceeded with the lovemaking, Stulwig found himself mentally shaking his head. . . . Those voluminous S'danza skirts, he thought, conceal more than slender flesh—his sudden impression was that, in fact, Illyra was on the plump side. And that obviously she wore the skirts to hide a considerably heavier body than she wanted onlookers to know about. Not hard to do, with her face so thin and youthful.

No mind. She was a woman who had not been easy to capture. And here she was, actually responding. Interesting, also, that her skin felt unusually warm, almost as if she had a temperature.

He was coming to the climax. And so the size of her was temporarily blanked out. Thus, the awareness of a transformation of her plump body into that of an Amazon, was like coming out of a glorious dream into a nightmare.

His sudden impossible impression: he was

lying on top of a woman over six feet tall, with hips that spread out beneath him at least a foot wider than he was.

His stunned thought, immediately spoken: "Illyra, what is this? Some sorceress' trick?"

In a single, sliding motion he disengaged from that massive female body. Slid off onto the floor. And scrambled to his feet.

As he did so there was a flash of incredible brightness. It lit up the entire room, revealing an oversized, strange, naked woman in his couch, sitting up now.

And revealing, also, a man's huge lighted figure coming through a door that, before his father's death, had been a private entrance to Alten's bedroom. It was an entrance that he had, long ago now, sealed up. . . . Through it came the shining figure into the bedroom.

One incredulous look was all Stulwig had time for. And many, many desperate awarenesses: the glowing one, the being who shone with a fiery body brightness—was Vashanka.

By the time he had that thought, he had numbly grasped his stave. And, moments later, was backing naked through the doorway that led out to the greenhouse.

Inside the bedroom a god was yelling in a deep, baritone voice at the nude Amazon, who was still sitting on the edge of the bed. And the Amazon was yelling back in a voice that was like that of a male tenor. They spoke in a language that was not Ilsig.

In his time Stulwig had learned several hundred basic medically useful words in half a dozen dialects of the Rankan empire. So now, after a few familiar words had come through to him—suddenly, the truth.

The woman was Azyuma. And Vashanka was berating her for her infidelity. And she was yelling back, accusing him of similar infidelities with human women.

The revelation dazzled Stulwig. So the gods, as had so often been suggested in vague tales about them, were like humans in their physical needs. Fleshly contacts. Angry arguments. Perhaps even intake of food with the consequent digestion and elimination by stool and urination.

But much more important for this situation was the intimate act she had sought with a human male.... Trust a woman! thought Stulwig. Hating her incestuous relationship. Degraded. Sad. Hopeless. But nevertheless jealous when her god-husband-brother went off to earth, and, as gods have done since the beginning of time, lay with a human woman. Or two. Or a hundred.

So she had got even. Had taken the form of a human woman. And had cunningly enticed a male—this time, himself; three and a half years ago, his father—to lie with her. Not too difficult to do in lustful Sanctuary.

And thus, Ten-Slayer, in his jealous rage, had become Eleven-Slayer—if humans like the elder Stulwig counted in the arithmetic of the divine ones.

Standing, now, in the center of the greenhouse, with no way at all that he could use as a quick escape (it always required a fair time to unbarricade his door) Stulwig braced himself. Clutched his stave. And waited for he knew not what.

He grew aware, then, that the word battle in the

bedroom had come to an ending. The woman was standing now, hastily wrapping the S'danza skirts around her huge waist. That was a momentary revelation. So such skirts could fit all female sizes without alteration.

Moments later, the woman came out. She had three of the filmy scarfs wrapped around her upper body. Her eyes avoided looking at Stulwig as she thudded past him on bare feet. And then he heard her at the door, removing the barricade.

That brought a sudden, wild hope to the man. Perhaps, if he backed in that direction, he also might make it through the doorway, once it was unblocked.

But his belief was: he dared not move. Dared not turn his head.

As Stulwig had that tense realization, the brightness—which had been slightly out of his line of vision—moved. There was an awesome sound of heavy, heavy footsteps. And then—

Vashanka strode into view.

There was no question in Stulwig's numbed mind. What he was seeing, suddenly, was clearly a sight not given to many men to observe so close up. The Rankan god, Vashanka. Maker of lightning in the sky. Master of weaponry. Killer of ten god-brothers. Murderer of Jutu Stulwig (father of Alten).

The mighty being stood now, poised in the doorway leading from the bedroom. And he literally had to stoop down so that his head did not strike the top of the door jamb.

He was a massive figure whose every stretch and fold of skin was lit up like a fire. The light that enveloped him from head to foot actually seemed to flicker, as if tiny tongues of white heat were burning there.

Those innumerable fires suffused the greenhouse with a brightness greater than daylight.

Clearly, a human confronted by a god should not rely on force alone. At no time was that realization a coherent thought in Stulwig's mind. But the awful truth of it was there in his muscles and bones. Every movement he made reflected the reality of a man confronting an overwhelming power.

Most desperately, he wanted to be somewhere, far away.

Which was impossible. And so—

Stulwig heard his voice stuttering out the first meaning of those defensive thought-feelings: "I'm innocent. I didn't know who she was."

It was purpose of a desperate sort. Avoid this incredible situation by explaining. Arguing. Proving.

The baleful eyes stared at him after he had spoken. If the being behind those eyes understood the words, there was no clear sign.

The man stammered on: "She came as a sorceress with whom I had arranged a rendezvous for this night. How could I know that it was a disguise?"

The Ilsig language, suddenly, did not seem to be a sufficient means of communication. Stulwig had heard that its verbal structure was despised by Rankans who had learned the speech of the conquered race. The verbs—it was said—were regarded by Rankans as lacking force. Whereas the conqueror's tongue was alive with verbs that expressed intense feeling, absolute purpose, uttermost determination.

Stulwig, fleetingly remembering those comparisons, had the thought: "To Vashanka it will seem as if I'm begging for mercy, whereas all I want is understanding."

Feeling hopeless, the man clung to his stave. It was all he had. So he held it up between himself and the great fire-god. But each passing instant he was recalling what Quag, the Hell Hound, had said—about Ils having failed his people of Sanctuary.

Suddenly, it was hard to believe that the minor magic of a failed god, as projected into a wooden stick—however tough the wood—could withstand even one blow from the mighty Vashanka.

As he had that cringing thought, Stulwig grew aware that the god had extended one hand. Instantly, the flame of the arm-hand grew brighter. Abruptly, it leaped. And struck the stave.

Utter confusion of brightness.

And confusion in his dazzled eyes as to what was happening, or what had happened.

Only one thing was clear: the attack of the god against the man had begun.

. . . He was still alive; that was Stulwig's first awareness. Alive with, now, a vague memory of having seen the lightning strike the stave. And of hearing a base-voiced braying sound. But of what exactly had happened at the moment of the fire interacting with the stave there was no afterimage in his eyes.

Uncertain, still somehow clinging miraculously to the stave, Stulwig took several steps backward before the awful brightness let go of his vision centers. And there, striding toward him, was the fire-god.

Up came the stave, defensively. But even as he was remembering the words of Cappen Varra, about holding the stave in front of him, Stulwig—the stave fighter—instinctively swung the stave in a hitting motion.

Swung it at the great being less than five feet away. And felt a momentary savage surge of hope, as mighty Vashanka actually ducked to avoid the blow.

Stave fighting! He had done a lot of it out there in the wilderness, where he either tended wild herbs, or gathered herbs for his greenhouse. Amazing how often a wandering nomad or two, seeing him alone, instantly unsheathed swords and came in for the kill.

In such a battle it would be deathly dangerous merely to prod with the stave. Used as a prod, the stave could be snatched. At which, it was merely a tussle of two men tugging for possession. And virtual certainty that some wild giant of a man would swiftly wrestle it away from the unwise person who had mistakenly tried to use it as if it also were a sword.

By Ils—thought a jubilant Stulwig—there is power in this stave. And he, the lightning-god, perceives it as dangerous.

With that realization, he began to swing with all the force he could muster: whack, whack, whack! Forgotten was Cappen Varra's admonition to use the stave only as a barrier.

It was fascinating—and exciting—to Stulwig to notice that Vashanka jumped back from the stave whenever it swung toward him. Once, the god actually leaped way up to avoid being hit. The stave went by almost two foot-lengths beneath his lowest extremity.

—But why is he staying? Why isn't he trying to get away if the stave is dangerous to him? . . . That thought came suddenly, and at once brought a great diminishment to Stulwig's battle impulse.

The fear that hit the man abruptly was that there had to be a reason why Vashanka continued to fight by avoidance. Could it be that he expected the power in the stave to wear off?

The awful possibility brought back the memory of what Ils-Cappen Varra had said. The instant shock of what must already have happened to the stave's defense power sent Stulwig backing at top speed toward the hallway leading to the stairs. He gulped with joy, then, as he glanced back for just an instant, and saw that the normally barricaded door had been left wide open by Azyuna.

With that, he spun on his heels, and almost literally flung himself down the stairs, taking four, and once five, steps at a time. He came to the bottom. And, mercifully, that door also was open. It had been hard to see as he made his wild escape effort.

At that ultimate last moment, the entire stairwell suddenly lit up like day. And there was instantly no question but that the demon-god had belatedly arrived, and was in hot pursuit.

Out in that night, so dark near his entrance, Stulwig ran madly to the nearest corner. Darted around it. And then ran along the street until he came to a main thoroughfare. There he stopped, took up position with his back against a closed stall, and his stave in front of him.

Belated realization came that he was still stark naked.

There were people here even at this late hour. Some of them looked at Stulwig. But almost everybody stopped and stared in the direction from which Stulwig had come—where a great brightness shone into the sky, visible above a long, low building with a dozen projecting towers.

Everywhere, now, voices were expressing amazement. And then, even as Stulwig wondered if Vashanka would actually continue his pursuit—abruptly, the brilliant light winked out.

It took a while, then, to gather his courage. But the feeling was: even though I made the mistake of fighting, I won—

Returning took a while longer. Also, the streets were darker again; and so his nakedness was not so obvious. Passersby had to come close before, in a city where so many were skimpily dressed, they could see a naked man at night. Thus he was able to act cautiously, without shame.

'Finally, then, holding his stave in front of him, Stulwig climbed the stairs up to his darkened quarters. Found the candle that was always lit (and replaced, of course, at proper intervals) at the bottom of a long tube in his office. And then, when he had made certain that the place was, indeed, free of intruders, he hastily replaced the barricade.

A little later.

Stulwig lay sprawled on his bed, unable to sleep. He considered taking one of the herbs he normally prescribed for light sleepers. But that

might send him off into a drugged unconsciousness. And for this night that seemed a last resort.
Not to be done casually.

Lying there, tossing, he grew aware that there
were sounds coming to him out of the night.
Voices. Many voices. A crowd of voices.

Huh!

Up and over into the greenhouse. First, removing a shutter. And then, looking out and down.

The streets that he could see from his second
floor were alive with torchlights. And, everywhere, people. Several times, as passersby went
beneath his window, Stulwig leaned out and
called stentoriously: "What is it? What's happening?"

From the replies that were yelled back, totalling
at least as many as he could count on the fingers of
both hands, he was able to piece together the
reason for the celebration—for that was what it
was.

The people of Sanctuary celebrating a victory.

What had occurred: beginning shortly after the
brilliance of Vashanka had dwindled to darkness
in a puff of vanishment, messengers began to run
along the streets of the Maze and through all the
lesser sections of the city.

The messengers were Jubal's spies and informants. And as a result of the message they
spread—

Myrtis' women whispered into the ears of
males, as each in turn received that for which he
had paid. An electrifying piece of information it
was, for the men flung on their clothes, grabbed
their weapons, and charged off into the night dis-
tances of the Maze.

The worshipers at the bar of the Vulgar Unicorn suddenly drained their cups. And they, also, took to their heels—that was the appearance. An astonished barkeep ventured to the door. Peered out. And, hearing the pad of feet and the rustle of clothing, and seeing the torches, hastily locked up and joined the throngs that were streaming in one direction: toward the temple of Ils.

From his open shutter Stulwig could see the temple with its gilded dome. All the portions that he could see were lit up, and the light was visible through numerous glass reflectors. A thousand candles must be burning inside for there to be so many shining surfaces.

And inside the temple the priests were in a state of excitement. For the message that Jubal's informants carried to all Sanctuary was that Ils had engaged in battle with the lightning god of the Rankans, and had won.

There would be exultant worshipping until the hour of dawn: that was the meaning that Stulwig had had shouted up to him.

As the meaning finally came to him, Stulwig hastily closed the shutter. And stood there, shivering. It was an inner cold, not an outer one. Was this wise?—he wondered. Suppose the people in the palace came out to learn what all the uproar was? Suppose Vashanka, in his rage at being made to appear a loser, sent his lightning bolts down upon the city. Come to think of it, the sky above had already started to look very cloudy and threatening.

His entire body throbbing with anxiety, Stulwig nonetheless found himself accepting the celebration as justified. It was true. Ils was the victor. And he had deliberately sought the opportunity. So it could be that the ancient god of Ilsig was at long last ready for—what?

What could happen? How could the forces of the Rankan empire be persuaded to depart from Sanctuary?

Stulwig was back in bed, the wonder and the mystery of it still seething inside him.

And he was still awake, later, when there came a gentle knock on his outer door.

Instant shock. Fear. Doubt. And then, trembling, he was at the vent asking the question: "Who is it?"

The voice of Illyra answered softly, "I am here, Alten, as we agreed this morning, to pay my debt in kind."

Long pause. Because the doubt and shock, and the beginning of disappointment, were absolutely intense. So long a pause that the woman spoke again: "My blacksmith, as you call him, has gone to the temple of Ils and will not be back until morning."

On one level—the level of his desire—it had the ring of truth. But the denying thought was stronger. Suppose this was Azyuna, forced by her shamed brother-lover to make one more entrance into the home of the healer; so that the brother could use some mysterious connection with her to penetrate hard walls. Then, when death had been dealt, Ils would again be disgraced.

Thinking thus, a reluctant Stulwig said, "You are freed of your promise, Illyra. Fate has worked once more to deny me one of the great joys of life. And once more enabled you to remain faithful to that hulking monster."

The healer uttered a long sigh; finished: "Perhaps, I shall have better fortune next time."

As he returned to his sheepskin he did have the male thought that a night when a man made love to a goddess, could surely not be considered a total loss.

In fact—

Remembering, suddenly, that the affair had also included embracing, in its early stages, an Illyra look-alike, Stulwig began to relax.

It was then that sweet sleep came.

VASHANKA'S MINION

Janet Morris

1

The storm swept down on Sanctuary in unnatural fury, as if to punish the thieves for their
misdeeds. Its hailstones were large as fists. They
pummeled Wideway and broke windows on the
Street of Red Lanterns and collapsed the temple of
Ils, most powerful of the conquered Ilsigs' gods.

The lightning it brought snapped up from the
hills and down from the devilish skies and
wherever it spat the world shuddered and rolled.
It licked round the dome of Prince Kadakithis's
palace and when it was gone, the Storm God Vashanka's name was seared into the stone in huge
hieratic letters visible from the harbor. It slithered
in the window of Jubal's walled estate and circled
round the slavetrader's chair while he sat in it,
turning his black face blue with terror.

It danced on a high hill between the slaver's
estate and the cowering town, where a mercenary
named Tempus schooled his new Syrese horse in
the art of death. He had bought the tarnished
silver beast sight unseen, sending to a man whose
father's life he had once saved.

"Easy," he advised the horse, who slipped in a sharp turn, throwing mud up into his rider's face. Tempus cursed the mud and the rain and the hours he would need to spend on his tack when the lesson was done. As for the screaming, stumbling hawk-masked man who fled iron-shod hooves in ever-shortening circles, he had no gods to invoke—he just howled.

The horse wheeled and hopped; its rider clung tightly, reins flapping loose, using only his knees to guide his mount. If the slaver who kept a private army must flaunt the fact, then the mercenary-cum-Guardsman would reduce its ranks. He would teach Jubal the overweening flesh merchant that he who is too arrogant, is lost. He saw it as part of his duty to the Ranke Prince-Governor he was sworn to protect. Tempus had taken down a dozen hawk-masks. This one, stumbling gibbering, would make thirteen.

"Kill," suggested the mercenary, tiring of his sport in the face of the storm.

The flattened ears of the misty horse flickered, came forward. It lunged, neck out. Teeth and hooves thunked into flesh. Screaming. Then screaming stopped.

Tempus let the horse pummel the corpse awhile, stroking the beast's neck and cooing soft praise. When bones showed in a lightning flash, he backed the horse off and set it at a walk toward the walled city.

It was then that the lightning came circling round man and mount.

"Stand, stand." The horse, though he shook like a newborn foal, stood. The searing red light violated Tempus's tight-shut lids and made his eyes tear. An awful voice rang inside his head, deep and thunderous: *"You are mine."*

"I have never doubted it," grated the mercenary.

"You have doubted it repeatedly," growled the voice querulously, if thunder can be said to carp. *"You have been unruly, faithless though you pledged me your troth. You have been, since you renounced your inheritance, a mage, a philosopher, an auditing Adept of the Order of the Blue Star, a—"*

"Look here, God. I have also been a cuckold, a footsoldier in the ranks, a general at the end of that. I have bedded more iron in flesh than any ten other men who have lived as long as I. Now you ring me round with thunder and compass me with lightning though I am here to expand Your worship among these infidels. I am building Your accursed temple as fast as I can. I am no priest, to be terrified by loud words and bright manifestations. Get Thee hence, and leave this slum unenlightened. They do not deserve me, and they do not deserve You!"

A gust sighed fiercely, flapping Tempus's woolens against his mail beneath.

"I have sent you hither to build me a temple among the heathens, O sleepless one! A temple you will build!"

"A temple I will build. Yes, sir, Vashanka, lord of the Edge and the Point. If You leave me alone to do it." Damn pushy tutelary god. "You blind my horse, O God, and I will put him under Your threshold instead of the enemies slain in battle Your ritual demands. Then we will see who comes to worship there."

"Do not trifle with me, Man."

"Then let me be. I am doing the best I can. There is no room for foreign gods in the hearts of these Sanctuarites. The Ilsig gods they were born under have seen to that. Do something amazing: strike the fear of You into them."

"I cannot even make you cower, O impudent human!"

"Even Your visitations get old, after three hundred-fifty years. Go scare the locals. This horse will founder, standing hot in the rain."

The thunder changed its tune, becoming canny. *"Go you to the harbor, My son, and look upon what My Majesty hath wrought! And into the Maze, where I am making My power known!"*

With that, the corral of lightning vanished, the thunder ceased, and the clouds blew away on a west wind, so that the full moon shone upon the land.

"Too much krrf," the mercenary who had sold himself for a Hell Hound sighed. "Hell Hound" was what the citizenry called the Prince's Guard; as far as Tempus was concerned, Sanctuary was Hell. The only thing that made it bearable was krff, his drug of choice. Rubbing a clammy palm across his mouth, he dug in his human-hide belt until searching fingers found a little silver box he always carried. Flipping it open, he took a pinch of black Caronne krrf and, clenching his fist, piled the dust into the hollow between his first thumb joint and the fleshy muscle leading to his knuckle. He sniffed deeply, sighed, and repeated the process, inundating his other nostril.

"Too much damn krrf," he chuckled, for the krrf had never been stepped on—he did not buy

adulterated drugs—and all six and a half feet of
him tingled from its kiss. One of these days he
would have to stop using it—the same day he lay
down his sword.

He felt for its hilt, patted it. He had taken to
calling it his "Wriggly-be-good," since he had
come to this Godforsaken warren of magicians
and changelings and thieves. Then, the initial
euphoria of the drug past, he kneed his horse
homeward.

It was the krrf, not the instructions of the lightning or any fear of Vashanka, that made him go by
way of the harbor. He was walking out his horse
before taking it to the stable the Hell Hounds
shared with the barracks personnel. What had
ever possessed him to come down-country among
the Ilsigs? It was not for his fee, which was exor-
bitant, that he had come, for the sake of those
interests in the Rankan capital who underwrote
him—those who hated the Emperor so much that
they were willing to back such a loser as
Kadakithis, if they could do it without becoming
the brunt of too many jokes. It was not for the
temple, though he was pleased to build it. It was
some old, residual empathy in Tempus for a
prince so inept as to be known far and wide as
"Kitty" which had made him come. Tempus had
walked away from his primogeniture in Azehur,
a long time ago, leaving the throne to his brother,
who was not compromised by palace politics. He
had deposited a treatise on the nature of being in
the temple of a favored goddess, and he had left.
Had he ever, really, been that young? Young as
Prince Kadakithis, whom even the Wrigglies dis-
paraged?

Tempus had been around in the days when the Ilsigs had been the Enemy: the Wrigglies. He had been on every battlefield in the Rankan/Ilsíg conflict. He had spitted more Ilsigs than most men, watched them writhe soundlessly until they died. Some said he had coined their derogatory nickname, but he had not, though he had doubtless helped spread it. . . .

He rode down Wideway, and he rode past the docks. A ship was being made fast, and a crowd had gathered round it. He squeezed the horse's barrel, urging it into the press. With only four of his fellow Hell Hounds in Sanctuary, and a local garrison whose personnel never ventured out in groups of less than six, it was incumbent upon him to take a look.

He did not like what he saw of the man who was being helped from the storm-wracked ship that had come miraculously to port with no sail intact, who murmured through pale cruel lips to the surrounding Ilsigs, then climbed into a Rankan litter bound for the palace.

He spurred the horse. "Who?" he demanded of the eunuch-master whose path he suddenly barred.

"Aspect, the archmage," lisped the palace lackey, "if it's any business of yours."

Behind the lackey and the quartet of ebony slaves the shoulder-borne litter trembled. The viewcurtain with Kitty's device on it was drawn back, fell loose again.

"Out of my way, Hound," squeaked the enraged little pastry of a eunuch-master.

"Don't get flapped, Eunice," said Tempus, wishing he were in Caronne, wishing he had never met a god, wishing he were anywhere else. *Oh, Kitty, you have done it this time.* Alain Aspect, yet! Alchemist extraordinaire, assassin among magicians, dispeller of enchantments, in a town that ran on contract sorcery?

"Back, back, back," he counseled the horse, who twitched its ears and turned its head around reproachfully, but obeyed him.

He heard titters among the eunuchs, another behind in the crowd. He swung round in his saddle. "Hakiem, if I hear any stories about me I do not like, I will know whose tongue to hang on my belt."

The bent, news-nosed storyteller, standing amid the children who always clustered round him, stopped laughing. His rheumy eyes met Tempus's. "I have a story I would like to tell you, Hell Hound. One you would like to hear, I humbly imagine."

"What is it, then, old man?"

"Come closer, Hell Hound, and say what you will pay."

"How can I tell you how much it's worth until I hear?" The horse snorted, raised his head, sniffed a rank, evil breeze come suddenly from the stinking Downwind beach.

"We must haggle."

"Somebody else, then, old man. I have a long night ahead." He patted the horse, watching the crowd of Ilsigs surging round, their heads level with his hips.

"That is the first time I have seen *him* backed off!": a stage-whisper reached Tempus through the buzz of the crowd. He looked for the source of it, could not find one culprit more likely than the rest. There would be a lot more of that sort of talk, when word spread. But he did not interfere with sorcerers. Never again. He had done it once, thinking his tutelary god could protect him. His hand went to his hip, squeezed. Beneath his dun woolens and beneath his ring-mail he wore a woman's scarf. He never took it off. It was faded and it was ragged and it reminded him never to argue with a warlock. It was all he had left of her, who had been the subject of his dispute with a mage.

Long ago in Azehur. . . .

He sighed, a rattling sound, in a voice hoarse and gravelly from endless battlefield commands. "Have it your way tonight, then, Wriggly. And hope you live 'til morning." He named a price. The storyteller named another. The difference was split.

The old man came close and put his hand on the horse's neck. "The lightning came and the thunder rolled and when it was gone the temple of Ils was no more. The Prince has bought the aid of a mighty enchanter, whom even the bravest of the Hell Hounds fears. A woman was washed up naked and half drowned on the Downwinders' beach and in her hair were pins of diamond."

"Pins?"

"Rods, then."

"Wonderful. What else?"

"The redhead from Amoli's Lily Garden died at moonrise."

He knew very well what whore the old man meant. He did not like the story, so far. He growled. "You had better astound me, quick, for the price you're asking."

"Between the Vulgar Unicorn and the tenement on the corner an entire building appeared on that vacant lot, where once the Black Spire stood— you know the one."

"I know it."

"Astounding?"

"Interesting. What else?"

"It is rather fancy, with a gilded dome. It has two doors, and above them two signs that read, 'Men,' and 'Women.' "

Vashanka had kept his word, then.

"Inside it, so the patrons of the Unicorn say, they sell weapons. Very special weapons. And the price is dear."

"What has this to do with me?"

"Some folk who have gone in there have not come out. And some have come out and turned one upon the other, dueling to the death. Some have merely slain whomsoever crossed their paths. Yet, word is spreading, and Ilsig and Rankan queue up like brothers before its doors. Since some of those who were standing in line were hawk-masks, I thought it good that you should know."

"I am touched, old man. I had no idea you cared." He threw the copper coins to the story-teller's feet and reined the horse sideways so abruptly it reared. When its feet touched the ground, he set it at a collected canter through the crowd, letting the rabble scatter before its iron-shod hooves as best they might.

2

In Sanctuary, enchantment ruled. No sorcerer believed in gods. But they believed in the Law of Correspondences, and they believed in evil. Thus, since every negative must have its positive, they *implied* gods. Give a god an inch and he will take your soul. That was what the commoners and the second-rate prestidigitators lined up outside the Weaponshop of Vashanka did not realize, and that was why no respectable magician or Hazard Class Enchanter stood among them.

In they filed, men to Tempus's left, toward the Vulgar Unicorn, and women to his right, toward the tenement on the corner.

Personally, Tempus did not feel it wise or dignified for a god to engage in a commercial venture. From across the street, he took notes on who came and went.

Tempus was not sure whether he was going in there, or not.

A shadow joined the queue, disengaged, walked toward the Vulgar Unicorn in the tricky light of fading stars. It saw him, hesitated, took one step back.

Tempus leaned forward, his elbow on his pommel, and crooked a finger. "Hanse, I would like a word with you."

The youth cat-walked toward him, errant torchlight from the Unicorn's open door twinkling on his weapons. From ankle to shoulder, Shadowspawn bristled with armaments.

"What is it with you, Tempus? Always on my tail. There are bigger frogs than this one in Sanctuary's pond."

"Are you not going to buy anything tonight?"

"I'll make do with what I have, thanks. I do not swithe with sorcerers."

"Steal something for me?" Tempus whispered, leaning down. The boy had black hair, black eyes, and blacker prospects in this desperados' demesne.

"I'm listening."

"Two diamond rods from the lady who came out of the sea tonight."

"Why?"

"I won't ask you how, and you won't ask me why, or we'll forget it." He sat up straight in his saddle.

"Forget it, then," toughed Shadowspawn, deciding he wanted nothing to do with this Hell Hound.

"Call it a prank, a jest at the expense of an old girlfriend."

The thief edged around where Tempus could not see him, into a dapple of deepest dark. He named a price.

The Hell Hound did not argue. Rather, he paid half in advance.

"I've heard you don't really work for Kitty. I've heard your dues to the mercenaries' guild are right up to date, and that Kitty knows better than to give you any orders. If you are not arguing about my price, it must be too low."

Silence.

"Is it true that you roughed up that whore who died tonight? That Amoli is so afraid of you that you do whatever you want in her place and never pay?"

Tempus chuckled, a sound like the cracking of dry ice. "I will take you there, when you deliver, and you can see for yourself what I do."

There was no answer from the shadows, just a skittering of stones.

Yes, I will take you there, young one. And yes, you are right. About everything. You should have asked for more.

3

Tempus lingered there still, eating a boxed lunch from the Unicorn's kitchen, when a voice from above his head said, "The deal is off. That girl is a sorceress, if a pretty one. I'll not chance ensorcelment to lift baubles I don't covet, and for a pittance!"

Girl? The woman was nearly his own age, unless another set of diamond rods existed, and he doubted that. He yawned, not reaching up to take the purse that dangled over the lee of the roof, "I am disappointed. I thought Shadowspawn could steal."

The innuendo was not lost on the invisible thief. The purse was withdrawn. An impalpable something told him he was once again alone, but for the clients of Vashanka's Weaponshop. Things would be interesting in Sanctuary, for a good little while to come. He had counted twenty-three purchasers able to walk away with their mystical armaments. Four had died while he watched, intrigued.

It was possible that a career Hell Hound such as Zalbar might have intervened. But Tempus wore Vashanka's amulet about his neck, and, if he did not agree with Him, he would at least bear with his god.

The woman he was waiting for showed there at dusk. He liked dusk; he liked it for killing and he liked it for loving. Sometimes if he was very lucky, the dusk made him tired and he could nap. A man who has been cursed by an archmage and pressed into service by a god does not sleep much. Sleep was something he chased like other men chased women. Women, in general, bored him, unless they were taken in battle, or unless they were whores.

This woman, her black hair brushing her doe-skin-clad shoulders, was an exception.

He called her name, very softly. Then again: "Cime." She turned, and at last he was sure. He had thought Hakiem could mean no other: he had not been wrong.

Her eyes were gray as his horse. Silver shot her hair, but she was yet comely. Her hands rose, hesitated, covered a mouth pretending to hardness and tight with fear. He recognized the aborted motion of her hands: toward her head, forgetful that the rods she sought were no longer there.

He did not move in his saddle, or speak again. He let her decide, glance quickly about the street, then come to him.

When her hand touched the horse's bridle, he said: "It bites."

"Because you taught it to. It will not bite me."
She held it by the muzzle, squeezing the pressure
points that rode the skin there. The horse raised
his head slightly, moaned, and stood shivering.

"What seek you in there?" He inclined his head
toward Vashanka's; a lock of copper hair fell over
one eye.

"The tools of my trade were stolen."

"Have you money?"

"Some. Not enough."

"Come with me."

"Never again."

"You have kept your vow, then?"

"I slay sorcerers. I cannot suffer any man to
touch me except a client. I dare no love; I am
chaste of heart."

"All these aching years?"

She smiled. It pulled her mouth in hard at its
corners and he saw aging no potion or cosmetic
spell could hide. "Every one. And you? You did
not take the Blue Star, or I would see it on your
brow. What discipline serves your will?"

"None. Revenge is fruitless. The past is only
alive in us. I am not meant for sorcery. I love logic
too well."

"So, you are yet damned?"

"If that is what you call it, I suppose—yes. I
work for the Storm God, sometimes. I do a lot of
wars."

"What brought you here, Cle—"

"Tempus, now. It keeps me in perspective. I am
building a temple for Him." He pointed to Vashanka's Weaponshop, across the street. His finger
shook. He hoped she had not seen. "You must not
ply your trade here. I have employment as a Hell

Hound. Appearances must be preserved. Do not pit us against one another. It would be too sour a memory."

"For whomever survived? Can it be you love me still?" Her eyes were full of wonder.

"No," he said, but cleared his throat. "Stay out of there. I know His service well. I would not recommend it. I will get you back what you have lost. Meet me at the Lily Garden tonight at midnight, and you will have them. I promise. Just take down no sorcerers between now and then. If you do, I will not return them, and you cannot get others."

"Bitter, are you not? If I do what you are too weak to do, what harm is there in that?" Her right eyebrow raised. It hurt him to watch her.

"We are the harm. And we are the harmed, as well. I am afraid that you may have to break your fast, so be prepared. I will reason with myself, but I promise nothing."

She sighed. "I was wrong. You have not changed one bit."

"Let go of my horse."

She did.

He wanted to tell her to let go of his heart, but he was struck mute. He wheeled his mount and clattered down the street. He had no intention of leaving. He just waited in a nearby alley until she was gone.

Then he hailed a passing soldier, and sent a message to the palace.

When the sun danced above the Vulgar Unicorn's improbably engaged weather vane, support troops arrived, and Kadakithis's new warlock, Aspect, was with them.

"Since last night, and this is the first report you have seen fit to make?" The sorcerer's pale lips flushed. His eyes burned within his shadowed cowl.

"I hope you and Kadakithis had a talk."

"We did, we did. You are not still angry at the world after all these years?"

"I am yet living. I have your kind to blame or thank, whichever."

"Do you not think it strange that we have been thrown together as—equals?"

"I think that is not the right word for it, Aspect. What are you about, here?"

"Now, now, Hell Hound—"

"Tempus."

"Yes, Tempus. You have not lost your fabled sense of irony. I hope it is a comfort."

"Quite, actually. Do not interfere with the gods, guildbrother of my nemesis."

"Our prince is justifiably worried. Those weapons—"

"—equal out the balance between the oppressors and the oppressed. Most of Sanctuary cannot afford your services, or the prices of even the lowliest members of the Enchanters' Guild. Let it be. We will get the weapons back, as their wielders meet their fates."

"I have to report to Kitt—to Kadakithis."

"Then report that I am handling it." Behind the magician, he could see the ranks whispering. Thirty men, the archmage had brought. Too many.

"You and I have more in common than in dispute, Tempus. Let us join forces."

"I would sooner bed an Ilsig matron."

"Well, I am going in there." The archmage

shook his head and the cowl fell back. He was
pretty, ageless, a blond. "With or without you."

"Be my guest," Tempus offered.

The archmage looked at him strangely. "We do
the same services in the world, you and I. Killing,
whether with natural or supernatural weapons, is
still killing. You are no better than I."

"Assuredly not, except that I will outlive you.
And I will make sure you do not get your requisite
burial ritual."

"You would not!"

"Like you said, I yet bear my grudge—against
every one of you."

With a curse that made the ranks clap their
hands to their helmeted ears, the archmage
swished into the street, across it, and through the
door marked "Men" without another word. It was
his motioned command which made the troops
follow.

A waitress Tempus knew came out when the
gibbous moon was high, to ask him if he was
hungry. She brought him fish and he ate it, watching the doors.

When he had just about finished, a terrible
rumble crawled up the street, tremors following
in its wake. He slid from his horse and held its
muzzle, and the reins up under its bit. The doors
of Vashanka's Weaponshop grew shimmery,
began taking color. Above, the moon went behind
a cloud. The little dome on the shop rocked, grew
cracks, crazed, steamed. The doors were ruby red,
and melting. Awful wails and screams and the
smell of sulphur and ozone filled the night.

Patrons began streaming out of the Vulgar Unicorn, drinks in hand. They stayed well back from
the rocking building, which howled as it stressed

larger, growing turgid, effluescing spectrums which sheeted and snapped and snarled. The doors went molten white, then they were gone. A figure was limned in the left-hand doorway, and it was trying to climb empty air. It flamed and screeched, dancing, crumbling, facing the street but unable to pass the invisible barrier against which it pounded. It stank: the smell of roasting flesh was overwhelming. Behind it, helmets crumpled, dripped onto the contorted faces of soldiers whose mustaches had begun to flare.

The mage who tried to break down the invisible door had no fists; he had pounded them away. The ranks were char and ash in infalling effigy of damnation. The doors which had been invisible began to cool to white, then to gold, then to red.

The street was utterly silent. Only the snorts of his horse and the squeals of the domed structure could be heard. The squeals fell off to growls and shudders. The doors cooled, turned dark.

People muttered, drifted back into the Unicorn with mumbled wardings, tracing signs and taking many backward looks.

Tempus, who could have saved thirty innocent soldiers and one guilty magician, got out his silver box and sniffed some krrf.

He had to be at the Lily Garden soon.

When he got there, the mixed elation of drug and death had faded.

What if Shadowspawn did not appear with the rods? What if the girl Cime did not come to get them back? What if he still could hurt, as he had not hurt for more than three hundred years?

He had had a message from the palace, from Prince Kadakithis himself. He was not going up there, just yet. He did not want to answer any questions about the archmage's demise. He did not want to appear involved. His only chance to help the Prince-Governor effectively lay in working his own way. Those were his terms, and under those terms Kitty's supporters in the Rankan capital had employed him to come down here and play Hell Hound and see what he would do. There were no wars, anywhere. He had been bored, his days stretching out never-ending, bleak. So he had concerned himself with Kitty, for something to do. The building of Vashanka's temple he oversaw for himself more than Kadakithis, who understood the necessity of elevating the state cult above the Ilsig gods, but believed only in wizardry, and his noble Ranke blood.

He was not happy about the spectacle at Vashanka's Weaponshop. Sloppy business, this sideshow melting and unmelting. The archmage must have been talented, to make his struggles visible to those outside.

Wisdom is to know the thought which steers all things through all things, a friend of his who was a philosopher had once said to him. The thought that was steering all things through Sanctuary was muddled, unclear.

That was the hitch, the catch, the problem with employing the supernatural in a natural milieu. Things got confused. With so many spells at work, the fabric of causality was overly strained. Add the gods, and Evil and Good faced each other across a board game whose extent was the phenomenal world. He wished the gods would stay in their heavens and the sorcerers in their hells.

Oh, he had heard endless persiflage about simultaneity; iteration—the constant redefining of the now by checking it against the future—; alchemical laws of consonance. When he had been a student of philosophy and Cime had been a maiden, he had learned the axiom that Mind is unlimited and self-controlled, but all other things are connected; that nothing is completely separated off from any other thing, nor are things divided one from the other, except Mind.

The sorcerers put it another way: they called the consciousness of all things into service, according to the laws of magic.

Not philosophy, nor theology, nor thaumaturgy held the answer for Tempus; he had turned away from them, each and all. But he could not forget what he had learned.

And none of the adepts like to admit that no servitor can be hired without wages. The wages of unnatural life are unnatural death.

He wished he could wake up in Azehur, with his family, and know that he had dreamed this impious dream.

But instead he came to Amoli's whorehouse, the Lily Garden. Almost, but not quite, he rode the horse up its stairs. Resisting the temptation, he reflected that in every age he had ever studied, doom-cryers abounded. No millenium is attractive to the man immured in it; enough prophecies have been made in antiquity that one who desires, in any age, to take the position that Apocalypse is at hand can easily defend it. He would not join that dour Order; he would not worry about anything but Tempus, and the matter awaiting his attention.

Inside Amoli's, Hanse the thief sat in full swagger, a pubescent girl on each knee.

"Ah," he waved. "I have something for you."

Shadowspawn tumbled both girls off of him, and stood, stretching widely, so that every arm-dagger and belted sticker and thigh-sheath creaked softly. The girls at his feet stayed there, staring up at Tempus wide-eyed. One whimpered to Shadowspawn and clutched his thigh.

"Room key," Tempus snapped to no one in particular, and held out his hand. The concierge, not Amoli, brought it to him.

"Hanse?"

"Coming." He extended a hand to one girl.

"Alone."

"You are not my type," said the thief, suspicious.

"I need just a moment of your evening. You can do what you wish with the rest."

Tempus looked at the key, headed off toward a staircase leading to the room which bore a corresponding number.

He heard the soft tread of Shadowspawn close behind.

When the exchange had been made, the thief departed, satisfied with both his payment and his gratuity, but not quite sure that Tempus appreciated the trouble to which he had put himself, or that he had gotten the best of the bargain they had made.

He saw the woman he had robbed before she saw him, and ended up in a different girl's room than the one he had chosen, in order to avoid a scene. When he had heard her steps pass by, stop before the door behind which the big Hell Hound waited, he made preclusive threats to the woman whose mouth he had stopped with the flat of his hand, and slipped downstairs to spend his money somewhere else, discreetly.

If he had stayed, he might have found out what the diamond rods were really worth; he might have found out what the sour-eyed mercenary with his high brow, suddenly so deeply creased, and his lightly carried mass, which seemed tonight too heavy, was worried about. Or perhaps he could have fathomed Tempus's enigmatic parting words:

"I would help you if I could, backstreeter," Tempus had rumbled. "If I had met you long ago, or if you liked horses, there would be a chance. You have done me a great service. More than that pouch holds. I am seldom in any man's debt, but you, I own, can call me anytime."

"You paid me, Hell Hound. I am content," Hanse had demurred, confused by weakness where he had never imagined it might dwell. Then he saw the Hell Hound fish out a snuffbox of krrf, and thought he understood.

But later, he went back to Amoli's and hung around the steps, cautiously petting the big man's horse, the krrf he had sniffed making him willing to dodge the beast's square, yellow teeth.

4

She had come to him, had Cime. She was what she was, what she had always been.

It was Tempus who was changed: Vashanka had entered into him, the Storm God who was Lord of Weapons who was Lord of Rape who was Lord of War who was Lord of Death's Gate.

He could not take her, gently. So spoke not his

physical impotence, as he might have expected, but the cold wash of wisdom: he would not despoil her; Vashanka would accept no less.

She knocked and entered and said, "Let me see them," so sure he would have the stolen diamonds that her fingers were already busy on the lacings of her Ilsig leathers.

He held up a hide-wrapped bundle, slimmer than her wrist, shorter than her forearm. "Here. How were they thieved?"

"Your voice is hoarser than I have ever heard it," she replied, and: "I needed money; there was this man . . . actually, there were a few, but there was a tough, a streetbrawler. I should have known—he is half my apparent age. What would such as he want with a middle-aged whore? And he agreed to pay the price I asked, without quibbling. Then he robbed me." She looked around, her eyes, as he remembered them, clear windows to her thoughts. She was appalled.

"The low estate into which I have sunk?"

She knew what he meant. Her nostrils shivered, taking in the musty reek of the soiled bedding on which he sprawled fully clothed, smelling easily as foul. "The devolution of us both. That I would be here, under these circumstances, is surely as pathetic as you."

"Thanks. I needed that. Don't."

"I thought you wanted me." She ceased unlacing, looked at him, her tunic open to her waist.

"I did. I don't. Have some krrf." On his hips rode her scarf; if she saw it, then she would comprehend his degradation too fully. So he had not removed it, hoping its presence would remind him, if he weakened and his thoughts drowned in lust, that this woman he must not violate.

She sat on the quilt, one doe-gloved leg tucked under her.

"You jest," she breathed, then, eyes narrowed, took the krrf.

"It will be ill with you, afterward, should I touch you."

Her fingers ran along the flap of hide wrapped over her wands. "I am receiving payment." She tapped the package. "And I may not owe debts."

"The boy who pilfered these, did it at my behest."

"Must you pander for me?"

He winced. "Why do you not go home?" She smelled of salt and honey and he thought desperately that she was here only because he forced the issue: to pay her debt.

She leaned forward, touched his lips with a finger. "For the same reason that you do not. Home is changed, gone to time."

"Do you know that?" He jerked his head away, cracking it against the bed's wooden headboard.

"I believe it."

"I cannot believe anything, any more. I surely cannot believe that your hand is saying what it seems to be saying."

"I cannot," she said, between kisses at his throat he could not, somehow, fend off, "leave . . . with . . . debts . . . owing."

"Sorry," he said firmly, and got out from under her hands. "I am just not in the mood."

She shrugged, unwrapped the wands, and wound her hair up with them. "Surely, you will regret this, later."

"Maybe you are right," he sighed heavily. "But that is my problem. I release you from any debt. We are even. I remember past gifts, given when you still knew how to give freely." There was no way in the world he was going to hurt her. He would not strip before her. With those two constraints, he had no option. He chased her out of there. He was as cruel about it as he could manage to be, for both their sakes.

Then he yelled downstairs for service.

When he descended the steps in the cool night air, a movement startled him, on the gray's off side.

"It is me, Shadowspawn."

"It is I, Shadowspawn," he corrected, huskily. His face averted, he mounted from the wrong side. The horse whickered disapprovingly. "What is it, snipe?"

As clouds covered the moon, Tempus seemed to pull all night's shadows round him. Hanse might have the name, but this Tempus had the skill. Hanse shivered. There were no Shadow Lords any longer. . . . "I was admiring your horse. Bunch of hawk-masks rode by, saw the horse, looked interested. I looked proprietary. The horse looked mean. The hawk-masks rode away. I just thought I'd see if you showed soon, and let you know."

A movement at the edge of his field of vision warned him, even as the horse's ears twitched at the click of iron on stone. "You should have kept going, it seems," said Tempus quietly, as the first of the hawk-masks edged his horse out past the intersection, and others followed. Two. Three. Four. Two more.

"Mothers," whispered Cudget Swearoath's prodigy, embarrassed at not having realized that he was not the only one waiting for Tempus.

"This is not your fight, junior."

"I'm aware of that. Let's see if they are."

Blue night: blue hawk-masks: the sparking thunder of six sets of hooves rushing toward the two of them. Whickering. The gleam of frothing teeth and bared weapons: iron clanging in a jumble of shuddering, straining horses. The kill-trained gray's challenge to another stallion: hooves thudding on flesh and great mouths gaped, snapping; a blaring death-clarion from a horse whose jugular had been severed. Always watching the boy: keeping the gray between the hawk-masks and a thief who just happened to get involved; who just happened to kill two of them with thrown knives, one through an eye and the other blade he recalled clearly, sticking out of a slug-white throat. Tempus would remember even the whores' ambivalent screams of thrill and horror, delight and disgust. He had plenty of time to sort it out:

Time to draw his own sword, to target the rider of his choice, feel his hilt go warm and pulsing in his hand. He really did not like to take unfair advantage. The iron sword glowed pink like a baby's skin or a just-born day. Then it began to react in his grip. The gray's reins, wrapped around the pommel, flapped loosely; he told it where he wanted it with gritted words, with a pressing knee, with his shifting weight. One hawk-mask had a greenish tinge to him: protected. Tempus's sword would not listen to such talk: it slit charms like butter, armor like silk. A blue wing whistled above his head, thrown by a compatriot of the man who fell so slowly with his guts pouring out over his saddle like cold molasses. While that hawk-mask's horse was in midair between two strides, Tempus's sword licked up and changed the color of the foe-seeking boomerang. Pink, now, not blue. He was content to let it return its death to the hand that threw it. That left just two.

One had the thief engaged, and the youth had drawn his wicked, twenty-inch Ibarsi knife, too short to be more than a temporizer against the hawk-mask's sword, too broad to be thrown. Backed against the Lily Garden's wall, there was just time for Tempus to flicker the horse over there and split the hawk-mask's head down to his collarbones. Gray brains splattered him. The thrust of the hawk-mask, undiminished by death, shattered on the flat of the long, curved knife Shadowspawn held up in a two-fisted, desperate block.

"Behind you!"

Tempus had known the one last hawk-mask was there. But this was not the boy's battle. Tempus had made a choice. He ducked and threw his weight sideways, reining the horse down with all his might. The sword, a singing one, sonata'd over his head, shearing hairs. His horse, overbalanced, fell heavily, screaming, pitching, rolling onto his left leg. Pinned for an instant, he saw white anguish, then the last hawk-mask was leaping down to finish him, and the gray scrambled to its feet. "Kill," he shouted, his blade yet at ready, but lying in the dirt. His leg flared once again, then quieted. He tried it, gained his knees, dust in his eyes. The horse reared and lunged. The hawk-mask struck blindly, arms above his head, sword reaching for gray, soft underbelly. He tried to save it. He tried. He tackled the hawk-mask with the singing sword. Too late, too late: horse fluids showered him. Bellows of agony pealed in his ears. The horse and the hawk-mask and Tempus went down together, thrashing.

When Tempus sorted it out, he allowed that the horse had killed the hawk-mask at the same time the hawk-mask had disemboweled the horse.

But he had to finish it. It lay there thrashing pathetically, deep groans coming from it. He stood over it uncertainly, then knelt and stroked its muzzle. It snapped at him, eyes rolling, demanding to die. He acceded, and the dust in his eyes hurt so much they watered profusely.

Its legs were still kicking weakly when he heard a movement, turned on his good leg, and stared.

Shadowspawn was methodically stripping the hawk-masks of their arms and valuables.

Hanse did not notice Tempus, as he limped away. Or he pretended he did not. Whichever, there was nothing left to say.

5

When he reached the weapons shop, his leg hardly pained him. It was numb; it no longer throbbed. It would heal flawlessly, as any wound he took always healed. Tempus hated it.

Up to the Weaponshop's door he strode, as the dawn spilled gore onto Sanctuary's alleys.

He kicked it; it opened wide. How he despised supernal battle, and himself when his preternatural abilities came into play.

"Hear me, Vashanka! I have had enough! Get this sidewalk stand out of here!"

There was no answer. Within, everything was dim as dusk, dim as the pit of unknowingness which spawned day and night and endless striving.

There were no weapons here for him to see, no counter, no proprietor, no rack of armaments pulsing and humming expectantly. But then, he already had his. One to a customer was the rule: one body; one mind; one swing through life.

He trod mists tarnished like the gray horse's coat. He trod a long corridor with light at its ending, pink like new beginnings, pink like his iron sword when Vashanka lifted it by Tempus's hand. He shied away from his duality; a man does not look closely at a curse of his own choosing. He was what he was, vessel of his god. But he had his own body, and that particular body was aching; and he had his own mind, and that particular mind was dank and dark like the dusk and the dusty death he dealt.

"Where are You, Vashanka, O Slaughter Lord?"

Right here, resounded the voice within his head. But Tempus was not going to listen to any internal voice. Tempus wanted confrontation.

"Materialize, you bastard!"

I already have; one body; one mind; one life— in every sphere.

"I am not you!" Tempus screamed through clenched teeth, willing firm footing beneath his sinking feet.

No, you are not. But I am you, sometimes, said the nimbus-wreathed figure striding toward him over gilt-edged clouds. Vashanka: so very tall with hair the color of yarrow honey and a high brow free from lines.

"Oh, no. . . ."

You wanted to see Me. Look upon Me, servant!

"Not so close, Pillager. Not so much resemblance. Do not torture me, my god! Let me blame it all on you—not be you!"

So many years, and you yet seek self-delusion?

"Definitely. As do You, if You think to gather worshipers in this fashion! O Berserker God, You cannot roast their mages before them: they are all dependent on sorcery. You cannot terrify them thusly, and expect them to come to You. Weapons will not woo them; they are not men of the armies. They are thieves, and pirates, and prostitutes! You have gone too far, and not far enough!"

Speaking of prostitutes, did you see your sister? Look at me!

Tempus had to obey. He faced the manifestation of Vashanka, and recalled that he could not take a woman in gentleness, that he could but war. He saw his battles, ranks parading in endless eyes of storm and blood bath. He saw the Storm God's consort, His own sister whom He raped eternally, moaning on Her coach in anguish that Her blood brother would ravish Her so.

Vashanka laughed.

Tempus snarled wordlessly through frozen lips.

You should have let us have her.

"Never!" Tempus howled. Then: "O God, leave off! You are not increasing your reputation among these mortals, nor mine! This was an ill-considered venture from the outset. Go back to Your heaven and wait. I will build Your temple better without Your maniacal aid. You have lost all sense of proportion. The Sanctuarites will not worship one who makes of their town a battle-field!"

Tempus, do not be wroth with Me. I have My own troubles, you know. I have to get away every now and again. And you have not been warring, whined the god, *for so very long. I am bored and I am lonely.*

"And you have caused the death of my horse!" Tempus spat, and broke free of Vashanka, wrenching his mind loose from the mirror mind of his god with an effort of will greater than any he had ever mounted before. He turned in his steps and began to retrace them. The god called to him over his shoulder, but he did not look back. He put his feet in the smudges they had left in the clouds as he had walked among them, and the farther he trudged, the more substantial those clouds became.

He trekked into lighter darkness, into a soft, new sunrise, into a pink and lavender morning which was almost Sanctuary's. He continued to walk until the smell of dead fish and Downwind pollution assailed his nostrils. He strode on, until a weed tripped him and he fell to his knees in the middle of a damp and vacant lot.

He heard a cruel laugh, and as he looked up he was thinking that he had not made it back at all—that Vashanka was not through punishing him.

But to his right was the Vulgar Unicorn, to his left the palimpsest tenement wall. And before him stood one of the palace eunuchs, come seeking him with a summons from Kittycat to discuss what might be done about the weapons shop said to be manifesting next to the Vulgar Unicorn.

"Tell Kadakithis," said Tempus, arduously gaining his feet, "that I will be there presently. As you can see . . ." He waved around him, where no structure stood or even could be proved ever to have stood. ". . . there is no longer any weapons shop. Therefore, there is no longer any problem, nor any urgency to attend to it. There is, however, one very irritable Hell Hound in this vacant lot who wants to be left alone."

The blue-black eunuch exposed perfect, argent teeth. "Yes, yes, master," he soothed the honey-haired man. "I can see that this is so."

Tempus ignored the eunuch's rosy, out-stretched palm, and his sneer at the Hell Hound pretending to negotiate the humpy turf without pain. Accursed Wriggly!

As the round-rumped eunuch sauntered off, Tempus decided the Vulgar Unicorn would do as well as anyplace to sit and sniff krrf and wait for his leg to finish healing. It ought to take about an hour—unless Vashanka was more angry at him that he estimated, in which case it might take a couple of days.

Shying from that dismal prospect, he pursued diverse thoughts. But he fared little better. Where he was going to get another horse like the one he had lost, he could not conjecture, any more than he could recall the exact moment when the last dissolving wisps of Vashanka's Weaponshop blurred away into the mists of dawn.

SHADOW'S PAWN

Andrew Offutt

She was more than attractive and she walked with head high in pride and awareness of her womanhood. The bracelet on her bare arm flashed and seemed to glow with that brightness the gods reserve for polished new gold. She should have been walking amid bright lights illuminating the dancing waters of a fountain, turning its sparkling into a million diamonds and, with the aid of a bit of refraction, colorful other gemstones as well.

There was no fountain down here by the fish market, and the few lights were not bright. She did not belong here. She was stupid to be here, walking unescorted so late at night. She was stupid. Stupidity had its penalties; it did not pay.

Still, the watching thief appreciated the stupidity of others. It did pay; it paid him. He made his living by it, by his own cleverness and the stupidity of others. He was about to go to work. Even at the reduced price he would receive from a changer, that serpent-carved bracelet would feed him well. It would keep him, without the necessity of more such hard work as this damnable lurking, waiting, for—oh, probably a month.

Though she was the sort of woman men looked

upon with lust, the thief would not have her. He did not see her that way. His lust was not carnal. The waiting thief was no rapist. He was a businessman. He did not even like to kill, and he seldom had to. She passed the doorway in whose shadows he lurked, on the north side of the street.

"G'night Praxy, and thanks again for all that beer," he called to no one, and stepped out onto the planking that bordered the street. He was ten paces behind the quarry. Twelve. "Good thing I'm walking—I'm in no condition to ride a horse t'night!" Fourteen paces.

Laughing giddily, he followed her. The quarry.

She reached the corner of the deserted street and turned north, onto the Street of Odors. Walking around two sides of the Serpentine! She *was* stupid. The dolt had no business whatever with that fine bracelet. Didn't have proper respect for it. Didn't know how to take care of it. The moment she rounded the corner, the thief stepped off the boardwalk onto the unpaved street, squattted to snatch up his shoes the moment he stepped out of them, and *ran*.

Just at the intersection he stopped as if he had run into a wall, and dropped the shoes. Stepped into them. Nodded affably, drunkenly to the couple who came around off Stink Street—slat and slattern wearing three coppers' worth of clothing and four of "jewelry." He stepped onto the planking, noting that they noted little save each other. How nice. The Street of Odors was empty as far as he could see. Except for the quarry.

"Uhh," he groaned as if in misery. "Lady," he called, not loudly. "My lady?" He slurred a little, not overdoing. Five paces ahead, she paused and looked back. "H-hellp," he said, right hand clutching at his stomach.

She was too stupid to be down here alone at this time of night, all right. She came back! All solici-tious she was, and his hand moved a little to the left and came out with a flat-bladed knife while his left hand clamped her right wrist, the unbrace-leted one. The point of the knife touched the knot of her expensive cerulean sash.

"Do not scream. This is a throwing knife. I throw it well, but I prefer not to kill. Unless I have to, understand me? All I want is that nice little snake you're wearing."

"Oh!" Her eyes were huge and she tucked in her belly, away from the point of several inches of dull-silvery leaf-shape he held to her middle. "It—it was a gift. . . ."

"I will accept it as a gift. Oh you are smart, very smart not to try yelling. I just hate to have to stick pretty women in the belly. It's messy, and it could give this end of town a bad name. I hate to throw a knife into their backs, for that matter. Do you believe me?"

Her voice was a squeak: "yes"

"Good." He released her wrist and kept his hand outstretched, palm up. "The bracelet then. I am not so rude as to tear such a pretty bauble off a pretty lady's pretty wrist."

Staring at him as if entranced, she backed a pace. He flipped the knife, caught it by the tip. His left palm remained extended, a waiting recepta-cle. The right hefted the knife in a throwing at-titude and she swiftly twisted off the bracelet. Better than he had thought, he realized with a flash of green and gratification; the serpent's eyes appeared to be nice topazes! All right then, he'd let her keep the expensive sash.

She did not drop the bracelet into his palm; she placed it there. Nice hard cold gold, marvelously weighty. Only slightly warmed from a wrist the color of burnt sienna. Nice, nice. Her eyes leaped, flickered in fear when he flipped the knife to catch it by its leather-wrapped tang. It had no hilt, to keep that end light behind the weighted blade.

"You see?" he said, showing teeth. "I have no desire for your blood, understand me? Only this bauble."

The bracelet remained cold in his palm and when it moved he jerked his hand instinctively. Fast as he was he was only human, not a striking serpent; the bracelet, suddenly become a living snake, drove its fangs into the meaty part of his hand that was the inner part of his thumb. It clung, and it hurt. Oh it hurt.

The thief's smile vanished with his outcry of pain. Yet he saw her smile, and even as he felt the horror within him he raised the throwing knife to stab the filthy bitch who had trapped him.

That is, he tried to raise the knife, tried to shake his bitten hand to which the serpent clung. He failed. Almost instantly, the bite of that unnatural snake ossified every bone and bit of cartilage in his body and, stiffly, Gath the thief fell down dead.

His victim, still smiling, squatted to retrieve her property. She was shivering in excitement. She slipped the cold hard bracelet of gold onto her wrist. Its eyes, cold hard stones, scintillated. And a tremor ran all through the woman. Her eyes glittered and sparkled.

"Oooohh," she murmured with a shiver, all trembly and tingly with excitement and delight. "It was worth every piece of silver I paid, this lovely bauble from that lovely shop. I'm really glad it was destroyed. Those of us who bought these weapons of the god are so *unique*." She was trembling, excitement high in her and her heart racing with the thrill of danger faced and killing accomplished, and she stroked the bracelet as if it were a lover.

She went home with her head high in pride and continuing excitement, and she was not at all happy when her husband railed at her for being so late and seized her by the left wrist. He went all bright eyed and stiff and fell down dead. She was not at all happy. She had intended to kill only strangers for the thrill of it, those who deserved it.

Somewhere, surely, the god Vashanka smiled.

"The god-damned city's in a mess and busy as a kicked anthill and I think you had more than a whit to do with it," the dark young man said. (Or was he a youth? Street-wise and tough and hooded of eyes and wearing knives as a courtesan wore gems. Hair blacker than black and eyes nearly so above a nose almost meant for a bird of prey.)

" 'God-damned' city, indeed," said the paler, discomfitingly tall man, who was older but not old, and he came close to smiling. "You don't know how near you are to truth, Shadowspawn."

Around them in the charcoal dimness others neither heard nor were overheard. In this place, the trick was not to be overheard. The trick was to talk under everyone else. A bad tavern with a bad reputation in a bad area of a nothing town, the tavern called Vulgar Unicorn was an astonishingly quiet place.

"Just call me Hanse and stop being all cryptic and fatherly," the dark young man said. "I'm not looking for a father. I had one—I'm told. Then I had Cudget Swearoath. Cudget told me all I—all he knew."

The other man heard; "fatherly" used to mean "patronizing," and the flash of ego in the tough called Shadowspawn. Chips on his shoulders out to here. The other man did not smile. How to tell Hanse how many Hanses he had known, over so many years?

"Listen. One night a while ago I killed. Two men." Hanse did not lower his voice for that statement-not-admission; he kept it low. The shadow of a voice.

"Not men, Hanse. Hawkmasks. Jubal's bravoes. Hardly men."

"They were men, Tempus. They were all men. So is Hanse and even Kadaki—the prince-governor."

"Kitty-Cat."

"I do not call him that," Hanse said, with austerity. Then he said, "It's you I'm not sure of, Tempus. Are you a man?"

"I'm a man," Tempus said, with a sigh that seemed to come from the weight of decades and decades. "Tonight I asked you to call me Thales. Go ahead, Hanse. You killed two men, while helping me. Were you, by the way? Or were you lurking around my horse that night thinking of laying hands on some krrf?"

"I use no drugs and little alcohol."

"That isn't what I asked," Tempus said, not bothering to refute.

Dark eyes met Tempus's, which impressed him. "Yes. That is why I was there, T—Thales. Why 'Thay-lees'?"

"Since all things are presently full of gods, why not 'Thales'? Thank you, Hanse. I appreciate your honesty. We can—"

"Honesty?" A man, once well built and now wearing his chest all over his broad belt and bulging under it as well, had been passing their small round table. "Did I hear something about Hanse's honesty? Hanse?" His laugh was a combination: pushed and genuine.

The lean youth called Shadowspawn moved nothing but his head. "How'd you like a hole in your middle to let out all that hot air, Abohorr?"

"How'd you like a third eye, Abohorr?" Hanse's tablemate said.

Abohorr betook himself elsewhere, muttering—and hurrying. Both Hanse's lean swift hands remained on the tabletop. "You know him, Thales?"

"No."

"You heard me say his name and so you said it right after me."

"Yes."

"You're sharp, Thales. Too . . . smart." Hanse slapped the table's surface. "I've been meeting too many sharp people lately. Sharp as . . ."

"Knives," Tempus said, finishing the complaint of a very very sharp young man. "You were mentioning that you were waiting for me to come out of that house-not-home, Hanse, because you knew I was carrying. And then Jubal's bravoes attacked—me—and you took down two."

"I was mentioning that, yes." Hanse developed a seemingly genuine interest in his brown-and-orange Saraprins mug. "How many men have you killed, Thales?"

"Oh gods. Do not ask."

"Many."

"Many, yes."

"And no scars on you."

Tempus looked pained. "No scars on me," he said, to his own big hands on the table. Bronzed, they were still more fair than Shadowspawn's. On a sudden thought, he looked up and his expression was of dawning revelation and disbelief. "Hanse? You saved my life that night. I saved yours—but they were after me to begin with. Hanse? How many men have you killed?"

Hanse looked away. Hair like a raven, nose of a young falcon. Profile carved out by a hand-ax sharper than a barber's razor, all planes and angles. A pair of onyxes for eyes, and just that hard. His look away was uncharacteristic and Tempus knew it. Tempus worked out of the palace and had access to confidential reports, one of which not even the prince-governor had seen. He wouldn't, either, because it no longer existed. Too, Tempus had dealt with this spawn of Downwind and the shadows. He was here in this murkily-lit tavern of humanity's dregs to deal with him again.

Hanse, looking away, said, "You are not to tell anyone."

Tempus knew just what to say. "Do not insult me again."

Hanse's nod was not as long as the thickness of one of his knives. (Were there five, or did he really

wear a sixth on one of his thighs? Tempus
doubted that; the strap wouldn't stay up.)

At last Hanse answered the question. "Two."

Two men. Tempus nodded, sighing, pushing
back to come as close to slumping on his bench as
his kind of soldier could. Damn. Who would have
thought it? The *reputation* he had, this dark surly
scary (to others, not the man currently calling
himself Tempus) youth from the gutters he doubtless thought he had risen so far above. Tempus
knew he had wounded a man or two, and he had
assumed. Now Shadowspawn said he had never
slain! That, from such a one, was an admission.
Because of me he has been blooded, Tempus
mused, and the weary thought followed: *Well,
he's not the first. I had my first two, once. I wonder
who they were, and where?* (But he knew, he
knew. A man did not forget such. Tempus was
older than anyone thought; he was not as world-
weary old as he thought, or thought he thought.)
Just now he wanted to put forth a hand and touch
the much younger man. He certainly did not.

He said, "How do you feel about it?"

Hanse continued to gaze assiduously at something else. How could a child of the desert with
such long long lashes and that sensuous, almost
pretty mouth look so grim and thin-lipped? "I
threw up."

"That proves you are human and is what you
did. How *do* you feel about it?"

Hanse looked at him directly. After a time, he
shrugged.

"Yes," Tempus sighed, nodding. He drained
his cup. Raised a right arm on high and glanced in
the general direction of the tap. The new night-

man nodded. Though he had not looked at the fellow, Tempus lowered his arm and looked at Hanse. "I understand," he said.

"Do you. A while ago I told the prince that it is a prince's business to kill, not a thief's. Now I have killed."

"What a wonderful thing to say to a bit of royalty! I wish you weren't so serious right now, so I could laugh aloud. Do not expect any gentle words from me about the kills, my friend. It happens. I didn't ask for your help—or for you to be waiting for me. You won't do that again."

"Not that way, no." Hanse leaned back while whatever-his-name-was (they called him "Two-Thumb") set two newly-filled mugs between them. He did not take the other two, or wait for payment. "I think things started when Bourne . . . died, and you came to Thieves' World."

"Thieves' World?"

Again that almost-embarrassed shrug. "It's what we call Sanctuary. Some of us. Now the whole city's in a mess and a turmoil and I think you have to do with that."

"I believe you said that."

"You led me astray, 'Thales.' That temple or store or whatever it was. It . . . collapsed?—erupted, like a volcano? Something. Next the prince—"

"You really do respect him, don't you?"

"I don't work for him though," Hanse pointed out; Tempus did. "He impounded the . . . the god-weapons?—that place sold, or tried to. Hell Hounds paying people for things they bought—or else! Things! New wealth in the city, because some of them had been stolen and now are bought

from thieves. People are laughing at dealing with
the new changer: the palace!"

Changer, Tempus knew, meant fence in this—
city? O my God Vashanka—this? A city?!

"Two ships sitting out there in the harbor,"
Hanse went on, "guarded up to here. I know those
Things, those dark weapons of sorcery, are being
loaded aboard. Then what? Out to sea and straight
to the bottom?"

"The very best place for them," Tempus said,
turning and slowly turning his glazed earthenware mug. This one was striped garishly in yellow waves. "Believe it. There is too much power
in those devices."

"Meanwhile some 'enforcers' from the mage-
guild have been trying to get hands on them first."

That Tempus also knew. Three of the toughs
had been eliminated in the past twenty hours,
unless another or two had been slain tonight,
by local Watchmen or those special guardsmen
called Hell Hounds. "Unions will try to protect
their members, yes. No matter what. A union is a
mindless animal."

"You paid me well—*fair*, to fetch you the
diamond wand-things that woman wears in her
hair. I did, and she has them back. You gave them
back."

Cime. Cime's diamond-rods in her fine wealth
of hair. "Yes. Did I?"

"You did. And strange things are happening in
Sanctuary. Those were sorcerous weapons those
hawk-masks used against you and me. A poor
thief tried to snatch a woman's bracelet the other
night, down in—never mind the street. She
shouldn't have been there. The bracelet turned

into a snake and killed him. I don't know what it did to him. He's dead and they say he weighs about twice as much as he did alive."

"It solidified his bones. It was obtained this morning. And when didn't strange things happen in Sanctuary, my friend?"

"That is twice you have called me that." Hanse's words had the sound of accusation about them.

"So I have. I must mean it, then."

Hanse became visibly uncomfortable. "I am Hanse. I was . . . apprentice to Cudget Swearoath. Prince Kitty-Cat had him hanged. I am Shadowspawn. I have breached the palace and because of me a Hell Hound is dead. I have no friends."

And you slip and call him "Kitty-Cat" when you think of your executed mentor, do you? Not seeking a father, eh? Do you know that all men do, and that I have mine, in Vashanka? Ah Hanse how you seek to be enigmatic and so cool—and are about as transparent as a pan of water caught from the sky!

Tempus waved a hand. "Save all that. Just tell me not to be your friend. Not to call you friend."

A silence fell over them like a struck banner and something naked stared out of Hanse's eyes. By the time he knew he must speak into the silence, it was too late. That same silence was Tempus' answer.

"Yes," Tempus said, considerately-cleverly changing the subject. "What old whatsisname Torchholder yammers about is true. Vashanka Came, and He claimed Sanctuary. His name is branded into the palace, now. The very temple of

Ils lies in rubble. Vashanka created the weapons shop, from nothing, and—"

"A pedlar-god?"

"I didn't think much of the tactic myself," Tempus said, hoping Vashanka heard him while noting how good the youth was at sneering. "And the weapons shop destroyed the mage the governor imported to combat him. Vashanka is not to be combatted."

Hanse snapped glances this way and that. "Say such things a time or two more in Sanctuary, my friend, and your body will be mourning the loss of its head."

The blond man stared at him. "Do you believe that?"

Hanse let that pass, while he rowed into the current of other conversations in the tavern. A current restless as a thief on a landing outside a window, and conversations just as stealthy and dark. He tuned it out again, stepping out of the flow yet flowing with it. Quietly.

"And how many of those fell Things do you think are still loose?"

"Too many. Two or four? You know our job is to collect them."

"Our?"

"The Hell Hounds."

"Who's your bearded friend, Hanse?"

The speaker stood beside the table, only a bit older than Hanse and just as cocky. Older in years only; he had not benefited from those years and would never be so much as Hanse. Self-conscious, he wore self-consciously tight black. Oh, a brilliant thief! About as unobtrusive as hives.

Hanse was staring at Tempus, who was pink

and bronze of skin, gold and honey of hair, lengthy and lengthy of legs, and smoothshaven as a pair of doeskin leggings. Hanse did not take his dark-eyed gaze off the Hell Hound, while his dark hand moved out to close on the (black-bracered) wrist of the other young man.

"What color would you say his beard is, Athavul?"

Athavul moved his arm and proved that his wrist would not come loose. His arrogance and mask of cocky confidence fled him faster than a street girl fled a man revealed poor. Tempus recognized Athavul's chuckle; nervousness and sham. Tempus had heard it a thousand or a million times. What was the difference? He reflected on temporarility, even while this boy Athavul temporized.

"You going blind, Shadowspawn? You think my self is, and testing he and I?" With a harsh short laugh and a slap with his other hand on his own chest, Athavul said, "Black as this. Black as this!" He slapped his black leather pants—self-consciously.

Tempus, leaning a bit forward, elbows on the little table, big swordsman's shoulders hunched, continued to gaze directly at Hanse. Into Hanse's eyes. His face looked open because he made it that way. Beardless.

"Same's his hair?" Hanse said, and his voice sounded brittle as very old harness-leather. His eyes glittered.

Athavul swallowed. "Hair. . . ." He swallowed again, looking from Hanse to Tempus to Hanse. "Ah . . . he's your, ah, friend, Hanse. Let go, will you? You twit him about his . . . head if

you want to, but I won't. Sorry I stopped and tried
to be civil."

Without looking away from Hanse, Tempus
said, "It's all right, Athavul. My name is Thales
and I am not sensitive. I've been this bald for
years."

Hanse was staring at Tempus, blond Tempus.
His hand opened. Athavul yanked his arm back so
fast he hit himself in his (nearly inexistent)
stomach. He made no pretense of grace; with a
dark glance at Hanse, he betook himself elsewhere, sullenly silent.

"Nicely done," Tempus said, showing his
teeth.

"Don't smile at me, stranger. What do you look
like?"

"Exactly what you see, Hanse. Exactly."

"And . . . what did he see?" Hanse's wave of
his arm was as tight as he had become inside.
"What do they see here, talking with Hanse?"

"He told you."

"Black beard, no hair."

Blond, beardless Tempus nodded.

Neither had taken his gaze off the other's eyes.
"What else?"

"Does it matter? I am in the employ of that
person we both know. What you people call a Hell
Hound. I would not come here in that appearance!
I doubt anyone else would be in this room, if they
saw me. I was here when you came in, remember?
Waiting for you. You were too cool to ask the
obvious."

"They call me spawn of the shadows," Hanse
said quietly, slowly, in a low tone. He was leaning
back as if to get a few more centimeters between

him and the tall man. "You're just a damned shadow!"

"It's fitting. I need your help, Shadowspawn."

Hanse said, enunciating distinctly, "Shit." And rising he added, "Sing for it. Dance in the streets for it." And he turned away, then back to add, "You're paying of course, Baldy," and then he betook himself elsewhere.

Outside, he glanced up and down the vermiform "street" called Serpentine, turned right to walk a few paces north. Automatically, he stepped over the broken plank in the boardwalk. He glanced into the tucked-in courtyard that was too broad and shallow to be dangerous for several hours yet. Denizens of the Maze called it variously The Outhouse, Tick's Vomitory, or, less seriously, Safehaven. From the pointed tail of the shortcloak on the man's back within that three-sided box, Hanse recognized Poker the Cadite. From the wet sounds, he made an assumption as to Poker's activity. The man with the piebald beard glanced around.

"Come on in, Shadowspawn. Not much room left."

"Looking for Athavul. Said he was carrying and said I could join him." Lying was more than easy to Shadowspawn; it was almost instinctive.

"You're not mad at him?" Poker dropped his tunic's hem and turned from the stained rearmost wall.

"No no, nothing like that."

"He went south. Turned into Slick Walk."

"Thanks, Poker. There's a big-bearded man in the Unicorn with no hair on top. Get him to buy you a cup. Tell him I said."

"Ah. Enemy of yours, Hansey?"

"Right."

Hanse turned and walked a few paces north toward Straight, his back to Slick Walk (which led into the two-block L whose real name no one remembered. Nary a door opened onto it and it stayed dark as a sorcerer's heart. It smelled perpetually sour and was referred to as Vomit Boulevard). When Poker said the weather was sunny, turn up your cloak's hood against rain. When Poker said right, head left.

Hanse cut left through Odd Birt's Dodge, angling around the corner of the tenement owned by Furtwan the dealer in snails for dye—who lived way over on the east side, hardly in tenement conditions. Instantly Hanse vanished into the embrace of his true friend and home. The shadows.

Because he had kept his eyes slitted while he was in the light filtering down from Straight Street, he was able to see. The darkness deepened with each of his gliding westward steps.

He heard the odd tapping sound as he passed Wrong Way Park. What in all the—a blind man? Hanse smiled—keeping his mouth closed against the possible flash of teeth. This was a wonderful place for the blind! They could "see" more in three-quarters of the Maze than anyone with working eyes. He eased along toward the short streetlet called Tanner, hearing the noises from Sly's Place. Then he heard Athavul's voice, out in the open.

"Your pardon, dear lady, but if you don't hand myself your necklace and your wallet I'll put this crossbow bolt through your left gourd."

Hanse eased closer, getting himself nearer the triple "corner" where Tanner sort of intersected with Odd Birt's Dodge and touched the north-south wriggle of the Serpentine as well. Streets in the Maze, it has been said, had been laid out by two love-struck snakes, both soaring on krrf. Hanse heard the reply of Ath's intended prey:

"You don't *have* a crossbow, slime lizard, but see what *I* have!"

The scream, in a voice barely recognizable as Athavul's, raised the hairs on the back of Hanse's neck and sent a chill running all the way down his coccyx. He considered freezing in place. He considered the sensible course of turning and running. Curiosity urged him to edge two steps farther and peek around the building housing Sly's. Curiosity won.

By the time he looked, Athavul was whimpering and gibbering. Someone in a long cloak the color of red clay, hood up, stepped around him and Hanse thought he heard a giggle. Cowering, pleading, gibbering in horribly obvious fear—of what?—Athavul fell to his knees. The cloak swept on along Tanner toward the Street of Odors, and Hanse swallowed with a little effort. A knife had got itself into his hand; he didn't throw it. He edged down a few more steps to see which way the cloak turned. Right. Hanse caught a glimpse of the walking stick. It was white. The way the person in that cloak was moving, though, she was not blind. Nor was she any big woman.

Hanse put up his knife and started toward Athavul.

"No! Please plehehehease!" On his knees, Ath clasped his hands and pleaded. His eyes were

wide and glassy with fear. Sweat and tears ran
down his face in such profusion that he must soon
have salt spots on his black jerkin. His shaking
was wind-blown wash on the line and his face
was the color of a priming coat of whitewash.

Hanse stood still. He stared. "What's the matter
with you, Ath? I'm not menacing you, you fugi-
tive from a dung-fueled stove! *Athavul!* What's
the *matter'th* you?"

"Oh please pleohplease no no oh ohh
ohohohono-o-o. . . ."

Athavul fell on his knees and his still-clasped
hands, bony rump in the air. His shaking had
increased to that of a whipped, starved dog.

Such an animal would have moved Hanse to
pity. Athavul was just ridiculous. Hanse wanted
to kick him. He was also aware that two or three
people were peering out of the dump still called
Sly's Place though Sly had taken dropsy and died
two years back.

"Ath? Did she hurt you? Hey! You little piece of
camel dropping—what did she *do* to you?"

At the angry, demanding sound of Hanse's
voice, Athavul clutched himself. Weeping loudly, he rolled over against the wall. He left little
spots of tears and slobber and a puddle from a
spasming sphincter. Hanse swallowed hard. Sorcery. That damned Enos Y—no, he didn't work
this way. Ath was absolutely terrified. Hanse had
always thought him the consistency of sparrow's
liver and chicken soup, with bird's eggs between
his legs. But *this*—not even this strutting ass
could be *this* hideously possessed by fear without
preternatural aid. Just the sight of it was scary.
Hanse felt an urge to stomp or stick Ath just to

shut him up, and that was awful.

He glanced at the thirty-one strands of dangling Syrese rope (each knotted thirty-one times) that hung in the doorway of Sly's. He saw seven staring eyeballs, six fingers, and several mismatched feet. Even in the Maze, noise attracted attention . . . but people had sense enough not to go running out to see what was amiss.

"BLAAAH!" Hanse shouted, making a horrid face and pouncing at the doorway. Then he rushed past the groveling, weeping Athavul. At the corner he looked up Odors toward Straight, and he was sure he saw the vermilion cloak. Maroon now, in the distance. Yes. Across Straight, heading north now past the tanners' broad open-front sheds, almost to the intersection with the Street Called Slippery.

Several people were walking along Odors, just walking, heading south in Hanse's direction. The lone one carried a lanthorn.

All six walkers—three, one, and two—passed him going in the opposite direction. None saw him, though Hanse was hurrying. He heard the couple talking about the hooded blind woman with the white staff. He crossed well-lighted Straight Street when the red clay cloak was at the place called Harlot's Cross. There Tanner's Row angled in to join the Street of Odors at its mutual intersection with the broad Governor's Walk. He passed the tiny "temple" of Theba and several shops to stop outside the entrance of the diminutive Temple of Eshi Virginal—few believed in that—and watched the cloak turn left. Northwest. A woman, all right. Heading past the long sprawl of the farmers' market? Or one of the little dwellings that faced it?

Heading for Red Lantern Road? *A woman who pretends to be blind and who put a spell of terror on Athavul like nothing I ever saw.*

He had to follow her. He was incapable of not following her.

He was not driven only by curiosity. He wanted to know the identity of a woman with such a devide, yes. There was also the possibility of obtaining such a useful wand. White, it resembled the walk-tap stick of a sightless woman. Painted though, it could be the swagger stick of . . . Shadowspawn. Or of someone with a swollen purse who could put it to good use against Hanse's fellow thieves.

He looked out for himself; let them.

Hanse did not follow. He moved to intersect, and could anyone have done it as swiftly and surefootedly, it must have been a child who lived hereabouts and had no supervision.

He ran past Slippery—fading into a fig-pedlar's doorway while a pair of City Watchmen passed—then ran through two vacant lots, a common back yard full of dog droppings and the white patches of older ones, over an outhouse, around a fat tree and then two meathouses and through two hedges—one spiny, which took no note of being cursed by a shadow on silent feet—across a porch and around a rain barrel, over the top of a sleeping black cat that objected with more noise than the two dogs he had aroused—one was still importantly barking, puffed up and hating to leave off—across another porch ("Is that you, Dadisha?

Where have you been?"), through someone's
scraps and—long jump!—over a mulchpile, and
around two lovers ("What was that, Wrenny?"),
an overturned outhouse, a rain barrel, a cow
tethered to a wagon he went under without even
slowing down, and three more buildings.

One of the lovers and one of the dogs actually
caught sight of the swift-fleeting shadow. No one
else. The cow might have wondered.

On one knee beside a fat beanberry bush at the
far end of Market Run, he looked out upon the
long straight stretch of well-kept street that ran
past the market on the other side. He was not
winded.

The hooded cloak with the walking stick was
just reaching this end of the long, long farmers'
market. Hanse crimped his cheeks in a little smile.
Oh he was so clever, so speedy! He was just in
time to—

—to see the two cloakless but hooded footpads
materialize from the deep jet shadows at the
building's corner. They pounced. One ran angling, to grasp her from behind, while his fellow
came at her face-on with no weapons visible.
Ready to snatch what she had, and run. She behaved surprisingly; she lunged to one side and
prodded the attacker in front. *Prodded*, that Hanse
saw; she did not strike or stab with the white staff.

Instantly the man went to his knees. He was
gibbering, pleading, quaking. A butterfly clinging to a twig in a windstorm. Or . . . Athavul.

Swiftly—not professionally fast, but swiftly for
her, a civilian, Hanse saw (he was moving)—she
turned to the one coming up behind her. He also
adjusted rapidly. He went low. The staff whirred

over his head while his partner babbled and
pleaded in the most abject fear. The footpad had
not stopped moving. (Neither had Hanse.) Up
came the hooded man from his crouch and his
right hand snapped out edge-on to strike her wrist
while his other fist leaped to her stomach. That
fist glittered in the moonlight, or something glittered in it. That silvery something went into her
and she made a puking gagging throaty noise and
while she fell the white stick slid from her reflexively opening fingers. He grabbed it.

That was surely ill-advised, but his hand closed
on the staff's handle without apparent effect on
him. He kicked her viciously, angrily—maybe she
felt it, gutted, and maybe she did not—and he
railed at his comrade. The latter, on his knees,
behaved as Athavul had when Hanse shouted at
him. He fell over and rolled away, assuming the
foetal posture while he wept and pled.

The killer spat several expletives and whirled
back to his victim. She was twitching, dying.
Yanking open the vermilion cloak, he jerked off
her necklace, ripped a twisted silver loop out of
each ear, and yanked at the scantling purse on her
girdle. It refused to come free. He sliced it with the
swift single movement of a practiced expert.
Straightening, he glanced in every direction, said
something to his partner—who rolled foetally,
sobbing.

"Theba take you, then," the thief said, and ran.

Back into the shadows of the market building's
west corner he fled, and one of the shadows
tripped him. As he fell, an elbow thumped the
back of his neck.

"I want what you've got, you murdering bastard," a shadow-voice said from the shadows, while the footpad twisted to roll over. "Your kind gives thieves a bad name."

"Take it then!" The fallen man rammed the white staff into the shadow's thigh as it started to bend over him.

Instantly fear seized Hanse. Vised him; encompassed him; possessed him. Sickening, stomach-fluttering fear. His armpits flooded and his sphincter fluttered.

Unlike the stick's victims he had seen, he was in darkness, and he was Shadowspawn. He did not fall to his knees.

He fled, desperately afraid, sniveling, clutching his gut, babbling. Tears flowed to blind him, but he was in darkness anyhow. Staggering, weeping, horribly and obscenely afraid and even more horribly knowing all the while that he had no reason to be afraid, that this was sorcery; the most demeaning spell that could be laid on a man. He heard the killer laugh, and Hanse tried to run faster. Hoping the man did not pursue to confront him. Accost him. Snarl mean things at him. He could not stand that.

It did not happen that way. The thief who had slain without intending to kill laughed, but he too was scared, and disconcerted. He fled, slinking, in another direction. Hanse stumbled-staggered-sniveled on, on. Instinct was not gone but was heightened; he clung to the shadows as a frightened child to its mother. But he made noise, noise.

Attracted at the same time as she was repulsed by that whining fearful gibbering, Mignureal came upon him. "What—it's Han—*what are you doing?*"

He was seriously considering ending the terror by ending himself with the knife in his fist. Anything to stop this enveloping, consuming agony of fear. At her voice he dropped the knife and fell weeping to his knees.

"Hanse—*stop that!*"

He did not. He could not. He could assume the foetal. He did. Uncomprehending, the garishly-dressed girl acted instinctively to save him. Her mother liked him and to Mignureal he was attractive, a figure of romance. In his state, saving him was easy, even for a thirteen-year-old. Though his hysterical sobbing pleas brought tears to her eyes, for him, Mignureal tied his wrists behind him. The while, she breathed prayers known only to the S'danzo.

"You come along now," she said firmly, leaking tears and gulping. "Come along with me!"

Hanse obeyed.

She went straight along the well-lit Governor's Walk and turned down Shadow Lane, conducting her bound, sniveling captive. At the corner of Shadow and Slippery, a couple of uniformed men accosted her.

"Why it's Moonflower's darter. What've you got there, Mineral?"

"Mignureal," she corrected. "Someone put a spell on him—over on the Processional," she said, choosing an area far from where she had found him. "My mother can help. Go with Eshi."

"Hmm. A spell of fear, huh? That damned Anus Yorl, I'll wager a cup! Who is it, sniveling under your shawl that way?"

Mignureal considered swiftly. What had happened to Hanse was awful. To have these City Watchmen know, and spread it about—that would be insupportable. Again Mignureal lied. It was her brother Antelope, she told them, and they made sympathetic noises and let her be on her way, while they muttered about dam' sorcerers and the nutty names S'danzo gave their get. Both men agreed; they would make a routine check of Awful Alley and stop in at the Alekeep, just down the street.

Mignureal led Hanse a half-block more and went into her parents' shop-and-living-quarters. They were asleep. The tautly overweight Moon-flower did not heed summonses and did not make house calls. Furthermore her husband was an irrepressibly randy man who bedded early and insisted on her company. At her daughter's sobbing and shaking her, the seer awoke. That gently-named collection of talent and adipose tissue and mammalia sufficient to nurse octuplets, simultaneously, sat erect. She reached comfortingly for her daughter. Soon she had listened, was out of bed, and beside Hanse. Mignureal had ordered him to remain on the divan in the shop.

"That just isn't Hanse, Mother!"

"Of course it isn't. Look on sorcery, and hate it."

"Name of Tiana Savior—it's awful, seeing him, hearing him this way. . . ."

"Fetch my shawl," Moonflower said, one by one relieving Hanse of his knives, "and do make some tea, sweetheart."

Moonflower held the quaking young man and crooned. She pillowed his tear-wet face in the vastness of her bosom. She loosed his wrists, drew his hands round, and held their wiry darkness in her large paler dimple-backed ones. And she crooned, and talked low, on and on. Her daughter draped her with the shawl and went to make tea.

The ray of moonlight that fell into the room moved the length of a big man's foot while the seer sat there with him, and more, and Hanse went to sleep, still shivering. She held his hands until he was still but for his breathing. Mignureal hovered close, all bright of eye, and knew the instant her mother went off. Sagging. Glassy-eyed. She began murmuring, a woman small inside and huge without; a gross kitten at her divining.

"A yellow-furred hunting dog? Tall as a tree, old as a tree . . . he hovers and with him is a god not of Ilsig. A god of Ranke—oh, it is a Hell Hound. Oh Hanse it is not wizard-sorcery but god-sorcery! And who is thi—oh. Another god. But why is Theba involved, who has so few adherents here? Oh!"

She shuddered and her daughter started to touch her; desisted.

"I see Ils Himself hiding His face . . . a shadow tall as a tree and another, not nearly so big. A shadow and its pawn? Why it has no head, this smaller shad—oh. It is afraid, that's it; it has no face left. It is Ha—I will not say even though he sleeps. Oh Mignue, there is a corpse on the street up in front of the farmers' market and—ahhh." Her relief was apparent in that great sigh. "Hanse did not kill her. Another did, and Theba hovers over her. Hmm. I see—I s—I will not say what I s . . . it fades, goes."

Again she sighed and sat still, sweating, overflowing her chair on both sides. Gazing at the sleeping Shadowspawn. "He has spoken with the governor who is the emperor's kinsman, Mignureal my dear, did you know that? He will again. They are not enemies, our governor and Shadowspawn."

"Oh." And Mignureal looked upon him, head to one side. Moonflower saw the look.

"You will go to bed and tomorrow you will tell me what you were doing abroad so late, Mignue. You will not come near Hanse again, do you understand?"

"Oh, mother." Mignureal met the level gaze only briefly. "Yes, mother. I understand." And she went to bed.

Moonflower did not; she stayed beside Hanse. In the morning he was all right and she told him what she had Seen. He would never be the same again, she knew, he who had met quintessential fear, Lord Terror himself, face to face. But he was Hanse again, and not afraid, and Moonflower was sure that within a few hours he would have his gliding swagger back. She did note that he was grim-facedly determined.

The message left at the little Watchpost at the corner of Shadow and Lizard's Way suggested that the "tall as a tree Hell-hound take a walk between stinky market and the cat storage" at the time of the fifth nightwatch "when the shadows are spawning fear in all hearts." The message was delivered to Tempus, who ordered the sub-prefect to forget it, and looked fierce. The wriggly agreed and got thence.

In private, his mind aided by a pinch of his

powdered friend, Tempus worked backward at
the cipher. The last line had to be the signature:
Shadowspawn. Hanse wanted to meet him very
privately, an hour past midnight. Good. So . . .
where? "Stinky market" could mean lots of
places. "Cat storage" meant nothing. Cat storage;
cat—the granaries?—where cats not only were
kept but migrated, drawn by the mice drawn by
the grain? No; there was no way to walk *between*
any of the granaries and anything deserving to be
characterized as stinky market beyond any other
stenchy place.

What stinks most? Easy, he answered himself.
The tanners—no! Don't be stupid, second thought
told him. *Fish stink worse than anything.* Hmm.
The fish market then, down on Red Clay
Street—which might as well be called Warehouse
Street. So all the natives called it. The stinking
fish market, then, and . . . *cat storage?* He stared
at the map.

Oh. Simple. The governor was called Kitty-Cat
and a warehouse was a place for storage. The
Governor's Warehouse then, down beside the fish
market. Not a block from the Watchpost at
Shadow and Lizard, the rascal! Tempus shook his
head, and hours and hours later he was there. He
made sure no one tried to "help" him; twice he
played thief, to watch his own trail. He was not
followed. Wrinkling his nose at the stench and
slipping on a discarded fishhead, he resolved to
get a clean-up detail down here, and recommend
a light as well.

"I am glad you look like you," the shadows
said, from behind and above him.

"A god has marked me, Hanse," Tempus

explained, without turning or looking up. "He helped me, in the Vulgar Unicorn. I didn't care to be seen there, compromising you. Did you leave the message because you have changed your mind?"

"There will be a bargain."

"I can appreciate that. Word is that you have bargained before, with my employer."

"That is as obviously impossible as breaking into the palace."

"Obviously. I am enpowered to bargain, Hanse."

"A woman was found dead on Farmer's Run just at the west end of the market," the shadows said quietly. "She wore a cloak the color of red clay."

"Yes."

"She had a walking stick. It has a . . . *horrible* effect on a man. Her killer stole it, after she used it on his partner. He abandoned him."

"No thief's corpse was found."

"It does not kill. Its effect is . . . *obscene*." A pause; while the shadow shuddered? "I saw it happen. They were hooded."

"Do you know who they are?"

"Not now. I can find out easily. Want the stick?"

"Yes."

"How many of those foul things remain in . . . circulation?"

"We think two. A clever fellow has done well for himself by counting the people who came out of the shop with a purchase, and recording the names of those he knew. What is the bargain, Hanse?"

"I had rather deal with him."

"I wish you would trust me. Setting up interviews with him takes time."

"I trust you, Tempus, just as you trust me. Get me something in writing from him, then. Signed. Give it to the seer, Moonflower. This is costing me time, pulling me away from my work—"

"Work?"

"—and I shall have to have compensation. Now."

O you damned arrogant boy, Tempus thought, and without a word he made three coins clink as he dropped them. He was sure Hanse's ears could distinguish gold from copper or silver by the sound of the clink. He also dropped a short section of pig's intestine, stitched at one end and tied off at the other. He said, "Oops."

"I want assistance in recovering something of mine, Tempus. Just labor, that's all. What's to be recovered is mine, I guarantee it."

"I'll help you myself."

"We'll need tools, a horse, rope, strength. . . ."

"Done. I will get it in writing, but it is done. Deliver and I deliver. We have a bond between us."

"So have he and I. I do want that paper signed and slipped to the S'danzo seer. Very well then, Tempus. We have bargained."

"By mid-afternoon. Good night, spawn of shadows."

"Good night, shadow-man. You didn't say 'pawn,' did you?"

"No." And Tempus turned and walked back up between the buildings to light, and less stenchy air. Behind him, soundlessly, the three gold coins and little bag of krrf he had dropped vanished, into the shadows.

Next day not long after dawn Hanse gave Moonflower a great hug and pretended to find a gold piece in her ear.

"I Saw for you, not for coin," she told him.

"I understand. I know. Why look, here's another in your other ear, for Mignureal. I give you the gold because I found it, not because you helped me. And a message will be given you today, for me."

Moonflower made both coins disappear beneath her shawl into what she called her treasure chest. "Don't frown; Mignue shall have the one as her very own. Will you do something for me I would prefer to coin, Hanse?"

Very seriously, relaxing for once, he nodded. "Without question."

"My daughter is very young and thinks you are just so romantic a figure. Will you just pretend she is your sister?"

"Oh you would not want *that*, Passionflower," he said, in one of those rare indications of what sort of childhood he must have had. "She is my friend's daughter and I shall call her cousin. Besides, she saw me . . . that way. I may not be able to look her in the eyes again."

She took those lean restless hands of a thief proud never to have hurt any he robbed. "You will, Hanse. You will. It was god-sorcery, and no embarrassment. Will you now be careful?"

"I will."

She studied his eyes. "But you are going to find him."

"I am."

The adherents of the most ancient goddess Theba went hooded to their little temple. This was their way. It also made it easier for the government to keep them under surveillance, and made it easy for Hanse to slip among them. A little tilt to his shoulder, a slight favoring of one leg under the dull brown robe, and he was not the lithely gliding Shadowspawn at all.

The services were dull and he had never liked the odor of incense. It made him want to sneeze and go to sleep, both at once. Insofar as he ever gave thought to religion, he leaned toward a sort of loyalty to the demigod Rander Rehabilitatus. He endured, and he observed. This goddess' worship in Sanctuary included two blind adherents. Both carried staffs. Though only one was white, it was not in the grip of a left-handed man.

Finding his quarry really was as simple as that. On deserting his partner, the murderous thief had sneered "Theba take you," and Moonflower had Seen that goddess, or at least the likeness of her icons and amulets. She had no more than forty worshipers here, and only this one (part-time) temple. The thief had also struck away the terrorstick with his right hand and used his left to drive the dagger into his victim—and to use the staff on Hanse.

There came the time of Communing In Her. Hanse watched what the others did. They mingled, and a buzz rose as they said nice silly loving peace-things to each other in the name of Her. The usual meaningless ritual; "peace" was a word and life and its exigencies were another matter. Hanse mingled.

"Peace and love to you, brother," a woman said from within her wine-dark cowl, and her hand slipped into Hanse's robe and he caught her wrist.

"Peace and defter fingers to you, sister," he said quietly, and went around her toward his goal. To be certain, he came cowl to cowl with the man with the white stick and, smiling, made a shamefully obscene gesture. The cowl and the staff did not move; a hand moved gently out to touch him.

"Her peace remain on you, my brother," the blind man said in a high voice, and Hanse mouthed words, then turned.

"You rotten slime," a cowl striped in green and red hissed. "Poor blind Sorad has been among us for years and no one ever made such a nasty gesture to him. Who are you, anyhow?"

"One who thinks that other blind man is not blind and not one of us, and was testing—brother. Have you ever seen him before?"

His accoster—burly, in that striped Myrsevadan robe, looked around. "Well . . . no. The one in the gloves?"

"Yes. I think they are because his stick—yes, peace to you too, sister—has just been painted."

"You think it's a disguised weapon? That he's from the . . . palace?"

"No. I think the prince-governor couldn't care a rat's whisker about us." Substituting the pronoun was a last instant thought, and Hanse felt proud of that touch. Playing "I'm just like you but *he* is bad" had got him out of several scrapes. "I do think he is a spy, though. That priest from Ranke, who thinks every temple should be closed down

except a glorious new one to Vash—Vashi—
whatever they call him. I'll bet that's his spy."

That made the loyal Thebite quiver in rage! He
went directly toward the man in the forest green
cloak, with the brown stick. Hanse, edging along
toward the entrance of what was by day a belt-
maker's shop, watched Striped Robe speak to the
man with the staff. An answer came, as Hanse
moved.

Hanse didn't hear the reply; he heard "May all
your days be bright in Her name and She take you
when you are tired of life, brother." This from the
fat man beside him, in a tent-sized cloak.

"Oh, thank you, brother. And on you, peace in
Her n—" Hanse broke off when the terrified
screaming began.

It was the big fellow in the robe of green and red
stripes, and his cowl fell back to show his fear-
twisted face. Naturally no one understood, and
other cries arose amid the milling of robed, face-
less people. Two did understand, and both moved
toward the door. One was closer. He hurried forth,
running—and outside, cut left out of view of the
doorway and swung swiftly back. He already had
the little jar of vinegar out of his dull brown robe,
and the cork pulled. Inside the temple: clamor.

The man with the gloves and brown walking
stick hurried through the door and turned left;
had he not, Hanse would have called. The fellow
had no time for anything before Hanse sent the
vinegar sloshing within his hood.

"Ah!" Naturally the man ducked his head as the
liquid drenched him and entered both eyes. Since
he was not blind and not accustomed to carrying a
staff as a part of him, he dropped it to rush both

hands to his face. Hanse swallowed hard before snatching up the stick by its handle. He kicked the moaning fellow in the kneecap, and ran. The god-weapon seemed hummingly *alive* in his hand, so much that he wanted to throw it down and keeping running. He did not, and it exerted no other effect on him. Just around the corner he paused for an importuning beggar, who soon had the gift of a nice brown, cowled robe. Since it was thrown over him as he sat, he never saw the generous giver. He had been swallowed by the shadows once the beggar got his head free of the encumbering woolen.

"Here, you little lizard, where do you think you're running to, hah?"

That from the brutish swaggering desert tradesman who grabbed at Hanse as he ran by. Well, he was not of the city, and did not know who he laid big hand on. Nor was he likely to aught but hie himself out of Sanctuary, once he returned to normal—doubtless robbed. Besides, a test really should be made to be sure, and Hanse poked him.

This was the staff of ensorcelment, all right.

Hurrying on his way, Hanse began to smile.

He had the stick and the murdering thief who had used it on him would not be too nimble for a long, long time, and the robe he had snitched off a drying line was in the possession of a beggar who would be needing it in a few months, and Hanse had his little message from the prince-governor. It avowed—so Hanse was told, as he did not read— that "he you specify shall lend full aid in the endeavor you specify, provided it is legal in full, in return for your returning another wand to us."

Hanse had laughed when he read that last; even

a prince had a sense of humor and could allude to
Hanse's having stolen his Savankh, rod of authority, less than a month ago. And now
Shadowspawn would have the aid of big strong
super-legal Tempus in regaining two bags of
silver coin from a well up in the supposedly
haunted ruins of Eaglenest. Hanse hoped Prince
Kadakithis would appreciate the humor in that,
too: the bagged booty had come from him, as
ransom for the official baton of his imperial authority in Sanctuary. Even Tempus' krrf had
brought in a bit of silver.

And now . . . Hanse's grin broadened. Suppose he just went about a *second* illicit entry of
the palace? Suppose a blind man showed up
among the swarm of alms-seekers to be admitted
into the courtyard two days hence, in accord
with Kadakithis' people wooing custom?
Shadowspawn would not only hand this awful
staff to the prince-governor, he would at the same
time provide graphic demonstration of the
palace's pitiable security.

Unfortunately, Tempus had taken charge of
security. The hooded blind beggar was challenged at the gate two days thence, and the Hell
Hound Quag suspiciously snatched the staff from
him. When the disguised Hanse objected, he was
struck with it. Well, at least that way it was proven
that he had brought the right stick in good faith,
and that way he did get to spend a night in the
palace, however unpleasant in his state of terror.

TO GUARD THE GUARDIANS

Robert Lynn Asprin

The Hell Hounds were now a common sight in Sanctuary so the appearance of one in the bazaar created little stir, save for the concealment of a few smuggled wares and a price increase on everything else. However, when two appeared together, as they did today, it was enough to silence casual conversation and draw uneasy stares, though the more observant vendors noted that the pair were engrossed in their own argument and did not even glance at the stalls they were passing.

"But the man has offended me. . . ." the darker of the pair snarled.

"He offends everyone," his companion countered, "it's his way. I tell you, Razkuli, I've heard him say things to the prince himself that would have other men flayed and blinded. You're a fool to take it personally."

"But, Zalbar. . . ."

"I know, I know—he offends you; and Quag bores you and Arman is an arrogant braggard. Well, this whole town offends me, but that doesn't give me the right to put it to the sword. Nothing Tempus has said to you warrants a blood feud."

"It is done." Razkuli thrust one fist against his other palm as they walked.

"It is not done until you act on your promise, and if you do I'll move to stop you. I won't have the men in my command killing each other."

The two men walked silently for several moments, each lost in his own dark thoughts.

"Look, my friend," Zalbar sighed, "I've already had one of my men killed under scandalous circumstances. I don't want to answer for another incident—particularly if it involves you. Can't you see Tempus is trying to goad you into a fight?—a fight you can't win."

"No one lives that I've seen over an arrow," Razkuli said ominously, his eyes narrowing on an imaginary target.

"Murder, Razkuli? I never thought I'd see the day you'd sink to being an assassin."

There was a sharp intake of breath and Razkuli faced his comrade with eyes that showed a glint of madness. Then the spark faded and the small man's shoulders relaxed. "You're right, my friend," he said, shaking his head, "I would never do that. Anger speeds my tongue ahead of reason."

"As it did when you vowed blood-feud. You've survived countless foes who were mortal; don't try the favor of the gods by seeking an enemy who is not."

"Then the rumors about Tempus are true?" Razkuli asked, his eyes narrowing again.

"I don't know, there are things about him which are difficult to explain by any other logic. Did you see how rapidly his leg healed? We both know men whose soldiering career was ended after they were caught under a horse—yet he was standing duty again within the week."

"Such a man is an affront against Nature."

"Then let Nature take vengeance on him," Zalbar laughed, clapping a friendly hand on his comrade's shoulder, "and free us for more worthwhile pasttimes. Come, I'll buy you lunch. It will be a pleasant change from barracks food."

Haakon, the sweetmeats vendor, brightened as the two soldiers approached him and waited patiently while they made their selections from his spiced-meat turnovers.

"That will be three coppers," he smiled through yellowed teeth.

"Three coppers?" Razkuli exclaimed angrily, but Zalbar silenced him with a nudge in the ribs.

"Here, fellow . . ." the Hell-Hound commander dropped some coins into Haakon's outstretched hand, "take four. Those of us from the Capitol are used to paying full value for quality goods—though I suppose that this far from civilization you have to adjust the prices to accommodate the poorer folk."

The barb went home and Zalbar was rewarded by a glare of pure hatred before he turned away, drawing Razkuli with him.

"Four coppers! You were being overcharged at three!"

"I know." Zalbar winked. "But I refuse to give them the satisfaction of haggling. I find it's worth the extra copper to see their faces when I imply that they're selling below value—it's one of the few pleasures available in this hellhole."

"I never thought of it that way," Razkuli said with a laugh, "but you're right. My father would have been livid if someone deliberately overpaid him. Do me a favor and let me try it when we buy the wine."

Razkuli's refusal to bargain brought much the same reaction from the wineseller. The dark mood of their conversation as they had entered the bazaar had vanished and they were ready to eat with calm humor.

"You provided the food and drink, so I'll provide the setting," Razkuli declared, tucking the wine-flask into his belt. "I know a spot which is both pleasant and relaxing."

"It must be outside the city."

"It is, just outside the Common Gate. Come on, the city won't miss our presence for an hour or so."

Zalbar was easily pursuaded though more from curiosity than belief. Except for occasional patrols along the Street of Red Lanterns he rarely got outside Sanctuary's North Wall and had never explored the area to the northwest where Razkuli was leading him.

It was a different world here, almost as if they had stepped through a magic portal into another land. The buildings were scattered, with large open spaces between them, in contrast to the cramped shops and narrow alleys of the city proper. The air was refreshingly free from the stench of unwashed bodies jostling each other in crowded streets. Zalbar relaxed in the peaceful surroundings. The pressures of patroling the hateful town slipped away like a heavy cloak, allowing him to look forward to an uninterrupted meal in pleasant company.

"Perhaps you could speak to Tempus? We

needn't like each other, but if he could find another target for his taunts, it would do much toward easing my hatred."

Zalbar shot a wary glance at his comrade, but detected none of the blind anger which he had earlier expressed. The question seemed to be an honest attempt on Razkuli's part to find a compromise solution to an intolerable situation.

"I would, if I thought it would help," he sighed reluctantly, "but I fear I have little influence on him. If anything, it would only make matters worse. He would redouble his attacks to prove he wasn't afraid of me either."

"But you're his superior officer," Razkuli argued.

"Officially, perhaps," his friend shrugged, "but we both know there are gaps between what is official and what is true. Tempus has the Prince's ear. He's a free agent here and follows my orders only when it suits him."

"You've kept him out of the Aphrodesia House. . . ."

"Only because I had convinced the prince of the necessity of maintaining the good will of that House before Tempus arrived," Zalbar countered, shaking his head. "I had to go to the prince to curb Tempus' ill-conduct and earned his hatred for it. You notice he still does what he pleases at the Lily Garden—and the prince looks the other way. No, I wouldn't count on my influence over Tempus. I don't think he would physically attack me because of my position in the Prince's bodyguard. I also don't think he would come to my aid if I were hard-pressed in a fight."

Just then Zalbar noticed a small flower garden

nestled beside a house not far from their path. A man was at work in the garden, watering and pruning. The sight created a sudden wave of nostalgia in the Hell Hound. How long had it been since he stood outside the Emperor's Palace in the Capitol, fighting boredom by watching the gardeners pampering the flowered grounds? It seemed like a lifetime. Despite the fact that he was a soldier by profession, or perhaps because he was a soldier, he had always admired the calm beauty of flowers.

"Let's eat there . . . under that tree," he suggested, indicating a spot with a view of the garden. "It's as good a place as any."

Razkuli hesitated, glancing at the gardened house and started to say something, then shrugged and veered toward the tree. Zalbar saw the mischievious smile flit briefly across his comrade's face, but ignored it, preferring to contemplate the peaceful garden instead.

The pair dined in the manner of hardened, but off-duty, campaigners. Rather than facing each other, or sitting side-by-side, the two assumed back-to-back positions in the shade of a spreading tree. The earthenware wine-flask was carefully placed to one side, but in easy reach of both. Not only did the arrangement give them a full circle of vision to insure that their meal would be uninterrupted, it also allowed a brief illusion of privacy for the individual—a rare commodity to those whose profession required that every moment be shared with at least a dozen colleagues. To further that illusion they ate in silence. Conversation would be neither attempted nor tolerated until both were finished with their meal. It was the stance of men who trusted each other completely.

Although his position allowed him a clear view of the flower garden, Zalbar found his thoughts wandering back to his earlier conversation with Razkuli. Part of his job was to maintain peace among the Hell Hounds, at least to a point where their personal differences did not interfere with the performance of their duties. To that end he had soothed his friend's ruffled feathers and forestalled any open fighting within the force . . . for the time being, at least. With peace thus preserved, Zalbar could admit to himself that he agreed wholeheartedly with Razkuli.

Loudmouthed bullies were nothing new in the army, but Tempus was a breed apart. As a devout believer in discipline and law, Zalbar was disgusted and appalled by Tempus' attitudes and conduct. What was worse, Tempus did have the prince's ear, so Zalbar was powerless to move against him despite the growing rumors of immoral and illegal conduct.

The Hell Hound's brow furrowed as he reflected upon the things he had heard and seen. Tempus openly used krrf, both on duty and off. He was rapidly building a reputation for brutality and sadism among the not easily shocked citizens of Sanctuary. There were even rumors that he was methodically hunting and killing the blue-masked sell-swords employed by the ex-gladiator, Jubal.

Zalbar had no love for that crime-lord who traded in slaves to mask his more illicit activities, but neither could he tolerate a Hell Hound taking it upon himself to be judge and executioner. But he had been ordered by the prince to allow Tem-

pus free rein and was powerless to even investigate the rumors: a fine state of affairs when the
law-enforcers became the lawbreakers and the
lawgiver only moved to shelter them.

A scream rent the air, interrupting Zalbar's re-
verie and bringing him to his feet, sword in hand.
As he cast about, searching for the source of the
noise, he remembered he had heard screams like
that before . . . though not on any battlefield. It
wasn't a scream of pain, hatred, or terror but the
heartless, soulless sounds of one without hope
and assaulted by horror too great for the mind to
comprehend.

The silence was completely shattered by a second scream and this time Zalbar knew the source
was the beautifully gardened house. He watched
in growing disbelief as the gardener calmly continued his work, not even bothering to look up
despite the now frequent screams. Either the man
was deaf or Zalbar himself was going mad, react-
ing to imaginary noises from a best-forgotten past.

Turning to Raskuli for confirmation, Zalbar was
outraged to find his friend not only still seated but
grinning ear-to-ear.

"Now do you see why I was willing to pass this
spot by?" the swarthy Hell Hound said with a
laugh. "Perhaps the next time I offer to lead you
won't be so quick to exert your rank."

"You were expecting this?" Zalbar demanded,
unsoothed by Razkuli's humor.

"Of course, you should be thankful it didn't
start until we were nearly finished with our
meal."

Zalbar's retort was cut off by a drawn out piercing cry that rasped against ear and mind and de-

fied human endurance with its length.

"Before you go charging to the rescue," Razkuli commented, ignoring the now fading outburst of pain, "you should know I've already looked into it. What you're hearing is a slave responding to its master's attentive care: a situation entirely within the law and therefore no concern of ours. It might interest you to know that the owner of that building is a. . . ."

"Kurd!" Zalbar breathed through taut lips, glaring at the house as if it were an archenemy.

"You know him?"

"We met once, back at the Capitol. That's why he's here . . . or at least why he's not still there."

"Then you know his business?" Razkuli scowled, a bit deflated that his revelations were no surprise. "I'll admit I find it distasteful, but there's nothing we can do about it."

"We'll see," Zalbar announced darkly, starting toward the house.

"Where're you going?"

"To pay Kurd a visit."

"Then I'll see you back at the barracks." Razkuli shuddered. "I've been inside that house once already, and I'll not enter again unless it's under orders."

Zalbar made no note of his friend's departure though he did sheathe his sword as he approached the house. The impending battle would not require conventional weapons.

"Ho there!" he hailed the gardener. "Tell your master I wish to speak with him."

"He's busy," the man snarled, "can't you hear?"

"Too busy to speak with one of the prince's

personal guard?" Zalbar challenged, raising an eyebrow.

"He's spoken to them before and each time they've gone away and I've lost pay for allowing the interruption."

"Tell him it's Zalbar . . ." the Hell Hound ordered, ". . . your master will speak with me, or would you like to deal with me in his stead?"

Though he made no move toward his weapons Zalbar's voice and stance convinced the gardener to waste no time. The gnome-like man abandoned his chores to disappear into the house.

As he waited Zalbar surveyed the flowers again, but knowledge of Kurd's presence had ruined his appreciation of floral beauty. Instead of lifting his spirits, the bright blossoms seemed a horrifying incongruity, like viewing a gaily colored fungus growing on a rotting corpse.

As Zalbar turned away from the flowers, Kurd emerged into the daylight. Though it had been five years since they had seen each other, the older man was sufficiently unchanged that Zalbar recognized him instantly: the stained dishevelled dress of one who sleeps in his clothes, the unwashed, unkempt hair and beard, as well as the cadaverously thin body with its long skeletal fingers and pasty complexion. Clearly Kurd had not discontinued his habit of neglecting his own body in the pursuit of his work.

"Good day . . . citizen," the Hell Hound's smile did not disguise the sarcasm poisoning his greeting.

"It *is* you," Kurd declared, squinting to study the other's features. "I thought we were done with each other when I left Ranke."

"I think you shall continue to see me until you see fit to change your occupation."

"My work is totally within the limits of the law." The thin man bristled, betraying, for a moment, the strength of will hidden in his outwardly feeble body.

"So you said in Ranke. I still find it offensive, without redeeming merit."

"Without redeeming. . . ." Kurd shrieked, then words failed him. His lips tightened, he seized Zalbar by the arm and began pulling him toward the house. "Come with me now," he instructed. "Let me show you my work and explain what I am doing. Perhaps then you will be able to grasp the importance of my studies."

In his career Zalbar had faced death in many guises and done it unflinchingly. Now, however, he drew back in horror.

"I . . . That won't be necessary," he insisted.

"Then you continue to blindly condemn my actions without allowing me a fair hearing?" Kurd pointed a bent, bony finger at the Hell Hound, a note of triumph in his voice.

Trapped by his own convictions, Zalbar swallowed hard and steeled himself. "Very well, lead on. But, I warn you—my opinions are not easily swayed."

Zalbar's resolve wavered once they entered the building and he was assaulted by the smells of its interior. Then he caught sight of the gardener smirking at him from the doorway and set his face in an expressionless mask as he was led up the stairs to the second floor.

All that the Hell Hound had ever heard or imagined about Kurd's work failed to prepare him for the scene which greeted him when the pale man opened the door to his workshop. Half a dozen large, heavy tables lined the walls, each set at a strange angle so their surfaces were nearly upright. They were not unlike the wooden frames court artists used to hold their work while painting. All the tables were fitted with leather harnesses and straps. The wood and leather, both, showed dried and crusted bloodstains. Four of the tables were occupied.

"Most so-called medical men only repeat what has gone before . . ." Kurd was saying, ". . . the few who do attempt new techniques do so in a slipshod, trial-and-error fashion borne of desperation and ignorance. If the patient dies, it is difficult to determine if the cause was the original affliction, or the new treatment itself. Here, under controlled conditions, I actually increase our knowledge of the human body and its frailties. Watch your step, please. . . ."

Grooves had been cut in the floor, running along beneath the tables and meeting in a shallow pit at the room's far end. As he stepped over one, Zalbar realized that the system was designed to guide the flow of spilled blood. He shuddered.

There was a naked man on the first table and when he saw them coming he began to writhe against his bonds. One arm was gone from the elbow down and he beat the stump against the tabletop. Gibberings poured from his mouth. Zalbar noted with disgust that the man's tongue had been cut out.

"Here," Kurd announced, pointing to a gaping wound in the man's shoulder, "is an example of my studies."

The man had obviously lost control of his bodily functions. Excretions stained his legs and the table. Kurd paid no attention to this, gesturing Zalbar closer to the table as he used his long fingers to spread the edges of the shoulder wound. "I have identified a point in the body which, if pressure like this. . . ."

The man shrieked, his body arching against the restraining straps.

"Stop!" Zalbar shouted, losing any pretense of disinterest.

It was unlikely he could be heard over the tortured sounds of the victim, but Kurd withdrew his bloody finger and the man sagged back on the table.

"Well, did you see it?" the pale man asked eagerly.

"See what?" Zalbar blinked, still shaken by what he had witnessed.

"His stump, man! It stopped moving! Pressure or damage to this point can rob a man of the use of his arm. Here, I'll show you again."

"No!" the Hell Hound ordered quickly, "I've seen enough."

"Then you see the value of my discovery?"

"Ummm. . . . where do you get your . . . subjects?" Zalbar evaded.

"From slavers, of course." Kurd frowned. "You can see the brands quite clearly. If I worked with anythign but slaves . . . well, that would be against Ranken law."

"And how do you get them onto the tables? Slaves or not, I should think they would fight to the death rather than submit to your knives."

"There is a herbalist in town," the pale man

explained, "he supplies me with a mild potion that renders them senseless. When they awaken, it's too late for effective resistance."

Zalbar started to ask another question, but Kurd held up a restraining hand. "You still haven't answered my question: do you now see the value of my work?"

The Hell Hound forced himself to look around the room again. "I see that you genuinely believe the knowledge you seek is worthwhile," he said carefully, "but I still feel subjecting men and women to this, even if they are slaves, is too high a price."

"But it's legal!" Kurd insisted. "What I do here breaks no Ranken laws."

"Ranke has many laws, you should remember that from our last meeting. Few live within all of them and while there is some discretion exercised between which laws are enforced and which are overlooked, I tell you now that I will be personally watching for anything which will allow me to move against you. It would be easier on both of us if you simply moved on now . . . for I won't rest while you are within my patrol-range."

"I am a law-abiding citizen." The pale man glared, drawing himself up. "I won't be driven from my home like a common criminal."

"So you said before." The Hell Hound smiled as he turned to go. "But, you are no longer in Ranke—remember that."

"That's right," Kurd shouted after him, "we are no longer in Ranke. Remember that yourself, Hell Hound."

Four days later Zalbar's confidence had ebbed

considerably. Finishing his night patrol of the city he turned down the Processional toward the wharves. This was becoming a habit with him now, a final off-duty stretch-of-the-legs to organize his thoughts in solitude before retiring to the crowded barracks. Though there was still activity back in the Maze, this portion of town had been long asleep and it was easy for the Hell Hound to lose himself in his ponderings as he paced slowly along the moon-shadowed street.

The prince had rejected his appeal, pointing out that harassing a relatively honest citizen was a poor use of time, particularly with the wave of killings sweeping Sanctuary. Zalbar could not argue with the prince's logic. Ever since that weapons shop had appeared, suddenly, in the Maze to dispense its deadly brand of magic, killings were not only more frequent but of an uglier nature than usual. Perhaps now that the shop had disappeared the madness would ease, but in the meantime he could ill afford the time to pursue Kurd with the vigor necessary to drive the vivisectionist from town.

For a moment Kurd's empassioned defense of his work flashed across Zalbar's mind, only to be quickly repressed. New medical knowledge was worth having, but slaves were still people. The systematic torture of another being in the name of knowledge was. . . .

"Cover!"

Zalbar was prone on the ground before the cry had fully registered in his mind. Reflexes honed by years in service to the Empire had him rolling, crawling, scrabbling along the dirt in search of shelter without pausing to identify the source of

the warning. Twice, before he reached the
shadows of an alley, he heard the unmistakable
hisss-pock of arrows striking nearby: ample proof
that the danger was not imaginary.

Finally, in the alley's relative security, he
snaked his sword from its scabbard and
breathlessly scanned the rooftops for the bowman
assassin. A flicker of movement atop a building
across the street caught his eyes, but it failed to
repeat itself. He strained to penetrate the darkness. There was a crying moan, ending in a cough;
moments later, a poor imitation of a night bird's
whistle.

Though he was sure someone had just died,
Zalbar didn't twitch a muscle, holding his position like a hunting cat. Who had died? The assassin? Or the person whose call had warned him
of danger? Even if it were the assassin there might
still be an accomplice lurking nearby.

As if in answer to this last thought a figure
detached itself from a darkened doorway and
moved to the center of the street. It paused, placed
hands on hips and hailed the alley wherein Zalbar
had taken refuge.

"It's safe now, Hell Hound. We've rescued you
from your own carelessness."

Regaining his feet Zalbar sheathed his sword
and stepped into the open. Even before being
hailed he had recognized the dark figure. A blue
hawk-mask and cloak could not hide the size or
coloring of his rescuer, and if they had, the Hell
Hound would have known the smooth grace of
those movements anywhere.

"What carelessness is that, Jubal?" he asked,
hiding his own annoyance.

"You have used this route three nights in a row, now," the ex-gladiator announced. "That's all the pattern an assassin needs."

The Negro crime-lord did not seem surprised or annoyed that his disguise had been penetrated. If anything, Jubal gave an impression of being pleased with himself as he bantered with the Hell Hound.

Zalbar realized that Jubal was right: on duty or off, a predictable pattern was an invitation for ambush. He was spared the embarrassment of making this admission, however, as the unseen savior on the rooftops chose this moment to dump the assassin's body to the street. The two men studied it with disdain.

"Though I appreciate your intervention," the Hell Hound commented drily, "it would have been nice to take him alive. I'll admit a passing curiosity as to who sent him."

"I can tell you that." The hawk-masked figure smiled grimly. "It's Kurd's money that filled that assassin's purse, though it puzzles me why he would bear you such a grudge."

"You knew about this in advance?"

"One of my informants overheard the hiring in the Vulgar Unicorn. It's amazing how many normally careful people forget that a man can hear as well as talk."

"Why didn't you send word to warn me in advance?"

"I had no proof." The black man shrugged. "It's doubtful my witness would be willing to testify in court. Besides, I still owed you a debt from our last meeting . . . or have you forgotten you saved my life once?"

"I haven't forgotten. As I told you then, I was only doing my duty. You owed me nothing."

". . . And I was only doing my duty as a Ranken citizen in assisting you tonight." Jubal's teeth flashed in the moonlight.

"Well, whatever your motive, you have my thanks."

Jubal was silent a moment. "If you truly wish to express your gratitude," he said at last, "would you join me now for a drink? There's something I would like to discuss with you."

"I . . . I'm afraid I can't. It's a long walk to your . . . house and I have duties tomorrow."

"I was thinking of the Vulgar Unicorn."

"The Vulgar Unicorn?" Zalbar stammered, genuinely astonished. "Where my assassination was planned. I can't go in there."

"Why not?"

"Well . . . if for no other reason that I am a Hell Hound. It would do neither of us any good to be seen together publicly, much less in the Vulgar Unicorn."

"You could wear my mask and cloak. That would hide your uniform and face. Then, to any onlooker it would only appear that I was having a drink with one of my men."

For a moment Zalbar wavered in indecision, then the audacity of a Hell Hound in a blue hawk-mask seized his fancy and he laughed aloud. "Why not?" he agreed, reaching for the offered disguise. "I've always wondered what the inside of that place looked like.

Zalbar had not realized how bright the moonlight was until he stepped through the door of the

Vulgar Unicorn. A few small oil lamps were the only illumination and those were shielded toward the wall, leaving most of the interior in heavy shadow. Though he could see figures huddled at several tables as he followed Jubal into the main room, he could not make out any individual's features.

There was one, however, whose face he did not need to see, the unmistakably gaunt form of Hakiem the storyteller slouched at a central table. A small bowl of wine sat before him, apparently forgotten, as the tale-spinner nodded in near-slumber. Zalbar harbored a secret liking for the ancient character and would have passed the table quietly, but Jubal caught the Hell Hound's eye and winked broadly. Withdrawing a coin from his sword-belt, the slaver tossed it in an easy arch toward the storyteller's table.

Hakiem's hand moved like a flicker of light and the coin disappeared in mid-flight. His drowsy manner remained unchanged.

"That's payment enough for a hundred stories, old man," Jubal rumbled softly, "but tell them somewhere else . . . and about someone else."

Moving with quiet dignity, the storyteller rose to his feet, bestowed a withering gaze on both of them, and stalked regally from the room. His bowl of wine had disappeared with his departure.

In the brief moment that their eyes met, Zalbar had felt an intense intelligence and was certain that the old man had penetrated both mask and cloak to coldly observe his true identity. Hastily revising his opinion of the gaunt tale-spinner, the Hell Hound recalled Jubal's description of an informant whom people forgot could hear as well as

see and knew whose spying had truly saved his
life.

The slaver sank down at the recently vacated
table and immediately received two unordered
goblets of expensive qualis. Settling next to him,
Zalbar noted that this table had a clear view of all
entrances and exits of the tavern and his estimation of Hakiem went up yet another notch.

"If I had thought of it sooner, I would have
suggested that your man on the rooftop join us,"
the Hell Hound commented. "I feel I owe him a
drink of thanks."

"That man is a woman, Moria; she works the
darkness better than I do . . . and without the
benefits of protective coloration."

"Well, I'd still like to thank her."

"I'd advise against it." The slaver grinned. "She
hates Rankens, and the Hell Hounds in particular.
She only intervened at my orders."

"You remind me of several questions." Zalbar
set his goblet down. "Why did you act on my
behalf tonight? And how is it that you know the
cry the army uses to warn of archers?"

"In good time. First you must answer a question
of mine. I'm not used to giving out information for
free, and since I told you the identity of your
enemy, perhaps now you can tell me why Kurd
would set an assassin on your trail?"

After taking a thoughtful sip of his drink, Zalbar
began to explain the situation between himself
and Kurd. As the story unfolded, the Hell Hound
found he was saying more than was necessary,
and was puzzled as to why he would reveal to
Jubal the anger and bitterness he had kept secret
even from his own force. Perhaps, it was because,

unlike his comrades whom he respected, Zalbar saw the slaver as a man so corrupt that his own darkest thoughts and doubts would seem commonplace by comparison.

Jubal listened in silence until the Hell Hound was finished, then nodded slowly. "Yes, that makes sense now," he murmured.

"The irony is that at the moment of attack I was bemoaning my inability to do anything about Kurd. For a while, at least, an assassin is unnecessary. I am under orders to leave Kurd alone."

Instead of laughing, Jubal studied his opposite thoughtfully. "Strange you should say that." He spoke with measured care. "I also have a problem I am currently unable to deal with. Perhaps we can solve each other's problems."

"Is that what you wanted to talk to me about?" Zalbar asked, suddenly suspicious.

"In a way. Actually this is better. Now, in return for the favor I must ask, I can offer something you want. If you address yourself to my problem, I'll put an end to Kurd's practice for you."

"I assume that what you want is illegal. If you really think I'd. . . ."

"It is not illegal!" Jubal spat with venom. "I don't need your help to break the law, that's easy enough to do despite the efforts of your so-called elite force. No, Hell Hound, I find it necessary to offer you a bribe to do your job—to enforce the law."

"Any citizen can appeal to any Hell Hound for assistance." Zalbar felt his own anger grow. "If it is indeed within the law, you don't have to. . . ."

"Fine!" the slaver interrupted. "Then, as a Ranken citizen I ask you to investigate and stop a wave of murders—someone is killing my people; hunting blue-masks through the streets as if they were diseased animals."

"I . . . I see."

"And I see that this comes as no surprise," Jubal snarled. "Well, Hell Hound, do your duty. I make no pretense about my people, but they are being executed without a trial or hearing. That's murder. Or do you hesitate because it's one of your own who's doing the killing?"

Zalbar's head came up with a snap and Jubal met his stare with a humorless smile.

"That's right, I know the murderer, not that it's been difficult to learn. Tempus has been open enough with his bragging."

"Actually," Zalbar mused drily, "I was wondering why you haven't dealt with him yourself if you know he's guilty. I've heard hawk-masks have killed transgressors when their offense was far less certain."

Now it was Jubal who averted his eyes in discomfort. "We've tried," he admitted, "Tempus seems exceptionally hard to down. Some of my men went against my orders and used magical weapons. The result was four more bloody masks to his credit."

The Hell Hound could hear the desperate appeal in the slaver's confession.

"I cannot allow him to continue his sport, but the price of stopping him grows fearfully high. I'm reduced to asking for your intervention. You, more than the others, have prided yourself in performing your duties in strict adherence to the codes of justice. Tell me, doesn't the law apply equally to everyone?"

A dozen excuses and explanations leapt to Zalbar's lips, then a cold wave of anger swept them away. "You're right, though I never thought you'd be the one to point out my duty to me. A killer in uniform is still a killer and should be punished for his crimes . . . all of them. If Tempus is your murderer, I'll personally see to it that he's dealt with."

"Very well." Jubal nodded. "And in return, I'll fill my end of the bargain—Kurd will no longer work in Sanctuary."

Zalbar opened his mouth to protest. The temptation was almost too great—if Jubal could make good his promise—but, no, "I'd have to insist that your actions remain within the law," he murmured reluctantly. "I can't ask you to do anything illegal."

"Not only is it legal, it's done! Kurd is out of business as of now."

"What do you mean?"

"Kurd can't work without subjects," the slaver smiled, "and I'm his supplier—or I was. Not only have I ended his supply of slaves, I'll spread the word to the other slavers that if they deal with him I'll undercut their prices in the other markets and drive them out of town as well."

Zalbar smiled with new distaste beneath his mask. "You knew what he was doing with the slaves and you dealt with him anyway?"

"Killing slaves for knowledge is no worse than having slaves kill each other in the arena for entertainment. Either is an unpleasant reality in our world."

Zalbar winced at the sarcasm in the slaver's voice, but was unwilling to abandon his position.

"We have different views of fighting. You were forced into the arena as a gladiator while I freely enlisted in the army. Still, we share a common experience: however terrible the battle: however frightful the odds, we had a chance. We could fight back and survive—or at least take our foemen with us as we fell. Being trussed up like a sacrificial animal, helpless to do anything but watch your enemy—no, not your enemy—your tormentor's weapon descend on you again and again. . . . No being, slave or freedman, should be forced into that. I cannot think of an enemy I hate enough to condemn to such a fate."

"I can think of a few," Jubal murmured, "but then, I've never shared your ideals. Though we both believe in justice we seek it in different ways."

"Justice?" the Hell Hound sneered, "that's the second time you've used that word tonight. I must admit it sounds strange coming from your lips."

"Does it?" the slaver asked. "I've always dealt fairly with my own or with those who do business with me. We both acknowledge the corruption in our world, Hell Hound. The difference is that, unlike yourself, I don't try to protect the world— I'm hard-pressed to protect myself and my own."

Zalbar set down his unfinished drink. "I'll leave your mask and cloak outside," he said levelly, "I fear that the difference is too great for us to enjoy a drink together."

Anger flashed in the slaver's eyes. "But you will investigate the murders?"

"I will," the Hell Hound promised, "and as the complaining citizen you'll be informed of the results of my investigation."

Tempus was working on his sword when Zalbar and Razkuli approached him. They had deliberately waited to confront him here in the barracks rather than at his favored haunt, the Lily Garden. Despite everything that had or might occur, they were all Army and what was to be said should not be heard by civilians outside their elite club.

Tempus favored them with a sullen glare, then brazenly returned his attention to his work. It was an unmistakable affront as he was only occupied with filing a series of saw-like teeth into one edge of his sword: a project that should run a poor second to speaking with the Hell Hound's captain.

"I would have a word with you, Tempus," Zalbar announced, swallowing his anger.

"It's your prerogative," the other replied without looking up.

Razkuli shifted his feet, but a look from his friend stilled him.

"I have had a complaint entered against you," Zalbar continued. "A complaint which has been confirmed by numerous witnesses. I felt it only fair to hear your side of the story before I went to Kadakithis with it."

At the mention of the prince's name, Tempus raised his head and ceased his filing. "And the nature of the complaint?" he asked darkly.

"It is said you're commiting wanton murder during your off-duty hours."

"Oh, that. It's not wanton. I only hunt hawkmasks."

Zalbar had been prepared for many possible responses to his accusations: angry denial, a mad dash for freedom, a demand for proof or witnesses. This easy admission, however, caught him totally off-balance. "You . . . you admit your guilt?" he managed at last, surprise robbing him of his composure.

"Certainly. I'm only surprised anyone has bothered to complain. No one should miss the killers I've taken . . . least of all you."

"Well, it's true I hold no love for Jubal or his sell-swords," Zalbar admitted, "but, there are still due processes of law to be followed. If you want to see them brought to justice you should have. . . ."

"Justice?" Tempus laughed. "Justice has nothing to do with it."

"Then why hunt them?"

"For practice," Tempus informed them, studying his serrated sword once more. "An unexercised sword grows slow. I like to keep a hand in whenever possible and supposedly the sell-swords Jubal hires are the best in town—though, to tell the truth, if the ones I've faced are any example, he's being cheated."

"That's all?" Razkuli burst out, unable to contain himself any longer. "That's all the reason you need to disgrace your uniform?"

Zalbar held up a warning hand, but Tempus only laughed at the two of them.

"That's right, Zalbar, better keep a leash on your dog there. If you can't stop his yapping, I'll do it for you."

For a moment Zalbar thought he might have to restrain his friend, but Razkuli had passed explosive rage. The swarthy Hell Hound glared at Tempus with a deep, glowering hatred which Zalbar knew could not be dimmed now with reason or threats. Grappling with his own anger, Zalbar turned, at last, to Tempus.

"Will you be as arrogant when the prince asks you to explain your actions?" he demanded.

"I won't have to." Tempus grinned again. "Kitty-Cat will never call me to task for anything. You got your way on the Street of Red Lanterns, but that was before the prince fully comprehended my position here. He'd even reverse that decision if he hadn't taken a public stance on it."

Zalbar was frozen by anger and frustration as he realized the truth of Tempus' words. "And just what *is* your position here?"

"If you have to ask," Tempus laughed, "I can't explain. But you must realize that you can't count on the prince to support your charges. Save yourselves a lot of grief by accepting me as someone outside the law's jurisdiction." He rose, sheathed his sword and started to leave, but Zalbar blocked his path.

"You may be right. You may indeed be above the law, but if there is a god—any god—watching over us now, the time is not far off when your sword will miss and we'll be rid of you. Justice is a natural process. It can't be swayed for long by a prince's whims."

"Don't call upon the gods unless you're ready to accept their interference." Tempus grimmaced. "You'd do well to heed that warning from one who knows."

Before Zalbar could react, Razkuli was lunging forward, his slim wrist-dagger darting for Tempus's throat. It was too late for the Hell Hound captain to intervene either physically or verbally, but then, Tempus did not seem to require outside help.

Moving with lazy ease, Tempus slapped his left hand over the speeding point, his palm taking the full impact of Razkuli's vengence. The blade emerged from the back of his hand and blood spurted freely for a moment, but Tempus seemed not to notice. A quick wrench with the already wounded hand and the knife was twisted from Razkuli's grip. Then Tempus' right hand closed like a vise on the throat of his dumbfounded attacker, lifting him, turning him, slamming him against a wall and pinning him there with his toes barely touching the floor.

"Tempus!" Zalbar barked, his friend's danger breaking through the momentary paralysis brought on by the sudden explosion of action.

"Don't worry, Captain," Tempus responded in a calm voice. "If you would be so kind?"

He extended his bloody hand toward Zalbar and the tall Hell Hound gingerly withdrew the dagger from the awful wound. As the knife came clear the clotting ooze of blood erupted into a steady stream. Tempus studied the scarlet cascade with distaste, then thrust his hand against Razkuli's face.

"Lick it, dog," he ordered. "Lick it clean, and be thankful I don't make you lick the floor as well!"

Helpless and fighting for each breath, the pinned man hesitated only a moment before extending his tongue in a feeble effort to comply with the demand. Quickly impatient, Tempus wiped his hand in a bloody smear across Razkuli's face and mouth, then he examined his wound again.

As Zalbar watched, horrified, the seepage from the wound slowed from flow to trickle and finally to a slow ooze—all in the matter of seconds.

Apparently satisfied with the healing process, Tempus turned dark eyes to his captain. "Every dog gets one bite—but the next time your pet crosses me, I'll take him down and neither you nor the prince will be able to stop me."

With that he wrenched Razkuli from the wall and dashed him to the floor at Zalbar's feet. With both Hell Hounds held motionless by his brutality, he strode from the room without a backward glance.

The suddenness and intensity of the exchange had shocked even Zalbar's battlefield reflexes into immobility, but with Tempus' departure, control flooded back into his limbs as if he had been released from a spell. Kneeling beside his friend, he hoisted Razkuli into a sitting position to aid his labored breathing.

"Don't try to talk," he ordered, reaching to wipe the blood smear from Razkuli's face, but the grasping man jerked his head back and forth, refusing both the order and the help.

Gathering his legs under him, the short Hell Hound surged to his feet and retained the upright position, though he had to cling to the wall for support. For several moments, his head sagged weakly as he drew breath in long ragged gasps, then he lifted his gaze to meet Zalbar's.

"I must kill him. I cannot . . . live in the same world and . . . breathe the same air with one who . . . shamed me so . . . and still call myself a man."

For a moment, Razkuli swayed as if speaking

had drained him of all energy, then he carefully lowered himself onto a bench, propping his back against the wall.

"I must kill him," he repeated, his voice steadying. "Even if it means fighting you."

"You won't have to fight me, my friend," Zalbar sat beside him, "instead accept me as a partner. Tempus must be stopped, and I fear it will take both of us to do it. Even then we may not be enough."

The swarthy Hell Hound nodded in slow agreement. "Perhaps if we acquired one of those hellish weapons that have been causing so much trouble in the Maze?" he suggested.

"I'd rather bed a viper. From the reports I've heard they cause more havoc for the wielder than for the victim. No, the plan I have in mind is of an entirely different nature."

The bright flowers danced gaily in the breeze as Zalbar finished his lunch. Razkuli was not guarding his back today: that individual was back at the barracks enjoying a much earned rest after their night's labors. Though he shared his friend's fatigue, Zalbar indulged himself with this last pleasure before retiring.

"You sent for me, Hell Hound?"

Zalbar didn't need to turn his head to identify his visitor. He had been watching him from the corner of his eyes throughout his dusty approach.

"Sit down, Jubal," he instructed. "I thought you'd like to hear about my investigations."

"It's about time," the slaver grumbled, sinking to the ground. "It's been a week—I was starting to doubt the seriousness of your pledge. Now, tell me why you couldn't find the killer."

The Hell Hound ignored the sneer in Jubal's voice. "Tempus is the killer, just as you said," he answered casually.

"You've confirmed it? When is he being brought to trial?"

Before Zalbar could answer a terrible scream broke the calm afternoon. The Hell Hound remained unmoved, but Jubal spun toward the sound. "What was that?" he demanded.

"That," Zalbar explained, "is the noise a man makes when Kurd goes looking for knowledge."

"But I thought. . . I swear to you, this is not my doing!"

"Don't worry about it, Jubal." The Hell Hound smiled and waited for the slaver to sit down again. "You were asking about Tempus' trial?"

"That's right," the black man agreed, though visibly shaken.

"He'll never come to trial."

"Because of *that*?" Jubal pointed to the house. "I can stop. . . ."

"Will you be quiet and listen! The court will never see Tempus because the prince protects him. That's why I hadn't investigated him before your complaint!"

"Royal protection!" The slaver spat. "So he's free to hunt my people still."

"Not exactly." Zalbar indulged in an extravagant yawn.

"But you said. . . ."

"I said I'd deal with him, and in your words 'it's done.' Tempus won't be reporting for duty today . . . or ever."

Jubal started to ask something, but another

scream drowned out his words. Surging to his feet he glared at Kurd's house. "I'm going to find out where that slave came from, and when I do. . . ."

"It came from me, and if you value your people you won't insist on his release."

The slaver turned to gape at the seated Hell Hound. "You mean. . . ."

"Tempus," Zalbar nodded. "Kurd told me of a drug he used to subdue his slaves, so I got some from Stulwig and put it in my comrade's *krrf*. He almost woke up when we branded him . . . but Kurd was willing to accept my little peace offering with no questions asked. We even cut out his tongue as an extra measure of friendship."

Another scream came—a low animal moan which lingered in the air as the two men listened.

"I couldn't ask for a more fitting revenge," Jubal said at last, extending his hand. "He'll be a long time dying."

"If he dies at all," Zalbar commented, accepting the handshake. "He heals very fast, you know."

With that the two men parted company, mindless of the shrieks that followed them.

THE LIGHTER SIDE OF SANCTUARY

The reader response to the first volume of THIEVES' WORLD has been overwhelming and heartwarming. (For those of you who were not aware of it: you can write to me or any other author in care of their publisher.) The volume of correspondence helped to sell volumes two and three and prompted a THIEVES' WORLD wargame soon to be released from the Chaosium. It seems that none of our THIEVES' WORLD readers realize that anthologies in general don't sell and that fantasy anthologies specifically are sudden death.

While the letters received have been brimming with enthusiasm and praise, there has been one comment/criticism which has recurred in much of the correspondence. Specifically, people have noted that Sanctuary is incredibly grim. It seems that the citizens of the town never laugh, or when they do it is forcefully stiffled . . . like the time Kitty-Cat spilled wine down the front of his tunic while trying to toast the health of his brother, the emperor.

This is a valid gripe. First of all because no town is totally dismal. Second, because those readers familiar with my other works are accustomed to finding *some* humor buried in the pages—even in a genocid a war between lizards and bugs. What's worse, in reviewing the stories in this second volume, I am painfully aware that the downward spiral of Sanctuary has continued rather than reversing itself.

As such I have taken it upon myself as editor to provide the reader with a brief glimpse of the bright side of the town—the benefits and advantages of living in the worst hell hole in the Empire.

To this end let us turn to a seldom seen, never quoted document issued by the Sanctuary Chamber of Commerce shortly before it went out of business. The fact that Kitty-Cat insisted the brochure contain some modicum of truth doubtless contributed to the document's lack of success. Nonetheless, for your enjoyment and edification, here are selected excerpts from

SANCTUARY
VACATION CAPITOL OF
THE RANKAN EMPIRE

Every year tourists flock to Sanctuary by the tens, drawn by the rumors of adventure and excitement which flourish in every dark corner of the Empire. They are never disappointed that they chose Sanctuary. Our city is everything it is rumored to be—and more! Many visitors never leave and those that do can testify that the lives to which they return seem dull in comparison with the heartstopping action they found in this personable town.

If you, as a merchant, are looking to expand or relocate your business consider scenic Sanctuary. Where else can you find all these features in one locale?

BUSINESS OPPORTUNITIES

PROPERTY—Land in Sanctuary is cheap! Whether you want to build in the swamplands to the east of town, or west in the desert fringes, you'll find large parcels of land available at temptingly low prices. If you seek a more central location for your business, just ask. Most shop owners in Sanctuary are willing to surrender their building, stock and staff for the price of a one-way passage out of town.

LABOR—There is no shortage of willing workers in Sanctuary. You'll find most citizens are for hire and will do anything for a price. Moreover, the array of talents and skills available in our city is nothing short of startling. Abilities you never thought were marketable are bought and sold freely in Sanctuary—and the price is always right!

For those who prefer slave labor, the selection available in Sanctuary is diverse and plentiful. You'll be as surprised as the slaves themselves are by who shows up on the auction block. There, as everywhere in Sanctuary, bargains abound for one with a sharp eye . . . or sword.

MATERIALS—If the remoteness of the town's location makes you hesitate—never fear. Anything of value in the Empire is sold in Sanctuary. In fact, commodities you may have been told were not for sale often appear in the stalls and shops of this amazing town. Don't bother asking the seller how he got his stock. Just rest assured that in Sanctuary no one will ask how you came by yours, either.

LIFESTYLES

SOCIAL LIFE—As the ancients say, one does not live by bread alone. Similarly, a citizen of the Rankan Empire requires an active social life to balance his business activity. Here is where Sanctuary truly excels. It has often been said that day to day life in Sanctuary is an adventure without parallel.

RELIGIONS—For those with an eye for the after-life, the religious offerings in a given area must withstand close scrutiny. Well, our town welcomes such scrutinizers with open arms. Every Rankan deity and cult is represented in Sanctuary, as well many not in open evidence elsewhere in the Empire. Old gods and forgotten rites exist and flourish alongside the more accepted traditions, adding to the town's quaint charm. Nor are our temples reserved for devout true-believers only. Most shrines welcome visitors of other beliefs and many allow—nay, require—audience participation in their curious native rituals.

NIGHT LIFE—Unlike many cities in the Empire which roll up their streets with the setting sun, Sanctuary comes to life at night. In fact, many of its citizens exist for the night life to a point where you seldom see them by the light of day. However conservative or jaded your taste in entertainment might be, you'll have the time of your life in the shadows of Sanctuary. Our Street of Red Lanterns alone offers a wide array of amusements, from the quiet elegance of the Ambrosia House to the more bizarre pleasures available at the House of Whips. If slumming is your pleasure, you need look no further than your own doorstep.

SOCIAL STATUS—Let's face it: everybody likes to feel superior to somebody. Well, nowhere is superiority as easy to come by as it is in Sanctuary. A Rankan citizen of moderate means is a wealthy man by Sanctuary standards, and will be treated as such by its inhabitants. Envious eyes will follow your passing and people will note your movements and customs with flattering attentiveness. Even if your funds are less than adequate in your own opinion, it is still easy to feel that you are better off than the average citizen of Sanctuary—if only on a moral scale. We can guarantee, without reservation, that however low your opinion of yourself might be, there will be somebody in Sanctuary you will be superior to.

A WORD ABOUT CRIME—You have probably heard rumors of the high crime rate in Sanctuary. We admit to having had our problems in the past, but that's behind us now. One need only look at the huge crowds that gather to watch the daily hangings and impalements to realize that the citizens of Sanctuary's support for law and order is at an all-time high. As a result of the new Governor's anti-crime program, we are pleased to announce that last year the rate of reported crime, per day, in Sanctuary was not greater than that of cities twice our size.

IN SUMMARY

Sanctuary is a place of opportunity for a far-thinking opportunist. Now is the time to move. Now, while property values are plummeting and the economy and the people are depressed. Where better to invest your money, your energies and your life than in this rapidly growing city of the future? Even our worst critics acknowledge the potential of Sanctuary when they describe it as a "town with nowhere to go but up!"

MURDER, MAYHEM, SKULDUGGERY..
AND A CAST OF CHARACTERS
YOU'LL NEVER FORGET!

THIEVES' WORLD™

EDITED BY
ROBERT LYNN ASPRIN and LYNN ABBEY

. . . .

FANTASTICAL ADVENTURES

One Thumb, the crooked bartender at the Vulgar Unicorn...*Enas Yorl,* magician and shape changer ...*Jubal,* ex-gladiator and crime lord...*Lythande the Star-browed,* master swordsman and would-be wizard...these are just a few of the players you will meet in a mystical place called Sanctuary.™ This is *Thieves' World.* Enter with care.

__80584-1	**THIEVES' WORLD**	**$2.95**
__80585-X	**TALES FROM THE**	**$2.95**
	VULGAR UNICORN	
__80586-8	**SHADOWS OF SANCTUARY**	**$2.95**
__78713-4	**STORM SEASON**	**$2.95**
__80587-6	**THE FACE OF CHAOS**	**$2.95**
__80588-4	**WINGS OF OMEN**	**$2.95**

Prices may be slightly higher in Canada.

Available at your local bookstore or return this form to:

ACE SCIENCE FICTION
Book Mailing Service
P.O. Box 690, Rockville Centre, NY 11571

Please send me the titles checked above. I enclose _____ Include 75¢ for postage and handling if one book is ordered; 25¢ per book for two or more not to exceed $1.75. California, Illinois, New York and Tennessee residents please add sales tax.

NAME _____

ADDRESS _____

CITY _____ STATE/ZIP _____

(allow six weeks for delivery)   **SF 2**

FRITZ LEIBER

☐ 11749-X	**CONJURE WIFE**	$2.75
☐ 64417-1	**OUR LADY OF DARKNESS**	$2.50

FAFHRD AND THE GRAY MOUSER SAGA

☐ 79191-3	**SWORDS AND DEVILTRY**	$2.95
☐ 79190-5	**SWORDS AGAINST DEATH**	$2.75
☐ 79192-1	**SWORDS IN THE MIST**	$2.95
☐ 79189-1	**SWORDS AND ICE MAGIC**	$2.75

Prices may be slightly higher in Canada.

URSULA K. LE GUIN

27 million Americans can't read a bedtime story to a child.

It's because 27 million adults in this country simply can't read.

Functional illiteracy has reached one out of five Americans. It robs them of even the simplest of human pleasures, like reading a fairy tale to a child.

You can change all this by joining the fight against illiteracy.

Call the Coalition for Literacy at toll-free **1-800-228-8813** and volunteer.

Volunteer Against Illiteracy. The only degree you need is a degree of caring.